In the Flickering Candlelight of the Perfume-scented Chamber . . .

Verony became a temptress. Her wide indigo eyes, veiled by thick lashes, glowed with a fire Curran had not seen before. Her ripe mouth parted slightly with the urgent rise and fall of her breasts. Beneath the transparent silk, he saw her nipples harden and marveled at the thought that his nearness alone could so move her.

Long, lithe strides ate up the distance separating them as he tracked Verony around the bed. Her back was against the wall before he stopped. Heavily muscled arms shot out on either side to hold her trapped.

The lambent flame in his gray-green eyes warned her that the first stage of preliminaries was over. But Verony was not distressed. She had much, much more planned for her ardent husband. . . .

Dear Reader,

We, the editors of Tapestry Romances, are committed to bringing you two outstanding original romantic historical novels each and every month.

From Kentucky in the 1850s to the court of Louis XIII, from the deck of a pirate ship within sight of Gibraltar to a mining camp high in the Sierra Nevadas, our heroines experience life and love, romance and adventure.

Our aim is to give you the kind of historical romances that you want to read. We would enjoy hearing your thoughts about this book and all future Tapestry Romances. Please write to us at the address below.

The Editors
Tapestry Romances
POCKET BOOKS
1230 Avenue of the Americas
Box TAP
New York, N.Y. 10020

Rebellious Love

Maura Seger

A TAPESTRY BOOK
PUBLISHED BY POCKET BOOKS NEW YORK

To Meredith Bernstein,
who pointed me in the right direction
at the right time
and has kept me heading there
ever since

An *Original* publication of TAPESTRY BOOKS

 A Tapestry Book published by
POCKET BOOKS, a Simon & Schuster division of
GULF & WESTERN CORPORATION
1230 Avenue of the Americas, New York, N.Y. 10020

ISBN: 0-671-46379-9

First Tapestry Books printing April, 1983

10 9 8 7 6 5 4 3 2 1

POCKET and colophon are registered trademarks
of Simon & Schuster.

TAPESTRY is a trademark of Simon & Schuster.

Printed in the U.S.A.

Chapter One

"RUN, LADY VERONY! RUN!" THE BOY GASPED. "Don't let them catch you."

Verony ignored him. Her small but strong hands continued to work fiercely at the snare. If she could only loosen it a little more . . .

The baying of hounds interrupted her. Looking up, she realized how very close their pursuers were. The boy's plea took on new urgency. "For God's sake, my lady, leave me! You don't know what they'll do to you if they find you like this!"

In fact, Verony knew full well her likely fate. She had not lived in her father's house for seventeen years without becoming aware of men's seemingly limitless capacity for cruelty and the particular delight they could take in tormenting helpless women. But still she did not flee. In her slender, almost

1

fragile form there was steel. Her hands worked faster.

Endless moments passed. She was aware of nothing but the ever closer sounds of dogs and horses, her own desperate heartbeat and the boy's sobs. He was barely eight, the only son of the people who had first sheltered her when she fled the manor. Even if she had not been born to lead and protect, she still could not have left him.

Dark red-gold hair fell into indigo-blue eyes. She pushed it back impatiently. That hair was her only remaining vanity. She refused to cut it and, to the horror of the serfs who shunned water, washed it frequently along with the rest of her now undernourished but still lovely body. Just then, however, she wished she had hacked it all off.

Her hands were cut and bleeding from her efforts to untangle the snare. In the chill dampness of late summer, she shivered without being aware that she did so. Discomfort was second nature now. It did not impinge on her furious will to survive. The baying grew louder. She could almost feel the hot, moist breath of the dogs on her back . . . sense their razor-sharp teeth digging into her soft flesh. . . .

The snare broke. Verony gasped as the toughened leather came apart in her hands. It took them both a moment to realize the boy was free. When they did so, Verony leaped to her feet, carrying him with her.

"Run!" she hissed. "Cross the stream. The dogs will lose your scent. Go on!" She gave him a little push, turning in the opposite direction.

The boy hesitated. In his shy, child's way, he loved

2

the Lady Verony. She was a mysterious creature of incomprehensible beauty and grace somehow fallen into their world from another, far higher life. But she was also the voice of authority. Generations of obedience won out. The boy turned and fled.

Verony gave him a moment before dashing through the nearby copse of gnarled oaks. She was very tired and the thick underbrush made for hard going, but she ran swiftly. With rape and death in pursuit, her flight was desperate.

She had always been a strong girl, despite her delicate bones and slender stature, and the hardships of the last few months had brought out strength she had not guessed she possessed. Despite the chronic lack of food and the toll taken by harsh weather and miserable shelter, she was still in good condition. If she could mislead the dogs, send them chasing a false scent, she might have a chance.

Beyond the copse was a small pond. Verony hoped to wade through it. But time was running out. She could hear the pounding hoofbeats and the jovial shouts of the men sensing a kill. Like most of the young women of her former rank, Verony had hunted often. But only recently had she learned what it meant to be the prey. A hard fist of fear grew in her stomach as her breath came in labored gasps. Damn Curran d'Arcy! Damn him and the other men who chased her! Damn every one of the noble lords who cared nothing for the anguish they inflicted.

The pond was only yards away when a twist of root thrust up from an oak tree tripped her. Verony fell heavily. Her head struck a stone and the breath was knocked out of her. Long, precious moments were lost before the whirling lights and plummeting darkness faded enough for her to realize what had happened. By then it was too late. As she tried frantically to rise, a huge mastiff hurled itself at her. The dog knocked Verony to the ground, his front paws pinning her shoulders as his teeth gripped the back of her neck.

The animal was well-trained. He did not bite, but merely held her immobile until the riders reached them. Face down on the earth, Verony could do nothing but listen helplessly as the men laughed, congratulating the dog and themselves.

"Well done, boy! Back off now. Let's see what we've caught."

"Not much of a catch. Doesn't look as though he's got any meat on him."

"Ran fast, though. Surprising. Most of these serfs are a lumberous lot. Hardly stir themselves."

"Down, boy! That's it. We may feed him to you later, but for now . . ."

Verony was hauled upright, grasped in hard hands that bruised her shoulders through the coarse wool cloak she wore. "Small," a deep voice commented. "Not more than a lad."

Her hood fell back, revealing the tumult of red-gold hair hiding her face. She felt, as well as heard, the gasp of the man holding her. "A wench! And a comely one at that! Our luck's in after all!"

The men pressed closer to get a look at her. She could smell the mead and ale drunk at breakfast mingling with the stench of sweat and horses. More hands reached for her, grasping at the thin cloak still sheltering most of her body from their greedy eyes. Before the garment could be ripped from her, their leader intervened.

"Bring her here," the deep voice commanded.

Her captors hesitated, but only for a moment. Hoisted off her feet, Verony was deposited roughly before the large shape of a man just dismounting from a roan stallion. Struggling to catch her breath, she kept her head down, the cloak gathered tightly around her. This was even worse than she had feared. There were so many of them—at least half a dozen—harsh, powerful men she did not doubt would readily take their pleasure before killing her.

Tears rose in Verony's blue eyes, only to be determinedly forced back. She did not want to die! Life, hard as it was, could still be sweet. There was so much she had never done or seen. Never lain in a man's arms and known the delight of love, never held a child of her own. Too late, her mind warned. She had already survived longer than anyone would have guessed. But her luck had run out. Caught poaching on the lands of Curran d'Arcy, she could expect only one punishment.

Verony's back stiffened. So be it. If she was to die, it would be with honor. Even as the deep-voiced one's hand reached to force her chin up, her own fingers were feeling for the dagger hidden in her tunic.

Her resolve faltered momentarily when her eyes met the compelling gaze of the man holding her. He was so tall that she had to strain to see the top of him. Massive shoulders clad in chain mail blotted out the sky. Hair dark as a raven's wing tumbled around his well-shaped head. His forehead was wide, matching the long, straight line of his nose, chiseled lips and strong jaw. But it was the deep-set eyes beneath thick brows that caught Verony. Their pure gray-green hue held her in a web of intense scrutiny unlike anything she had ever known.

Her own deep-blue eyes glinted silver against her alabaster skin, the tumult of her red-gold hair framing delicately perfect features. The total lack of color in her face in no way detracted from high-boned cheeks, a small, uptilted nose and a lushly curved mouth. The man's gaze lingered there, drawn by the tiny mole at one corner of her lips. He had difficulty tearing his gaze from it to scan the ivory column of her throat, just visible above the all-enveloping cloak. His breath came more quickly as a cold, mailed hand moved to grasp her slender shoulders.

"Not a serf," he growled. "Too beautiful . . . and too clean." Harshly he demanded: "Who are you?"

Verony hesitated. She had little hope of being able to keep her identity secret, nor did she see any real purpose in trying. But she had to weigh the odds that, knowing who she was, he would decide to let her die easily or make her punishment even harsher.

Only when impatience tightened the rugged features before her did she murmur: "I am Verony . . . de Langford. . . ."

The exclamations of the other men smothered anything further she might have said.

"De Langford's whelp! Who could have guessed she was alive?"

6

"All these months! Few men would endure. How did a mere girl manage?"

"She's not lying," an older man proclaimed. The grizzled veteran moved closer to stare at her. "I saw her once at court, about a year ago. It's her all right."

"I know that," the leader said quietly. "You are not the only one to remember the lady, Sir Lyle."

Laughter rippled through the band, fractionally relieving the tension. "Trust you, my lord, to recall a comely wench. And trust the d'Arcy luck to find one here. Perhaps the winter will not be as dreary as you expected, Lord Curran!"

Curran d'Arcy! Verony smothered a gasp of surprise. She should have guessed the leader would be none other than the new earl, come only weeks before to take possession of the lands that had been her father's. If the stories she remembered from court were anything to go by, Curran d'Arcy was not a man to let any usurp his authority. No one else would lead his knights, or protect that which was his.

With their families firmly planted on opposite sides of the interminable political struggles, Verony and Curran had never been formally introduced. But she had no difficulty recalling the glimpses she had of him on the training fields or in the lists. Her cheeks colored as she envisioned the brawny sweep of his unclothed chest and long, sinewy legs. Nor had she forgotten a word of the admiring stories told of him in the ladies' solar, where it was said his great prowess on the field no more than equaled his skills in bed.

At twenty-three, he was wealthy, powerful, admired, and at least as of a year ago, unwed. Though a second son of the feared d'Arcy clan, he held lands of his own and bowed to no man but the king, doing that only grudgingly. Since the death of Verony's father in a drunken brawl, Curran had risen to even greater strength. King John had granted the young earl all the lands once held by the Baron de Langford. All that lay within that demesne, and everyone dwelling on it, were his to do with as he would.

"What's to be done with her, my lord?" one of the men asked, echoing Verony's own thoughts. Gathering her courage, she looked directly at Curran, her eyes wide and luminous in the dim forest light.

He did not answer at once. Instead his grip on her tightened. "We found a deer some way back, slain by an arrow. Your trail led from there. Who was helping you poach?"

Not for the world would Verony tell him, and he would not have a chance to force the information from her. On that she was already determined. Facing him bravely, she insisted: "No one. I was alone."

Curran laughed. The sound was greatly at odds with his harsh demeanor. Verony stared fascinated at the gleam of white teeth against his stubble-roughened face. At court, she had never seen him unshaven. Was the current lack of a lady in his life responsible for such a lapse? Surely he could not be used to long periods of celibacy.

Steeling herself for what was certain to be a swift worsening of his temper, she insisted: "I shot the deer. There was no one else." Defiantly she added: "But God would surely forgive your people if they did poach, with the hunger so great. . . ."

She broke off. Curran's scowl frightened her more than she cared to admit. She was a fool to provoke him when he held her life in his hands.

"You would be wise to concentrate on your own predicament," he said coldly, "rather than try to excuse the serfs' crimes."

"It is no crime to want to live!" Verony exclaimed angrily. His careless dismissal of the starving men, women and children huddled in hovels across his land enraged her. Just as when confronted by her father's brutal callousness, she could not keep silent.

Her defiance earned a harsh shake that threatened to snap her collarbones. "I find you on my land, killing my deer, and you dare to challenge the condition of my serfs? Moreover, you dare lie to me! You shot that deer? I would sooner believe you charmed him into lying down and dying!"

Another shake, this one painful enough to make her bite back a moan of protest. "I will ask you only once more. Who helped you?"

"No one!" Rage and fear merged to block out all caution. "I will never say otherwise! You may know nothing of loyalty, but I will not betray those who sheltered and protected me when they had little enough for themselves. They are worth ten of you, Curran d'Arcy, nay a hundred!" Contempt shone clear in her blazing eyes and the proud stiffening of her body. The cold metal of her dagger pressed into her hand. Taking courage from it, she sneered openly. "You do not frighten me. I have faced far too much these last few months to tremble before an arrogant, pompous lout!"

Blank astonishment made Curran loosen, but not quite release, his grip on her. The fiery hellion before him was beyond anything he had ever encountered. Beauty, strength, pride all in what looked to be—at least from the neck up—a delectable package indeed. Through his mail glove, he could feel the fragility of her bones but poorly protected by the thin cloak. He became aware suddenly that she trembled, though whether from anger or fear he could not guess.

A reluctant smile quirked Curran's mouth. He forced it back determinedly. "Brave words. We'll see how far your courage lasts back at the keep," he challenged ominously.

Verony froze. She saw the eager light in the eyes of the men surrounding them and thought with sickening clarity of what was to come. Frantically, she twisted in his hold, her sudden movement surprising him. Managing to break free, Verony actually got a few paces away before Curran seized her, dragging her back against his steely length. "By God, you seem determined to provoke me!" he exclaimed. "Have you no sense at all?"

Verony was not listening. Despite the vast differences in their strength, which made all her efforts useless, she continued to struggle. Only one thing mattered: to get away. She was willing to accept escape in any form, even death. Her cloak slipped open, revealing the delicately rounded body but lightly clad in a worn tunic. When she fled the keep, Verony had been able to take few clothes. What little she did have had long ago been shared with the peasants.

Nothing remained of the beautiful wardrobe her father had grudgingly provided, not out of generosity but to increase her bridal worth. But she had never needed clothes to emphasize her loveliness. Not even the roughest garment could disguise the ripe fullness of her breasts, her small waist, and the gently rounded hips fashioned for a man's hand.

Perfectly formed, poised between innocence and sensuality, Verony had no conception of the impact she had on Curran. Nor did she glimpse the rare mingling of desire and gentleness that flickered in his gray-green eyes. She knew only the iron strength of his arms holding her to him, the implacable force of a heavily muscled male body and the growing excitement of his knights who stared at her lustfully.

Steel flashed in her small woman's hand. Steel, appearing where he had least expected it, darted past Curran's guard to slash at the metal links of his armor. Steel sharpened by months of careful use and wielded in profound desperation found a chink and drove deep, piercing skin and sinew.

She had her wish, Verony thought an instant later when she was hurled to the ground. The knights, seeing their lord attacked, responded instinctively. Not for them to wonder at her daring or spare even a moment to consider her fragility. Blows fell across her head and shoulders. A hand drove hard into her stomach, driving the air from her. Waves of pain washed over her, each greater than the last. She floundered on the edge of awareness before her last strength dissolved. A deep well awaited her, plummeting her far from all but the promise of release.

Chapter Two

VERONY RETURNED TO CONSCIOUSNESS RELUCTANT-
ly. Every inch of her body ached. A hammer pounded in her head, and her throat was painfully dry. She
stirred fitfully, a soft whimper escaping from between her clenched lips.

"There, there, dear, don't be trying to move," a
gentle voice murmured. "Just lie still. You'll be
better soon." Lifted, Verony felt the rim of a cup
pressed to her mouth. She drank greedily, the cool
water tasting like nectar. Only when she was lowered
again to the soft pillow did she dare to open her eyes.

She was lying in a small, sparsely furnished room
whose contours were as familiar to her as those of
her own face. Her old sleeping chamber. The room
she had grown up in, but which she had never
imagined seeing again.

Against one wall, a trestle table still held the

battered brass ewer she had kept filled with wild-flowers or dried herbs. A leather- and bronze-studded chest which had once held her clothes stood at the foot of the narrow bed. Glancing down, she recognized even the wool blanket covering her. It was one woven at the keep, dyed crimson with blossoms she herself had collected not two summers before. The bright color complemented those used in the tapestry done by her long-dead mother which hung opposite the bed. In the soft light filtering through the shuttered windows, the wall hanging had the gently muted aspect of an old friend.

"H-how . . . ?" Verony began, struggling upright. The hand on her shoulder stopped her.

"No, my lady, you must not try to move. Please. Rest is what you need." The voice grew coaxing. "Be a good girl now. Mayhap you'll be able to get up shortly."

Verony's eyes widened as she stared from the withered hand on her shoulder to the kindly, well-remembered face just above her. "Hilda! What are you doing here? It can't be . . . I must be dreaming. . . ."

The velvet-brown eyes of the woman who had cared for Verony since her birth filled with tears. "No, child," she murmured, "it's no dream. You're back where you belong, and mine to look after once again. So Lord Curran says, God bless him!"

This last piece of information, uttered with remarkable sincerity, shocked Verony to full awareness. Despite Hilda's restraining hand, the young girl straightened abruptly. "What are you saying?" she demanded. "Lord Curran brought me here? That can't be."

"And who else do you think could have carried you into this keep, right up to this very room," Hilda insisted tartly. Beneath the snow-white wimple framing her finely lined face, her expression regained much of its accustomed authority.

"But-but . . . I stabbed him," Verony breathed, struggling against a growing sense of unreality. "In the forest. I remember. He caught me with . . . That is, he caught me poaching. He was going to . . . I thought . . . his men . . ." A dull flush stained her cheeks. "I couldn't get away, so I stabbed him. I thought . . ."

"What did you think, child?" Hilda asked gently. Sitting down on the edge of the bed, she took both of Verony's hands in hers.

The young girl looked at her dazedly. Surely this was a dream? She could not be lying in her own room, with her old nurse tending her. She must be unconscious and dying, perhaps even dead. Yet everything about her proclaimed that she was very much alive and even safe, if only temporarily.

"I thought they were going to kill me for poaching," she explained in a low voice. "But I was afraid that before I died, they would rape me. So I tried to make them slay me right away. But it didn't work. I am here, and Lord Curran must be very angry." She broke off, struggling to hide her fear. If only she knew what punishment he intended for her, she would be better able to meet it courageously.

Looking up, Verony was startled by the sheen of

tears in her nurse's brown eyes. Hilda's chin wobbled precariously as she gathered her charge in a loving embrace. "Poor little thing! It was that father of yours who put such thoughts into your head. No wonder you expect the worst. But you must know, Lord Curran is not the same sort of man. He is—"

Hilda broke off, interrupted by a knock at the chamber door. She opened it to reveal two serving women carrying a tray of food and an ewer of steaming water.

"Well, don't just stand there," the nurse snapped. "Put those things on the table."

The women obeyed, gazing at Verony surreptitiously. She did not recognize them, but supposed they were members of the d'Arcy household sent to help look after their lord's comfort. Dimly she remembered that Curran's mother, the Lady Emelie d'Arcy, was renowned for the beauty and hospitality of her home. She would not be likely to let her son go off to the wilds of his new manor without proper servants.

Whoever had trained the women, Verony thought a moment later, had done the job well. Whereas she had always had to struggle against the servants' natural fear of her father and his men, and the general slovenliness the late Baron spread about him, these women showed neither timidity nor lack of skill.

Within minutes the table was laid with a clean cloth, the room filled with the scent of freshly baked bread and herbed chicken, and soap and fresh towels were put out next to a basin of hot water. Hilda surveyed the results critically before brusquely dismissing the women. They stole a final glance at Verony as they hurried away.

"They know what they're about here," the old nurse admitted grudgingly. "Had this place cleaned out and well stocked in no time." Wrapping a cloak around Verony's slender shoulders, she guided her to the table. "Now eat all of that," Hilda directed automatically. "The Lord knows you were never a big girl, but now you definitely need some weight put on you."

Verony hardly heard her. She was too busy staring at the meal laid out on the table. After so many months of only the poorest food and little enough of that, it looked like a feast. Her mouth watered and her stomach growled in pleasant anticipation, but still Verony held back. The hardships she had shared with those who protected her were far too fresh for her to enjoy such unexpected bounty.

As she had since the time Verony was a little child, Hilda seemed able to read her thoughts. Gently but firmly, she eased her into a chair. "Be sensible. There is no way for you to share this food, and you surely wish to regain your strength."

Hilda was right, of course, but knowing that did not make the young girl feel any less guilty. Hesitantly, she picked up a sliver of chicken. It melted on her tongue, prompting her to take another. She ate silently, concentrating on the food as she had never before had reason to do. Watching the slender little figure huddled in the cloak from which only one small hand emerged, Hilda was hard pressed to keep from weeping. Relief at her lady's safety coupled with a sensible understanding of what she must have suffered in the last year made the old nurse tremble. To hide her discomfort, she busied herself by laying out clothes.

By the time Verony had eaten all her shrunken stomach could hold, a complete outfit was spread over the bed. She stared at the soft linen chemise, blue silk tunic with bands of white satin, and the surcoat of white wool embroidered in gold. She had last worn those garments on her final visit to the royal court at London, just a few months before her father's death. The clothes, along with almost everything else she owned, had been left behind when she fled the keep. If she had thought about them at all in the intervening months, she would have presumed them looted or given away by the new lord. But instead there they were, freshly aired and pressed, waiting for her to don them.

"Come, lovey," Hilda murmured, "we must get you ready."

Numbed by a day already far too full of surprises, Verony did not even think to ask what she was being prepared for. It was a very subdued girl who allowed the old nurse to stand her in the center of the room near a lighted brazier whose heat dispelled the chill. Stripped of the stained, torn cloak and bedraggled tunic, she was gently washed clean.

Hilda winced as she saw the bruises inflicted by the knights and the other evidence of her young mistress' suffering, but she said nothing. When Verony was scrubbed and lightly perfumed with the scent of jasmine, Hilda wrapped her in a soft blanket before sitting her on a bench beside the bed. There she brushed the waist-length tresses until they shone like burnished copper in the fading light.

The linen chemise fell softly against Verony's skin, followed by the graceful tunic with long, tight sleeves buttoned from elbow to wrist. The sleeveless surcoat had a slight train, the weight of which pulled the fabric back far enough to reveal soft, pointed shoes of creamy leather. Intricately carved gold brooches that had belonged to Verony's mother were set at her shoulders, and a belt woven of golden strands tightly girded her small waist.

Her hair was left uncovered. Once she would have adorned it with a transparent veil held in place by a jeweled chaplet. But that was a symbol of rank she no longer felt able to wear. Hilda's efforts to persuade her otherwise had no effect. The old nurse gave up reluctantly, only after assuring herself that her charge looked every inch the lady even without further ornament.

The weariness and fear still all too evident in the young girl's eyes convinced Hilda not to argue further. "You are truly beautiful," she assured her gently. "Of course, you always were."

Verony smiled faintly, touched by her nurse's loyalty. If Hilda had been nearby the year before, when word came that the Baron de Langford was dead and his lands seized by the crown, she would undoubtedly have insisted on accompanying Verony.

Courage Hilda had aplenty, but the rigors of the

forest would certainly have been too much for her. Verony offered a silent prayer of thanks that her old nurse had survived. Whatever happened, she was grateful for this time with the woman who was as much her mother as the lady who had died giving her birth.

Recalled to herself by a sudden, sharp rap at the door, Hilda went swiftly to open it. Two men-at-arms stood in the corridor. Almost as tall and broad as their lord, the knights wore chain mail and carried longswords buckled at their sides. Their faces were grim as they surveyed the women.

"He wants her now," one informed Hilda gruffly.

Verony paled. So the brief interlude of comfort and care was over. She swallowed with difficulty, turning away to keep the old nurse from seeing how her shoulders trembled. Only long practice in discipline and courage enabled her to walk silently from the room.

Perhaps because she so desperately needed some distraction from her fear, Verony allowed her curiosity free rein as she walked through what had once been her home. She could see few changes, but that in itself was telling. The second-story gallery looking down on the Center Hall was swept clean and sweetly perfumed with fresh rushes. The torches set at regular intervals burned brightly without excessive smoke. The air above the hall was clear enough to indicate that the main chimney was being regularly swept.

To someone raised in the household of a lady of accomplishment such as Emelie d'Arcy, such amenities would be taken for granted. But Verony had been forced to battle filth and disorder to achieve even the smallest victories. She was glad to see that the household she had so laboriously raised to a proper standard was being well maintained.

Nor did the condition of the servants escape her notice. All were clean and well dressed, industriously occupied and seemingly adept at their various tasks. Some she recognized and of those a few were brave enough to discreetly nod or even dare a small smile. Most were new arrivals, and they seemed in command. Her suspicion that Lady Emelie ordered the smooth running of her son's household was strengthened.

Glancing downstairs, she saw that sleeping pallets were rolled neatly against the walls, trestle tables and benches still glistened from the sand and water rubbed into them after the midday meal, and few dogs were in sight. Those allowed in the hall were well behaved. They lay quietly by the huge fireplace, gnawing on bones or sleeping. Only one of the shaggy hounds lifted its head as Verony was led up the steep stone steps to the earl's private quarters.

There the knights paused. Standing between the massive men, hemmed in without actually being touched, she had to fight down the desperate urge to flee. They waited through long, seemingly endless moments until an aged knight came out to greet them.

A wave of Sir Lyle's hand was sufficient to dismiss the knights. Left alone, the grizzled warrior and the beautiful, frightened young girl faced each other.

Verony's eyes were unnaturally dark as she studied the man who had supported her identity.

White-thatched and black-eyed, he stood tall and supple despite what she guessed to be his sixty-five years. His face was tanned and seamed to the consistency of leather, but he had what under different circumstances might have been considered a kindly look. Certainly there was nothing threatening in his manner as he returned her scrutiny. At worst, his expression could be called stern.

Straightening under the careful gaze that seemed to see right through her, Verony forced herself to remain calm. Pride demanded that she meet whatever was to happen with dignity. But try though she did, she could not quite suppress all sign of her fear. Her delicate skin was ashen and a faint tremor made her shoulders quiver.

"Come on then," Sir Lyle said abruptly. Taking her arm, he half pushed, half pulled the young girl inside.

The high, stone room set just below the castle battlements was the private retreat of the resident lord. In the old baron's day, the chamber was the scene of drunken bouts and other activities better not discussed. Despite Verony's best efforts at cleanliness, the air always hung sodden with the stench of raw wine, and the furniture and floor were littered with debris. But now a quick glance told her all that had changed.

Even in the dim light of copper braziers, she could see that the room was immaculate. Like all the rest of the keep, it was swept clean and laid with fresh rushes. Tapestries warmed the walls. There was a sense of order about the single table set with a brace of candles, the chairs drawn in a circle for easy talk, the immaculate hangings around the bed.

The bed . . . Verony's throat tightened painfully. She was helpless to keep her gaze from the man lying there. Curran d'Arcy's powerful, bronzed arms lay crossed beneath his head. His naked torso gleamed in the firelight. Sculpted muscles rippled down the long line of his chest and flat abdomen, disappearing beneath the blanket that covered the rest of him.

He had been staring at the ceiling when she entered, but at the sound of the door opening his focus shifted. Gray-green eyes impaled her mercilessly.

Before the sheer impact of his gaze, Verony faltered. The breath caught in her lungs, and her heart hammered frantically. Never in her life had she been so aware of compelling masculinity. Curran's blatant regard, combining antagonism and lust, unleashed a response within her that she could barely credit. Slowly, irresistibly, the first glimmers of answering desire lit the dark shadows of her terror.

The gray-green eyes moved to Sir Lyle. "Leave us."

Dimly Verony thought she heard a faint chuckle as the knight withdrew. Resentment shot through her. There was nothing humorous about the situation. As the door clicked shut behind her, she stiffened in every muscle. He would get nothing, she vowed, without an all-out struggle. With luck, she would at least find the escape of unconsciousness before he raped her.

"Come here," Curran growled, sitting up in the bed.

Verony stood rooted where she was, refusing to move. Mutely she shook her head.

Slanted black eyebrows raised in astonishment. "You don't have any sense at all. Are you simple-minded?"

"Of course not!" she burst out indignantly before realizing he had meant to provoke her. Her soft, vermilion mouth drawn in an angry line, she turned away. Stubbornly, she focused on the corner of the room farthest from him.

Silence, but only for a moment. So softly that she had to strain to hear him, Curran said: "I told you to come here." There was no mistaking his ominous tone. He was holding on to his temper only by the thinnest edge.

Still Verony refused. Her mouth was dry, and her stomach clenched, but she would not move. "I am not some sheep to go placidly to my own slaughter! Whatever happens here will be by your will alone."

Much as he tried, Curran could not deny a spurt of admiration for her daring. A faint smile curved the corners of his sensual mouth before he abruptly recalled himself. Tauntingly, he demanded: "Would you prefer I come and get you?"

Verony backed up a pace, eyes widening as he began to pull aside the blanket. "N-no . . . !"

"Then pick up that medical kit and come over here."

Startled, Verony followed the direction of his pointing hand. There was a small wooden box on the table, as well as a basin of water and fresh towels. Uncertainly she glanced at him.

"If I have to tell you again . . ."

Without giving herself time to think, Verony crossed the room in rapid strides. Picking up the supplies, she carried them to the bed. Careful to stay just beyond the reach of Curran's long arm, she stared at him wide-eyed.

"Well . . ." he drawled, letting his gaze linger on her rounded breasts and the narrow curve of her waist. There was a slight stirring beneath the blanket which, mercifully, did not penetrate the young girl's confusion.

"I-I don't understand what you . . . want me to do. . . ."

With mock patience, drawing out each word, Curran explained. "I want you to repair the damage you did in the forest." When still she did not seem to understand he pointed at the angry slash on his left shoulder. "You wounded my pride, madam, as well as my flesh. I have never been so easily attacked."

"I did not mean to . . ." Verony began, only to break off. They both knew she had most certainly meant to wound him. It seemed futile to try to explain that the proof of her success sickened her. She had seen many wounds in her short life, but never before one she herself had inflicted. The sight of his torn skin surrounded by dried blood made her stomach reel. Helplessly Verony swayed.

"Don't you dare faint!" Curran snapped. "If you

try it, I'll know you're faking." His face darkened threateningly. "You're no shrinking maiden too shy and delicate to face the coarser side of life. Far from it! Never have I met such a hellion. You are a menace, madam, with or without a weapon!"

The muscles of his massive shoulders suddenly stiffened as a possibility occurred to him. "Damn it! For all I know, you may have armed yourself again."

Words of denial sprang to Verony's lips, but she was powerless to utter them, for in that instant Curran stepped swiftly from the bed, revealing the full magnificence of his bronzed male beauty. Looming over her, he snatched the supplies away, then yanked both her hands into one of his and drew her hard against his body.

A scream rose in Verony's throat. Frantically she tried to struggle. But iron bands locked her to his steely length. His arm tight around her tiny waist, his granite thighs pressed intimately to her softness, he filled her consciousness. The castle, the room, even the sense of her own being faded before the implacable onslaught of his sheer size and strength. Aching awareness flared within her as his large hand passed slowly, lingeringly over her curves.

Not an inch of her remained untouched, from her vulnerable white throat to her shapely thighs lightly covered by the surcoat and tunic. Savoring beauty more exquisite than any he had yet encountered, Curran deliberately allowed his skillful fingers to manipulate the hardening peaks of her breasts. Until a low, broken sob forced him to realize that her response was one of fear rather than desire.

Abruptly he released her, returning to the bed and pulling the covers back into place before he looked at her again. Verony stood with her slender arms wrapped tight around herself, futilely trying to shield her body from his eyes. Her head was bent, the red-gold curls spilling in a silken cascade of light. She trembled, moaning softly.

"Stop that!" Curran demanded, shame burning him. He was not one of those who found pleasure in the abuse of women. On the contrary. Such brutality filled him with disgust. Embarrassment followed hard upon his guilt, making him speak sharply. "Get control of yourself. I want this wound dressed right now."

For a terrifying moment, Verony thought she would not be able to comply. Shocked into abrupt awareness of her body, torn from the protection of innocence more complete than even Curran could guess, she quivered uncontrollably. But for the fear that he would come after her again, she could not have obeyed.

Clumsily she picked up the supplies. Her hands shook as she sat down beside him on the bed, watching him warily. Only the fact that his attention seemed once more focused on the ceiling allowed her to continue.

As Curran lay still beneath her hesitant touch, Verony bathed the wound before gently applying a salve. Satisfied that stitches were not needed, she folded a thin gauze bandage that would provide protection while allowing air to get through.

As she carefully tied the padding in place, their

glances locked. Verony faltered and looked away hastily. She missed the slight smile that softened Curran's rugged features.

"Th-there . . . that's the best I can do."

"I suppose I'll live," he grunted, his gaze on the small, white hands now in her lap. Never could he remember a woman's touch bringing such pleasure. His huge body resonated to her gentleness, shivers of desire running along his spine. Beneath the rough stubble of his beard he paled. Determined she would not know how greatly she stirred him, he flexed his knees, concealing the hardened urgency of his manhood.

"I'm sorry. . . ." Verony breathed, unaware that her sympathy over his wound might have been better directed.

"You ought to be."

"I've never done anything like that before. . . ."

"You mean you don't make it a practice of stabbing men?"

The sardonic challenge forced Verony to lift her head. Glaring, she bit out: "I was only trying to defend myself. Surely anyone has that right?"

Startled, Curran did not respond immediately. Since he never really intended to harm her, he was surprised to discover she had expected nothing else. But now that he thought about it, he had to admit that the circumstances would have led her to fear the worst.

Grudgingly, he advised: "In the future, try not to be so impulsive. Unless someone is actually coming at you with a weapon, take a few seconds to find out if he's a friend or an enemy."

Verony stared at him in blank astonishment. His words seemed to suggest there was some possibility they were not adversaries. Hesitantly she murmured, "Wh-which are you, Curran d'Arcy . . . ?"

The precarious hold he was keeping on his desires had tried his temper. He had neither the will nor the patience to play word games with her. "I am your master, and you would do well to remember it! This land and everything on it are mine."

Curran gripped her delicate chin and pulled her closer. "I could kill you for what happened in the forest. Or give you to my men, after having you myself. You are my property. I own you, body and soul." Abruptly he let her go, sending her sprawling across the bed near his feet.

Enraged, Verony forgot all caution. "You arrogant cur! I am no man's. I belong to myself. If you think for one minute that you can—"

Steel-hard arms lashed out, dragging her against his fully aroused body. Through the thin cover, Verony could not help but feel his need. At first the alien hardness against her belly meant nothing to her. She had never felt it before and knew of nothing similar in herself. When understanding dawned, she blushed fiercely.

"Shall I prove it to you, Verony? Shall I prove you belong to me?"

"N-nooo . . . !"

An instant longer Curran held her, making her acutely conscious of just how he wanted to possess her. Terrified, Verony writhed in his arms. Tears flooded her indigo eyes, trailing down her alabaster cheeks.

Without warning he thrust her from him. *"Sir Lyle!"*

The old knight entered instantly, having been waiting just beyond the door. He fought down a grin as he surveyed the two on the bed. "My lord?"

"Take Lady Verony back to her room and make sure she stays there!"

Shooting his master a chiding glance, Sir Lyle lifted the shaken young girl to her feet and led her gently away.

Chapter Three

THE NEXT FEW DAYS PASSED IN A CONFUSED DAZE for Verony. Though she was not permitted to leave her quarters without escort, she was otherwise treated as an honored guest. Certainly all her creature comforts were well seen to. In the security of her room, she dined lavishly, slept surprisingly well and even savored such luxuries as long, daily baths. Hilda hovered over her constantly, seeing to it that she did not exert herself in the slightest until the old nurse was convinced she had recovered from her ordeal.

Occasionally, she saw Curran going about his business on the demesne. Watching him from her narrow window, Verony felt again the mysterious stirrings within her that she had first experienced in his chamber. Bewildered by her own feelings, she found herself spending more and more time hoping for a glimpse of him.

A week after being found in the forest, her peaceful interlude abruptly ended. She was working in the castle herb garden when Sir Lyle came to find her. Looking up from her careful pruning of a clump of parsley, she found him staring at her.

The old knight had thought her lovely from the first moment he saw her. But now, after proper rest and care, she was exquisitely beautiful. Even with her red-gold hair slightly mussed from the soft summer breeze and a faint smattering of freckles on her uptilted nose, she could not be faulted.

Dismissing the men-at-arms who were guarding her, he smiled gently. "Good morning, my lady. I trust you are well."

Verony wiped her hands off a bit self-consciously before answering him. The herb garden had always been one of her special places, and she found great enjoyment working there. But she wasn't absolutely certain Lord Curran would approve. Cautiously she ventured: "Thank you, Sir Lyle. I am very well. I was just picking some seasonings for tonight's supper. . . ."

The knight nodded blandly. "Of course." Ever mindful of the courtesies, he said: "If you have enough, perhaps one of the servants could take your basket back to the keep." By way of explanation, he added: "Lord Curran would like to speak with you."

Some of the sun-warmed color Verony had recently acquired faded, but she nodded calmly. Only the glitter of her deep sapphire eyes revealed her puzzlement. Given the polite nature of the summons, Curran might be planning to discuss the weather or the likelihood of good crops. Perhaps he wanted advice on decorating his new home. Resisting an almost hysterical desire to laugh, she followed the knight.

They walked some little distance from the keep, across the bailey where blacksmiths, armorers, tanners and other castle workers shared space with the keepers of pigs and chickens, through the guardhouse where watchful men-at-arms saluted respectfully, and down the road toward the river. The day was fair enough for Verony to be quite comfortable. Warm clothes and good food added immeasurably to her well-being. She cast an appreciative look up at the clear blue sky mirroring the color of her eyes, unaware that Sir Lyle watched her with satisfaction. She was everything he had hoped, and more. The old knight's step was light as they rounded the last bend before the mill.

The rush of water and the clash of metal reached Verony simultaneously, followed quickly by the low, angry curses of men frustrated in their purpose. Sir Lyle sighed, meeting her puzzled look with a shrug. "The gearing must have cracked. What little grain we found in the keep was largely unground. Lord Curran ordered it milled at once, but it seems he is to be thwarted."

The irate mutterings continued from inside the low, wooden building beside the river. A channel cut decades before held the water wheel, connected by a horizontal shaft to gears turning the millstones. Each of the three stones was of a different size and could be set to grind oats or barley or rye to preference. Below the stones hung sieves, shaken by the river waters as they flowed back out of the mill. Lower still were the catch pans where the bran fell, leaving the flour behind.

When the mill worked properly, it greatly eased the labor of the peasants who depended on it. But neglect by the former earl, who saw no worth in anything but drinking, fighting and wenching, led to inevitable breakdowns. Verony sighed as she looked round at the unmistakable signs of neglect. Spider webs spanned the ceiling rafters. A thick powder of dust lay over the planked floor, making it difficult to breathe. The sieves had rotted through in places, though they seemed reparable enough.

About to say something of this to Sir Lyle, Verony broke off abruptly, all attention focused on the man standing beside the cracked gear. Curran d'Arcy was cursing long and fluently in a voice made none the less ominous by its inherently melodious quality. Out of armor, wearing only an unbleached tunic stained with sweat despite the cool air, he looked every bit as impressive and frightening as he had in their previous encounters.

Taller by at least half a head than any of the other men, his broad shoulders, muscular chest, tapered hips and long, corded legs radiated a barely controlled sense of raw power. He carried himself with the lithe grace of a man accustomed to hard work and fighting. The play of bunched muscle and sinew across his wide back and torso caught Verony's gaze, even as she noted that he had shaved recently.

His chiseled mouth was set in a hard line, and his firm jaw was clenched angrily. An ebony lock of hair fell across his forehead, brushed irritably aside as he caught sight of Verony.

Across the width of the mill, their eyes locked. Dazedly she puzzled over how a gaze as gray-green as a forest pond could blaze so hotly that her very skin felt burned. She shivered, but not with fear. Some other sensation, just as basic but far more pleasant, made her heart beat fiercely. Verony flushed, her eyes dropping with all the instinctive modesty and artless coquetry of a young girl who has never been troubled by anything more than the desire for a man's glance and touch.

For just an instant, Curran caught a glimpse of how she would have been if life had not so burdened her with a witless father and a brutal fate. The breath caught in his chest as he contemplated loveliness greater than any he had ever seen, made all the more poignant by the air of vulnerability so at odds with her inherent strength.

Then the memory of what that strength had led her to do intervened enough for him to manage a frown. "You picked a bad moment to join us, my lady," he snapped. "I have no time to talk with you now."

"I picked?" Verony repeated, surprise making her less than circumspect. "You summoned me, my lord, or have you forgotten I did not come here of my own choice?"

Despite himself, Curran felt a spurt of pleasure at her spirit. He could think of no woman, save his mother or sister-in-law, who could endure what this girl had and still emerge strong and defiant. Unwilling admiration warred with the irresistible male need to take her down a peg or two.

"I have forgotten nothing," he growled. "Nor am I likely to, at least while my shoulder still aches."

Verony bit her lip. How could she have been so stupid as to remind him of that? Hastily she said: "I am glad to see you are all right."

"That pleases you?" Curran demanded skeptically. "Somehow I got the impression you did not have my welfare at heart when you stabbed me."

"I . . . I . . ." Verony began, only to give up before the overwhelming futility of trying to explain herself. Surely he would not care in the least about her fears, or her desire to die without first being dishonored. Should she reveal such feelings to him, he might only take delight in assuring her that her worst dread would become reality all too soon. Already he seemed gratified by her discomfort, her fumbling attempt to answer earning a mirthless grin. Determined to banish his satisfaction, Verony asked firmly: "Why am I here?"

"Anxious to learn your fate?" Curran drawled, even as he knew a moment of shame for taunting her. The girl was clearly still frightened of him, though she hid it well. Comparing her to the pretty but empty-headed young ladies his father, normally the best of men, occasionally threatened him with, he decided she deserved better than his ill humor. More gently Curran said: "I do want to talk with you. We have much to discuss. But I can't spare the time right now, not with this new problem holding up the grinding. Perhaps this evening, if matters are settled here . . ."

He was serious, Verony realized with a start. The repair of the mill was—like everything else, it seemed—more important to Lord Curran than the punishment of the woman who had stabbed him. Even as she tried to puzzle out what manner of man would set such priorities, Verony heard herself murmur: "The grinding need not be greatly delayed. There is another gear."

In the act of turning back to the broken wheel, Curran froze. "What?"

"There is another gear," Verony explained patiently. "It was made last summer, when this one showed signs of cracking soon."

"And where is this new gear?"

"Under the mill," Verony admitted hesitantly. "Wrapped in straw. You will find it near the back entrance."

"You hid it?" Curran demanded. "Why?"

It was clear from his tone that he presumed she had secreted the new gear after learning of her father's death, although what she could have hoped to achieve by such a petty act of theft from the new lord he could not imagine. Nor did she impress him as the sort to engage in such subterfuge without ample reason. Seeing the fear that had leaped instantly to life within her eyes at the first sound of his suspicion, Curran softened. Taking a step toward her, he rephrased his question more gently. "Why did you hide the gear, Verony?"

"Because my father had not given permission for it to be made," she explained all in a rush. Her eyes meeting his in an unconscious plea, Verony went on: "When the miller told me about the gear, I asked for approval to replace it. But my father cared nothing for such things, and would not spend the coin for it."

37

"Yet the gear was made nonetheless," Curran prompted, growing more interested by the moment. There were depths to this girl he had not yet begun to explore.

"There was no choice. Without it the mill would not work, the grain could not be ground, and the people would go hungry. Just as is happening now. I thought to prevent that by having the gear fashioned and hiding it until such time as it was needed."

Hands on his hips, towering over her, Curran scowled with what he hoped was appropriate disapproval for her rashness. He could not quite carry it off. The old baron's utter disregard for the management of his estate, coupled with wanton brutality far beyond even the accepted limits of a savage age, were too well known not to applaud the courageous efforts of his daughter. He could only wonder in amazement how de Langford had managed to produce such a remarkable offspring. "Is there anything else hidden away, my lady? Barrels of beef, perhaps? Reams of cloth? Livestock?"

Eyes lowered before the force of his disapproval, Verony shook her head. "No, nothing like that. Only . . ."

"Only what?" Curran demanded incredulously. He could not believe his teasing sally was about to be returned by yet more revelations.

"Only new blades for the plows. They are in the stable rafters." Not daring to look at him, Verony took a deep breath. She decided it was wiser to make a clean breast of it all at once. "And replacement parts for the looms, behind the wine vats in the cellar. Most of a tanning press is down there, too. It was never finished, but could be quickly if you decided you wanted it." Her voice trailed off, smothered by the astonished exclamations of Curran, Sir Lyle and the other men who had been listening avidly to the whole exchange.

"Thank the Lord for those blades," the old knight muttered. "I thought for sure we would have to send to the Earl for aid before the plowing could begin."

"The blacksmith will be glad to know of that press," another said. "He was complaining just yesterday that there wasn't enough toughened leather."

Taking hold of her shoulder with one large hand, and her chin with the other, Curran forced her to meet his gaze. "You did all this without your father's approval?"

Verony nodded miserably. She had no doubt what he or any other man would think of her presumption. Women were expected to be docile, obedient and utterly submissive. They were passed from the control of a father to that of a husband without ever being permitted to make even the slightest decision ordering their own lives. All their time, thought and effort was supposedly devoted to family and church. Regarded as somewhat more valuable than dogs or horses, but certainly far less so than male children, they were looked upon with either indulgence or callousness, depending on the whim of their master. Never, under any circumstances, were they expected to take matters into their own hands to improve their lives and that of the miserable peasants surrounding them.

"He had no idea what you were doing?" Curran persisted, astonishment giving his voice a hard edge.

Verony's self-control, so sorely tried over the last few hours, snapped. "'No," she exclaimed angrily, "he did not! He and his men were far too busy fighting, drinking and making life miserable for any woman unlucky enough to come within their grasp. They could hardly be bothered to hunt meat for our table, so busy were they planning grand campaigns, let alone give a thought to the well-being of the serfs. Yet just once let a meal be served late or poorly, let fine clothes not be ready to wear to court, let iron be used for farm implements rather than yet more weapons, and their heavy hands fell on everyone." Lowering her head to hide the sheen of tears in her wide, deep eyes, Verony murmured: "So I traded off goods I thought he would not notice missing, lied about the production of metal from our mines, falsified even the crop tallies to keep him from starving our people." She shrugged hopelessly, no longer even feeling Curran's grip on her. "Add that to my list of crimes if you must, my lord. But surely it is already long enough to justify what you intend."

"What I intend?" Curran questioned, so softly that Verony glanced up in surprise. Her dark-indigo gaze was caught and irresistibly held by his own. Fascinated, she watched the play of emotions across his rugged face. Whatever else he might be, Curran d'Arcy was no stranger to tenderness. A smile curving his hard mouth, he brushed a gentle hand across her cheek. It came away wet. Contritely Curran tipped her head back farther, eyes riveted on the tears trailing silently down her alabaster skin. He cursed softly under his breath, a far different sound from what he had hurled at the recalcitrant mill gear.

"Since you have so speedily solved this problem for me, my lady," Curran said quietly, gesturing toward the new gear already being moved into position, "we will go and talk now. It seems there is even more for us to discuss than I thought." Taking her arm, he guided her outside, not releasing her as they started back up the path to the keep. Sir Lyle, Verony noted distantly, did not accompany them.

They walked in silence for some little way until, approaching the bailey wall, they spotted a large crowd gathering outside. Verony glanced at Curran in surprise, her bewilderment increasing when he muttered: "I have been expecting this."

Drawing closer, Verony was at first puzzled and then horrified to see that the crowd was made up of serfs from the demesne. They milled about silently, mostly men but with a few women and children, surveying the approach of their new lord with blank faces and watchful eyes.

"They must be here to greet you," Verony said swiftly, praying that it was so.

"Hardly that," Curran snorted, slowing his pace so that she could walk more easily. "They are here because of you."

"No!" Verony insisted, even as she feared he might be right. The peasants had neither the endurance nor the training to assert themselves for their own sakes; the struggle merely to stay alive demanded all their strength. But they could be fiercely loyal to those they thought deserving. Through her efforts to improve their lot, and the courage she had shown

41

over the last year, she had unwittingly earned their devotion. They would not stand by and see her slain, not while they could at least impress upon the earl their unhappiness with such an act.

Little details about the crowd, which she doubted Curran would notice, struck Verony forcibly. Great pains had been taken to scrub away at least some portion of the ubiquitous dirt and to don clothes which, rough though they appeared, were the best these people possessed. The women wore long, simply cut gowns of unbleached or russet wool girded at the waist and falling to their ankles. The men had put on the knee-length tunics normally reserved for church wear. Even the children, dressed like their elders, looked unusually neat and clean.

A lump rose in Verony's throat as she recognized the desperate pride that compelled her people to put the best possible face on a dangerous, even potentially deadly confrontation. More determined than ever to protect them, she took a step forward, only to be stopped by Curran's gentle but firm hand on her arm.

"I would hear what they have to say, my lady," he told her quietly, his tone making it clear he would brook no interference.

As Verony watched apprehensively, he addressed the crowd. "Is there one among you who will speak for the rest?"

A murmur ran through the little group, dying away quickly as an old man stepped forward. Verony bit back her instinctive protest. Not Father Dermond! Not the kindly, stalwart priest who struggled so hard to help his flock through the long years when England lay under papal interdict. She had known him all her life and esteemed him above any other holy man, most of whom seemed interested in nothing more than filling their bellies and taking their ease. Father Dermond's religious vocation was genuine, and his capacity for self-sacrifice seemed endless. Even now, with his stooped and bent body precariously supported by a gnarled cane, his eyes burned brightly and his voice was strong.

"These good people, my lord," he said firmly, "come out of love for one who has many times in the past put herself in danger for them." He looked at Verony gently, his own love and admiration written clear on his weathered face. "There is great concern that you may blame the Lady Verony for a crime she did not commit, and that she may therefore be unjustly punished when she is in fact deserving only of protection and care."

The crowd murmured its agreement, but Verony could no longer restrain her concern. "You are wrong to proclaim my innocence, Father. Lord Curran knows I am responsible for the poaching."

The priest shook his head sadly. "My child, you have already carried far more than your share of this life's burdens. We cannot stand by and see you assume more."

Verony opened her mouth to argue further, but Curran forestalled her. His compelling gaze swept the crowd, drawing respectful silence. "Despite the change that has occurred here, Lady Verony still regards you as her people. That being the case, it is her right to assume responsibility for your actions.

Should you truly wish to protect her, you will return now to your homes and in future you will not violate the forest laws."

"And the lady?" someone found the courage to demand. "What happens to her?"

"Aye, we can't just go off and leave her."

"She's done no harm, lord. Isn't right to blame her."

The men-at-arms, who surrounded the crowd as soon as it appeared, pressed forward. Fear ran through the helpless people, only to be eased as Curran raised his hand. "Enough. You have made your case, and I have heard it. The matter rests with me. Go home."

"Do as he says," Verony added quickly. "If you truly care for me, go now." Her voice dropped, but still rang clear. "There has already been so much suffering on this land. Do not add to it."

The crowd hesitated, but quickly accepted that there was nothing more to be done. Even on such short acquaintance, it was clear the new lord was very different from the old. Any attempt to challenge him would be at best futile and at worst disastrous. Realizing that their resistance would not serve the Lady Verony, they dispersed slowly.

Curran and his men-at-arms, whose ranks were swelled by knights drawn by word of what was happening, watched them go. Not until the last one vanished into the forest did they ease their guard. Back inside the bailey, Curran shook his head in amazement. "Extraordinary! I've never seen serfs behave like that."

"They are good people," Verony hastened to

assure him, "hard working and obedient. They will give you no trouble."

Curran grinned at her ruefully. "They gather themselves together to confront me, leaving no doubt that they hold you dear indeed, and you assure me they will be no trouble. I hope you are right, my lady." Thoughtfully he added: "I have no wish to keep the peace on my land harshly. But neither can I allow the peasants to think they have any say in my actions. . . ."

"They don't think that!" Verony exclaimed, unconsciously placing a small hand on his arm in a pleading gesture that did not go unnoticed by Curran. "Believe me, they are loyal and diligent. It is completely out of character for them to act like this. I still cannot quite believe they did it."

"I can believe it," he murmured, looking down at her gently. "They love you, to such a degree that they were willing to put themselves in danger to protect you." Leading her up the steps to the keep, he asked: "Tell me, how did you inspire such devotion? The priest suggested you had done much for them."

"I did very little," Verony murmured, blinking in the dimness of the Center Hall. "There was hardly any way to ease my father's cruelty, but when I did see a chance, I took it." Her chin lifted, showing much of the same defiance he had witnessed twice in her before. "I suppose you think it's wrong to care whether the peasants are hungry or ill, whether their work is excessive or they live in constant terror of capricious brutality. I know many fine lords insist those people out there aren't even human, but I know better. They are just like us, except that we have been raised differently. They laugh, cry, bleed, love . . . just like us. And they possess a spirit of generosity far beyond anything I ever saw at court or in the great homes. They shared everything with me, even to the extent of endangering themselves."

"I can't say I regard the peasants as you do," Curran admitted, gesturing Verony to sit down. Pouring two goblets of wine, he went on: "But I take no pleasure in hurting them." His eyes raked her intensely as he turned back to the table. "I am not like your father."

"Thank God for that," Verony breathed, accepting one of the goblets. She sipped the wine slowly, grateful for the chance to gather her thoughts. Nothing was going as she had expected. The mere fact that she was still alive and relatively unharmed was surprising enough. When she also considered her lack of confinement and Curran's remarkable courtesy, she could only wonder in bewilderment why he was acting this way. To one accustomed to gratuitous harshness at every turn, his behavior was inexplicable.

Curran watched her carefully, understanding much of her thoughts from the emotions mirrored by her lovely face. The sheer beauty of the girl distracted him somewhat, but he managed to concentrate well enough to at least guess most of what she was feeling. When he thought she had recovered enough from her worry over the peasants, he said gently: "Tell me how you came to be in the forest."

Verony looked at him in surprise. They sat close together on facing benches set around the main table. The hall was empty, although sounds filtered up from the kitchens indicating preparations for the evening meal were under way. So well ordered was the household that she sensed they would not be disturbed. The servants would contrive to avoid the hall until Lord Curran's business was concluded.

"Where else would I have gone?" she asked faintly. "When my father died without a male heir and our lands were ceded to the crown, I could not stay here. I knew King John would sell the estate— and me with it—to the highest bidder. Rather than submit to one of his brutish friends, I fled."

This much Curran could understand. The royal custom of selling orphaned girls and widows in marriage was a great bone of contention among the nobility. More often than not, estates went to the king's foreign cohorts, who then bled the land and its people dry. Growing opposition to such cavalier mismanagement lay behind the year-long delay in disposing of de Langford's estate. Verony was right in thinking King John had intended to sell both her and the manor to a grasping interloper who would undoubtedly have abused both. But the same men who were objecting to other royal excesses had put a stop to that, and insisted one of their own be named to the fiefdom.

"By why the forest?" Curran persisted. "Surely there were alternatives?"

"Like what? A convent? None would take me without the dowry price to buy my entrance. Or are you thinking I have some loving relatives who would have sheltered me? There are none." Verony shrugged, a gesture that revealed both bitterness and resignation. "The forest offered my only protection, and the people there gave me the only love and care I have received from anyone other than my old nurse. They took me in, shared what little they had and taught me the skills I needed to survive." A short laugh bubbled up in her throat. "I thought I knew so much, but running a manor and staying alive in the forest are two far different tasks. I was so clumsy at first, and they were so patient." Her eyes fell, settling on small hands that had once been soft and white but were now red and careworn. "I will never forget their kindness, and while there is breath in me I will do all I can to help them."

"A sentiment they apparently share," Curran said gruffly. For several minutes he concentrated on his wine, until he was certain the surge of fierce protectiveness set off by the girl's story was back under control. It would not do for her to see how deeply she affected him, at least not yet.

"So what's to be done with you?" he murmured at last, almost to himself.

Verony stiffened. This was the moment she dreaded. Her grip on the cup tightened as she dared all in a final, desperate effort to survive. "You could let me go . . ."

She spoke so softly that several moments passed before her words penetrated Curran's own thoughts. When they did, his head shot up. "You mean back to the forest? Don't be silly. That's out of the question."

The wine she had just sipped rose to burn the back of Verony's throat. He was right, of course. No man, however even-tempered and reasonable he seemed, would free a self-confessed poacher who had stabbed him. Grimly Verony blocked out of her mind the more brutal details of her father's favorite punishments. She had paced the floor of her room too many nights, helpless to aid the tormented prisoners who screamed their voices away in the dungeons below, not to be fully aware of how much a human being could be made to suffer. But she understood instinctively that Lord Curran did not go in for that sort of thing. When he killed, as he undoubtedly had many times, it would be done cleanly. Telling herself she had that much to be grateful for, Verony silently awaited his verdict.

When it came, such as it was, she stared at him in astonishment. "I'll have to think about it," Curran said tiredly. A smile softened his features as he gazed at her. "You pose quite a problem, my lady. But don't worry, I'll come up with something. In the meantime, may I suggest you take supper in your room and retire early?" His gaze narrowed. "You could do with some extra rest."

He was serious, Verony realized in hopeless frustration. Curran meant to leave her dangling at least another day while he decided her fate. She gazed at him in bewilderment, wondering if she had been wrong about his character. Was this cruelty deliberate, or did he honestly not understand that she would rather get her punishment over with?

No answer was forthcoming as Curran gravely escorted her to the foot of the stairs, bidding her a polite good night before going off to join his men.

Chapter Four

"YOUR FATHER MET WITH STEPHEN LANGTON AGAIN," Sir Lyle said, shifting himself more comfortably on the bench.

Curran raised an eyebrow. He was not surprised that the faithful old retainer would have this news before he himself received it. Sir Lyle had served the Earl Garrett d'Arcy so long and honorably, as both friend and vassal, that he was regarded almost as a brother. His loyalty was beyond doubt, as was his discretion.

"Where did they meet?" Curran inquired, refilling his wine cup.

"At London. In the same house where they met in August, although this time only the chief barons were present."

"And did the good Archbishop of Canterbury preach the same sermon?"

"Apparently," Sir Lyle said agreeably. "He wants a curtailing of the king's power and a return to the charter of Henry I guaranteeing the rights of Englishmen."

"Everyone knows that charter wasn't worth the paper it was written on," Curran complained. "In fact, there are damn few who will swear the thing is even genuine."

"That doesn't matter," Sir Lyle insisted, eyeing the greatly diminished level of the wine pitcher. "It's just a symbol, a goad if you will, to encourage us to stand up against the king."

"I have no argument with that," Curran grunted. "Was there ever a worse ruler?"

Sir Lyle laughed, knowing they were secure enough to speak frankly. "Not in my lifetime. Old Henry was a tyrant and reprobate, but he knew what was best for the country. Richard I never liked. Too fond of the boys, if you know what I mean. And he enjoyed killing just for the sake of it. Had no interest in the day-to-day running of the country. But compared to John he looks like a saint. God help us, the man grows worse each day."

"He can't fight, can't rule, can't give justice, can't even hold on to two pence at the same time," Curran argued, his speech just a bit slurred. "He wasn't content to bring the wrath of the Church down on us, putting England under interdict and getting himself excommunicated. Just when he's finally back in the Pope's good graces, he goes merrily on his way bedding the wives of his lords against their wills, taxing excessively, betraying every confidence and bond of faith . . ."

"But," Sir Lyle interjected, "he provides us with a great opportunity. John will not live forever, but while we still have him, we would be fools not to make the best of it."

Squinting into his almost empty cup, Curran tried to make sense of this. "What're you talking about?"

"I'm saying," the old knight explained patiently, "that John has the barons so angry they will join together to force concessions from him. Concessions that will endure long after he is gone."

"That's true," Curran allowed magnanimously. "But I'd fight John just for his own sake. Even that idiot de Langford had the sense to oppose him. Although strictly for the wrong reasons."

Wondering what had suddenly brought the late baron into the conversation, Sir Lyle gazed at his young friend closely. What he saw did not please him. In the dim light of the shadowed hall, Curran looked rather the worse for wear. His eyes were bloodshot and red-rimmed. His hair was tousled, and he seemed to be having trouble sitting up straight.

Sir Lyle had chosen this time for their talk because the rest of the household was asleep. Supper had been over for hours, the servants were all retired, and the knights and men-at-arms were snoring on their pallets well out of earshot. Even the embers in the great fireplace were burning down as the last torches flared and guttered. Soon the first faint rim of light would show above the eastern horizon and a new day would begin. But before that happened, he wanted to bring Curran up to date on his father's latest news, including the warning from the earl about what might be expected to happen in the next few months. It seemed, though, that such weighty discussion would have to wait.

Sir Lyle was well accustomed to seeing men less than sober; he was no stranger to that unfortunate state himself. But never could he remember seeing Curran, if not actually drunk, then perilously close to it. Cautiously he asked: "Just how much wine have you had?"

"Who knows?" Curran shrugged broadly. "Wha' dif'rence does it make?"

"None," Sir Lyle admitted. "You are a grown man, on your own lands drinking your own wine. You can make yourself as ill as you like. I merely wondered what lay behind this."

"Since when," Curran demanded belligerently, "does a man need a reason t'get drunk?"

"Many men don't. But you have always been moderate in your habits. I can't help but think something has disturbed you."

Curran shook his head vehemently, only to stop quickly as if it threatened to roll off. "No such thing. Jus' enjoying myself."

"If you say so," the old knight muttered skeptically. He kept his silence for several moments while working on the problem of what might be troubling his lord. The answer was not long in coming. Although many hours had passed since the Lady Verony was last in the hall, her perfume seemed to linger on the air. Sir Lyle had no difficulty conjuring up the image of her youthful loveliness, unparalleled for beauty and grace despite the desperate trial she had passed through.

53

A smile lit his eyes as he regarded his friend benevolently. "She's incredible, isn't she?" he asked innocently.

"Incredible doesn't come close to it!" Curran blurted before he could catch himself. Ruefully he added: "I don't understand how she survived, and I blame myself and the whole stupid system for subjecting her to such danger in the first place. I knew months ago John would give in and cede this land to me, to try to win my father's support. I could have done something. . . at least looked for her. . . . But I never even thought . . ."

"You thought she was dead, or sheltered somewhere with people of her own class," Sir Lyle said gently. "Exactly what any of us would think. You can't be blamed for not guessing the situation."

"Maybe not," Curran muttered doubtfully, "but it's *my* situation now. I've got to figure out what to do with her."

"That," Sir Lyle suggested, "should not be too difficult." He smiled encouragingly at the young man, who scowled in return.

"'Course it is. She's a noble woman, in the best possible sense of the word. But she has no legal position, no wealth, no protection. She's completely vulnerable, and the worst thing is she knows it. I half suspect she thinks I may punish her for stabbing me, though the Lord knows it was deserved under the circumstances. Doesn't take much to figure out what she thought was going to happen to her. Greater courage and spirit I haven't seen from any man. D'you know, she actually asked me to let her go back to the forest."

"You didn't agree!"

"'Course not! Think I'm crazy? I can't understand how she survived this long, but I'm not about to see how much she could take. No . . . I've got to come up with something else. . . ."

Long ago Sir Lyle had mastered the art of hiding his innermost feelings, a trait useful in all sorts of negotiations. But this present predicament almost undid him. Struggling against the almost over-whelming urge to laugh, he suggested: "A convent, perhaps? Surely that is the logical solution."

Curran choked on the wine he had just swallowed. "That's ridiculous! Verony, a nun? You'd condemn that beautiful, spirited girl to a life of prayer?"

"She might not look at it that way," Sir Lyle insisted placidly. "After all, what alternatives does she have?"

"Plenty!" Curran growled. He knew he was being deliberately provoked but was unable to prevent his response. "You know perfectly well she isn't meant for that sterile existence. She's warm and lovely and brave. Any man would be privileged to call her . . ." He broke off abruptly, stunned by what he had almost said.

"Yes . . ." Sir Lyle drawled encouragingly.

"Never mind! All I'm saying is that something has to be done with her. She needs a position . . . protection . . ."

"She needs a man."

"Don't let her hear you say that!" Curran advised vehemently. "I've got the idea she likes to take care of herself. Oh, she accepted help from the peasants, but that was only because she had helped them in return. Let her know you think she can't manage without a man and I hate to imagine what she'd do."

"I knew a lady once," the old knight began pensively, "beautiful, intelligent, courageous . . . the loveliest thing anyone could look upon. But fiercely independent. Until the right man came along. Then she was glad enough to share her life."

Curran sighed, knowing the reference was to his mother, who had led the greatest nobles of the kingdom a merry chase before being swept off her feet by his handsome, determined father. But their marriage had brought about the union of two great families, to the advantage of both. Lady Emelie had a vast dowry, which she still administered with a firm hand, only occasionally deigning to ask her loving husband for advice. Verony had nothing, and that meant it would be hard to convince her that she was marriageable.

That she must be made to see the sense of his plan, he had already decided. Marriage was the best solution to both their problems. After all, if Verony had remained on the manor and they had met in the natural course of events, he would undoubtedly have wed her when he took over the lands. Aside from her intrinsic value as a strong, courageous woman who would breed fine sons and her proven ability to keep the estate running smoothly, their union would go a long way toward legitimizing the transition of power in the eyes of rival nobles and peasants alike.

Pride, Curran knew, was the sticking point. Without property or position, Verony would be loath to come to him. He had to devise some means of making her want their union as much as he did. "It's not going to be easy," he muttered disconsolately.

Sir Lyle shrugged. "I'm sure you'll work it out."

Curran didn't reply. He was sunk in bleary thought as the old knight took his leave. An hour later, still thinking and still drinking, Curran sighed heavily. He was no nearer a solution than when he began. From time to time, he thought he had hit on something that might work, only to have been misled by the effects of raw wine dulling his reason.

He leaned back, remembering almost too late that he was perched on a bench, and just managed to catch his balance before toppling over. That struck him as funny, and he chuckled. Such good humor called for another drink, which he downed unhesitantly. What small portion of his brain had continued to warn he was going to regret such behavior ceased to function. Verony occupied all his mind, although that was by no means the only part of his body concerned with her.

Damn but she was beautiful! He couldn't remember when a woman had so affected him. The memory of her softness clasped against him lingered sweetly. His hands had told him no lies, he realized as he considered how she had looked dressed in clothes appropriate to her station. For all the hardships of the last months, her body was ripely slender, combining the lithesome grace of a young girl with the lush promise of womanhood. It wasn't difficult to imagine how she would look ungarbed. Not even all the wine he had drunk could suppress his body's natural reaction to that thought. Knowing that she lay just upstairs, within easy reach, brought an ache to his loins that made Curran groan.

He had not been with a woman in weeks, being too busy with his new lands and not inclined to take advantage of the peasant girls who would have all too willingly obliged him. But even if he had just tumbled half a dozen wenches, he would still have desired Verony. She was under his skin, in his blood, everywhere but where she belonged: joined in the delights of love.

And she was his, Curran told himself fiercely. After all, she was part of the demesne, wasn't she? Everything and everyone on it belonged to him. Why should she be an exception? With her brutish father and her closeness to the serfs, she was certainly no innocent. Virgin, most likely, but not unaware of what passed between a man and woman. If the truth were known, he advised himself sagely, she was probably lying up there right now wondering why he hadn't tried to take her.

That was it! Curran exclaimed to himself, smacking himself on the forehead with what would normally have been sufficient force to floor him. Why had he needed so long to see it? With Verony thoroughly compromised, it should require little effort to convince her to become his wife. Should pride still force her to refuse, he would simply set himself to getting her with child, a pleasant task the mere thought of which made him grin. Once carrying, she would drag *him* to the altar. Doing some swift if foggy calculating, Curran decided he could have her safely wed by Christmas.

Highly pleased by this plan that would achieve his

ultimate aims while giving immediate release to his ardor, he rose unsteadily.

It was very dark in the corridor. Curran had to find his way largely by touch, not particularly effective in his present condition. He walked into one pillar and stubbed his toes twice before at last locating Verony's room. Easing the door open, he peered fondly within.

The braziers had been allowed to go out, and the shutters were firmly closed, so there was little light. But he could make out the silhouette of a slender shape on the bed, nestled under piles of covers. Moving closer, he gazed on the silken strands of red-gold curls spread over the bolster, half hiding her face from his amorous appreciation.

The delicate rise and fall of her breasts beneath the blankets held his attention for several moments. Only with effort did he manage to refocus on the thick fringe of lashes fanning over her apricot-tinged cheeks, and the generous mouth parted slightly in sleep. Longing to touch those tender lips with his own, Curran leaned forward. Too far. He lost his balance, toppling across the bed, tangling in the covers, waking Verony, who sat up with a yelp.

"What! Who is it? Oh! Help . . . !" Drawing breath to scream, she was stopped by Curran's hand covering her mouth.

"Ssshhh . . . it's only me," he advised kindly.

She was not reassured. The huge male body sprawled over her filled Verony with terror. She began instinctively to struggle.

Curran misunderstood her movements. He laughed deep in his throat. "I'm not usually so dense with women, sweetling. But you . . . you do things to me I don't understand." Hot, moist lips trailed down the ivory column of her neck, lingering at the vulnerable pulse points. "Ver'ny . . . so beautiful . . ."

"H . . . umph . . . what' . . . m'lady . . . ?"

Curran stiffened, abruptly aware that the old nurse had resumed her traditional sleeping place on a pallet beside Verony's bed. Damn! This was hardly the setting to convince her of his passion. "C'mon," he said thickly, "we'll go to my room."

Verony opened her mouth to protest loudly, only to be stopped by Curran's impassioned kiss. Without releasing her, he lifted her easily and carried her from the chamber.

For all Curran's speculation about the degree of her experience, Verony had in fact never been kissed before. She was, however, rapidly discovering the sensation to be everything she had imagined and then some. By the time he kicked open the door to his room and deposited her gently on the bed, her heart was racing, and her mind whirled.

Even befuddled by drink, Curran was a highly skilled and considerate lover. As his hands cupped her breasts through the thin sleeping robe, his thumbs brushing over her rapidly hardening nipples, his mouth trailed a line of fire from her delicate earlobes to the corner of her mouth already aching for his touch.

Verony gasped as his tongue darted out to caress the tiny mole set at one corner of her lips. "I've wanted to do that since the first time I saw you,"

Curran groaned, his fingers unsteady as they began unlacing her robe.

Whatever this was, Verony thought dazedly, it could not be called rape. Having succeeded in stripping them both, Curran set himself to igniting every cell of her body into a fierce blaze only his possession could ease. With his hands tenderly stroking her hips and thighs, his mouth raining kisses from her erect nipples down to the very center of her womanhood, his strong, hard body pressed intimately to hers, Verony could only wonder at what she had feared.

She knew her behavior was wanton, but Curran's caresses managed to make that seem singularly unimportant. She should be fighting him, screaming for help, risking everything to preserve her honor. And she did try, at least a little. But the slightest movement brought her into even greater contact with his hair-roughened length and her traitorous body arched in pleasure. A moan broke from her when he gently parted her legs, his skillful fingers stroking upward as he murmured love words against her breasts.

Abandoning all thought of struggling, Verony embraced him passionately. Her hands caressed the bunched muscles of his back, each separate finger tip savoring the pure male beauty of him. She breathed in the crisp, sun-warmed scent of his hair, her tongue tasting the faintly salty smoothness of his skin.

A tiny dart of fear shivered through her when she felt the huge shaft of his manhood carefully probing her tiny entrance. But the gentleness he showed, and her own raging need, banished Verony's last hesitation. All pretense gone, she acknowledged that she wanted him completely, wanted to understand at last the mystery that lay between a man and woman who came to each other tenderly.

Her body arched to his, her slender legs parted, Verony breathed in deeply. All her senses more alive than they had ever been, she yearned for his possession.

Nothing. One moment Curran's fingers were gently opening her, the next his hand was stilled, his great body slumped over hers as all the strength and passion abruptly left him. Verony did not at first understand what had happened. She waited through several long breaths made difficult by the weight of him, before cautiously murmuring his name.

"Curran . . . ?"

Still nothing. He lay like one dead, utterly immobile and unresponsive.

Managing to free a hand, Verony shook him tentatively. "Curran . . ."

His answer was a faint snore. Disbelievingly, she stared at him. Vast quantities of wine far beyond any amount he had ever drunk before had at last done their work. The battle-toughened warrior lay blissfully unconscious, with Verony trapped under him.

Torn between hilarity and chagrin, she tried vainly to free herself. It took no great experience to know that come morning, Curran would not be fit company for anyone. Added to which her situation was more than a little embarrassing. If she should be found there . . .

Verony banished that thought. Better to concentrate all her energies on getting away. The waist-length tresses of her hair were caught under his torso, her breast still cupped in his hand and her legs pinned by his. Attacking one problem at a time, she tried to release her hair. After long, futile minutes during which she managed only to hurt herself, Verony gave up. Perhaps she could move Curran's arm. . . .

Conditioned to lift and wield a forty-pound battle sword for hours on end, the limb was corded from finger to shoulder by heavy muscle and sinew. Not for the life of her could Verony budge it. By the time she gave up, she was gasping for breath.

Her legs then, she thought. Free them and she could get better leverage for releasing the rest of herself. But the moment her thighs moved against Curran's, he muttered pleasantly in his sleep and drew her even closer.

"Ver'ny . . . so beautiful . . . have to take care of you . . ."

And a fine job you're making of it, she thought waspishly. Aroused to a peak of pleasure almost painful in its intensity, Verony was in no mood to sleep. But she had no choice. She certainly wasn't going anywhere, and morning, with all the problems it would bring, came quickly enough. Sighing, she snuggled more comfortably against him and drifted off.

A nasty sensation in his stomach woke Curran shortly after dawn. He opened an eye gingerly, unsure of where he was or what was happening to him. The movement was a mistake. Pain of a kind he had never before known slammed in at him, swiftly accompanied by nausea. Groaning, he hung his head over the edge of the bed and retched.

A cool hand stroked his forehead. "Easy . . . you'll be all right . . . just take it slowly . . ." The voice was soft but had an unmistakable edge of impatience.

He must be wounded, Curran decided, when with eyes once again safely closed his head was lowered back down on the bolster. The injury must be grievous to cause such agony. Yet he could remember no battle. . . .

He did, however, recall a tussle of a far different sort. Verony! Blocking out all other considerations, he sat up abruptly. The room spun, or perhaps it was the inside of his head revolving in the jellied mass his brain seemed to have become. His stomach twisted dizzily as someone hammered on his skull.

"I told you to take it slowly," Verony snapped. Wrapped in a blanket and crouched beside him on the bed, she looked little more than a child. Her cheeks were flushed, and her eyes glinted angrily. Glancing down, Curran could see her discarded night robe on the floor beside them.

"Oh, God! Verony . . . I'm sorry—" He broke off. How on earth did one apologize to a lady for taking advantage of her? That he had done so, Curran had no doubt. There was no boastfulness in the certain knowledge of his virility. From a rather precocious age he had enjoyed the company of women, and they had seemed at least equally pleased by him. But his mistresses were unfailingly experienced and wise in the ways of the world. Never had he forced an innocent, vulnerable young girl to share his bed.

Shame surged through Curran, blotting out at least for the moment his physical discomfort. What he had done was beneath contempt. He was lower than a worm. It required no effort to imagine what his father and brothers would say if they learned of his dishonor. Raised to respect and admire women, he had nothing but disdain for men who used physical strength or intimidation to enforce their will. Yet he was compelled to believe he had done just that.

Cursing himself for a drunken fool, he searched desperately for some way to make amends. "Last night . . . the wine . . . I got some crazy idea I should . . ." He shook his head sorrowfully, almost welcoming the pain he did not doubt was well deserved.

"Curran . . ." Verony began, feeling a bit more kindly disposed toward him as she witnessed his anguish.

"Let me finish," he entreated. "Don't worry about what happened. Believe me, I'll take care of everything. If I had been in my wits last night, I would have simply explained to you what must be. This only makes it more urgent." Meeting her eyes hesitantly, he repeated: "Don't worry, everything will be all right."

What was he talking about, Verony wondered? It was clear he sincerely regretted his behavior of the previous night for more reasons than simply the painful aftereffects he must be suffering. But she could not imagine what he meant to do.

"I'll talk to Sir Lyle," Curran continued. "He'll arrange for the necessary documents and the priest. That Father . . . Dermond, was it? He can perform the ceremony. We'll waive the bans, if you don't mind. I don't think we should wait any longer than we have to."

Ceremony? Bans? Verony's mouth dropped open. He was talking about getting married. To her. The two of them. Man and wife, just as though the events of the last year had never happened and she was still the eminently marriageable daughter of a noble house. Torn between the desire to laugh or cry, Verony exclaimed: "You're crazy! That wine curdled your brain. Just lie still. I'll get something to make you feel better."

She tried to slip off the bed, but Curran, even in his sad state, was too quick for her. A powerful hand grasped her wrist as he said: "I don't blame you for being upset. It couldn't have been . . . very pleasant for you. But Verony, I promise, it will be different when we're married. I'm not an . . . inconsiderate man. . . ." A dull flush darkened his high-boned cheeks as he struggled to convince her that however brutish her initiation might have been, he would make sure she found lovemaking a pleasure.

Verony's heart tightened. How did he manage to look so contrite and so handsome at the same time? With his raven hair mussed, his color grayish and his eyes looking as though an army had marched over them, he still sent shivers of desire radiating through her. He was a magnificent man, she thought wistfully. Strong, tender, noble, all she could ever have hoped for in a husband. And incredibly he wanted to marry her, despite her total lack of property and position. But only because he believed he had dishonored her. Biting her lip, Verony fought down the treacherous impulse to let him go on believing that until they could be wed. The temptation to reverse her desperate circumstances was almost overwhelming. Only a deeply rooted sense of honor as powerful as Curran's own stopped her.

Lowering her eyes, she murmured: "My lord, you mistake the situation. Your talk of marriage is unnecessary."

When he stared at her blankly, not understanding, Verony was forced to continue. "Nothing happened," she whispered, not quite managing to keep a note of regret from her voice.

Curran's bloodshot gaze widened. He shifted uneasily in the bed. "Nothing happened?"

Verony nodded, still not meeting his eyes.

"But I remember . . ." he began, breaking off as he tried to puzzle out her meaning. The truth came to him with a jolt, turning his face bright red. He remembered the ripe, sensual body pressed to his, the firm, uptilted breasts whose nipples blossomed in his mouth, the long, slender legs glowing like alabaster. He remembered his own intense excitement, the girl's hesitant but unmistakable response, the fierce sense of joy that had filled him as he moved to possess her. Then nothing.

Acute embarrassment surged through him, banishing the relief he should have felt. A few minutes before, when he was berating himself for a contemptible dolt, Curran would not have imagined he could feel worse. But he had not then discovered that remorse over ravaging a helpless woman was equaled by shame over having tried and failed. Impaled on this two-pronged horn of mortification, he hung his head.

Verony took advantage of his preoccupation by leaving the room. She sensed Curran needed some time alone, and she wanted to be back in her own chamber before the household became fully active. But her hope of regaining her own quarters unseen was not to be realized. A small gasp escaped her as she encountered the shape of a knight leaning against one wall of the corridor.

"Good morning, my lady," Sir Lyle said pleasantly, as though it was the most normal thing in the world to find her thus.

Taking refuge in bad temper, Verony snapped: "You are ever surprising me, Sir Lyle. Do you spend all your time skulking about?"

"No," he informed her good-naturedly.

His gentle smile made her regret her waspishness. Contritely Verony said: "I'm sorry. I'm just a little . . . confused this morning. . . . If you will excuse me, I was just going to . . ."

"To dress?" Sir Lyle interrupted. His tone was still pleasant, but with an undercurrent of sharpness that left no doubt he understood the meaning of her presence in the corridor at such an early hour and in such inappropriate garb.

Verony flushed, but still managed to hold her head high. "Lord Curran," she said calmly, "could use your attentions better than I, my lord. He is not well."

Sir Lyle snorted. "I should think not, given the quantity of wine that boy swallowed. And him not used to it. He's never been a drinking man, and somehow I don't think he'll become one now. But he will hurt for a while. Do him good," he concluded flatly.

"I doubt Lord Curran would agree with you," Verony said, barely suppressing a grin. She went to move past the old knight, only to hesitate. Impulsively she asked: "Have you no concern at all about what happened last night, Sir Lyle?"

"None, my lady," he declared succinctly. His expression softened as he explained: "You see, I've known Lord Curran all his life. And I've no doubt at all that drunk or sober he's just not capable of harming a woman. So that being the case, I figure whatever happened is between the two of you." A laugh crinkled his eyes. "You'll work it out, I'm sure. To all our benefit. But perhaps I had better see to the lad, just in case you're impatient for his company."

Bowing gracefully, Sir Lyle took himself off, leaving an astonished Verony to wonder if she had mistaken the glint of approval in his gaze.

By midmorning she had bathed, dressed and placated Hilda, who had woken panic-stricken to find her missing. With that done, she was at a loss as to how to occupy herself.

Curran had not yet put in an appearance, leading to much jocular ribbing on the part of his men. Their ribald talk ceased when Verony entered the hall.

Nodding at her respectfully, they hastened off about their tasks.

A rueful smile touched her lips as she realized the events of the previous night were hardly a secret. Yet no one seemed inclined to condemn her for what everyone must presume had happened. On the contrary. She was now considered to be under Curran's protection and was treated with the utmost regard.

Certainly the servants were well disposed to accept her initially hesitant and then more assured guidance. Without even being aware that she did so, Verony was slipping back into the daily routine she had followed before her father's death. Only this time supervising the household was a pleasure rather than a struggle.

The steward, trained by Curran's mother, seemed relieved to once again have a lady in charge. He cordially persuaded Verony to allow him to escort her around the manor so that she could evaluate the few changes that had been made and decide what else needed to be done. By the time Curran emerged from his chamber, Verony had set several women to weaving on the new loom and had helped set up the tanning press, after first determining that he had already approved such action. She looked forward to telling him all that had been accomplished, but was prevented from doing so by his foul mood.

Though he joined his men for supper, a meal Verony shared with them, Curran neither spoke nor looked at her. He sat morosely at the head of the table, picking at his food, and refused the offer of wine with a snarl. No sooner were the dishes removed than he went back upstairs, leaving his men to glance at each other uneasily.

Verony did not linger after him. Hurt by what she regarded as his coldness, she told herself he could be as childish as he liked. She didn't care. Going off to bed, she tossed and turned for a while. But the upheavals of the last few days quickly caught up with her and she slept soundly through the night, enjoying dreams she would later blush to remember.

Chapter Five

"THE NORTH FIELD WAS SOWN IN BARLEY LAST YEAR, my lord," the village elder explained. "So it lies fallow. The south field is seeded for wheat, may it please your lordship."

Curran nodded absently. He bent to pick up a clod of soil, pressing it between his fingers. Dark and moist, it crumbled easily. Satisfied, he nodded at the man who watched him so anxiously. "The land is well cared for."

"Aye, lord, we have done our best. All manure is gathered for fertilizer and we bring marl from the south to spread twice a year. That was the Lady Verony's doing. She understood why it was good for the crops and arranged the shipments."

"The Lady Verony," Curran noted drily, "must have kept very busy."

"Aye, sir. From the earliest age, she worked day

in and day out, dawn to dusk. Always cheerful and wise, always helping us. There isn't a man, woman or child on this land who doesn't hold her in the greatest esteem. May the good Lord bless and watch over her."

Though the words were said courteously enough, Curran did not miss the hint of warning. He would hardly be able to, considering that he had been receiving essentially the same message all day. In the hours he spent walking and riding over his land, he was informed over and over that the Lady Verony had made this improvement and that refinement . . . had arranged for these tools and those supplies . . . had advised on ways to improve the yield of crops, the fertility of livestock, even the health of the peasants themselves.

"Got us to whitewash the cottages, she did," the elder explained, pointing at the neat array of huts clustered just beyond the fields. "Couldn't see the sense of it myself. But when it was done, and everything swept out and kept tidy, there were less vermin. After a while, it began to seem that fewer people got sick. When she convinced us to carry the waste further from the houses and wash the clothes more often, there was less fever. 'Course, one thing might not have anything to do with the other."

His tone made it clear he believed otherwise. The Lady Verony was sage and trustworthy. Because of her, there was less illness and fewer people died. Children who would never have seen their first year lived to the joy of their parents. Daring her father's rage, she had worked hard to improve the life of her people, and they loved her for it.

The lady, Curran thought grimly, inspired strong feelings. Not the least of which was admiration. Her management of the estate would have merited great respect under any circumstances. But considering that she had at every step to combat her father's callousness and brutality, her achievements were nothing less than remarkable. He had expected to find barren fields, exhausted land and sullen serfs who would mulishly oppose him at every turn. Instead, he found the promise of good crops and hard-working people who showed themselves quite willing to cooperate with him, given the single proviso that he not harm their beloved mistress.

And all that was due to the lady he could not bring himself to face. All the last week, since that debacle in his bedchamber, he had studiously avoided her. Yet not for an instant did he manage to think of anything else. Beautiful, seductive, tantalizing Verony haunted him day and night. In the keep, he was eternally conscious of her graceful movements, the scent of her perfume, her soft laughter as she moved among the servants, competently overseeing every task.

Outside in the fields, where he finally sought refuge, her name was on all lips. He could no more force her from his mind than he could stop his body's incessant yearning for her. Having recovered from his embarrassing failure to compromise her, he was increasingly desperate to repair his botched proposal.

His men sensibly kept away from him. His temper was strained to breaking and he was liable to lash out at the slightest provocation. Only Sir Lyle main-

tained a patient watch over him, unobtrusively seeing to it that he ate and slept regularly. In this he was
aided by Verony, who quietly instructed the kitchens
to prepare Curran's favorite dishes, added fresh
clothes to his wardrobe and did a multitude of other
small things for his comfort.

Between the old knight and the young girl a ready
friendship had sprung up. They understood each
other perfectly without any need for words, and they
worked together smoothly out of love for Curran.
His manor might have been the happiest of places,
but for his own aching frustration.

Perhaps he could go fight somewhere, Curran
thought hopefully, only to immediately reject that
idea. He could hardly flee his own lands because an
exquisite woman held him in thrall. But neither
could he do what his body demanded and take her to
his bed. In all honor, she deserved better.

The village elder coughed discreetly, recalling his
lord's attention to matters more immediately at
hand. "The children, sir, are waiting to welcome
you."

A cluster of boys and girls, briefly freed from their
duties in the fields and workshops, stood before him.
Under the proud eyes of their parents, they chorused
thanks for the meat Curran and his men were
supplying to the village. Recognizing that Verony's
claim of great hunger among his people was not
exaggerated, he had set himself to remedy that
condition as quickly as possible. Dozens of deer,
boars and smaller game fell before their lances,
some designated for the manor kitchens but most
shared among the serfs.

Already a bloom of health could be seen on faces that had been pallid. Everyone moved with greater energy, the children in particular. They found the constant chores no hindrance to their eager games, their happy shrieks penetrating even Curran's gloom.

He smiled at them indulgently, encouraging the little girl chosen to offer the villagers' gift. In a tiny voice that gained strength as she realized the lordly giant would not harm her, she said: "'Twas carved by my father, sir, from wood my brothers found. My mother did the polishing, but I helped. . . ." Small hands thrust the cloth-wrapped package at him.

Curran opened it carefully. He was prepared to graciously accept whatever might be inside, but the first sight of the villagers' offering took his breath away. The statue of a woman glowed warmly in the sunlight. So precise was the work that the beautiful features, the set of the head, even the carriage of the slender, proud body were all unmistakable. The peasant artist had perfectly captured the face and form of Lady Verony.

"Do you like it?" the little girl whispered, daring greatly.

"Y-yes," Curran managed to get out. Unconsciously he turned the statue in his hands, almost as though he was caressing the woman herself. An idea began to form in the back of his mind.

"I hope you don't object, my lord," the village elder said cautiously. He thought he understood what lay behind the young lord's disquiet, and he wasn't absolutely sure they had acted wisely. Suppose he took offense at what might be regarded as presumption?

"No . . . I don't object. . . ." Curran said slowly, mulling over the thought that had just come to him. A tentative smile creased his handsome features. "I don't mind at all." Turning to the artist, he said sincerely: "You are highly talented. Even at court I have not seen work to equal this. My thanks."

A great sigh of relief rippled through the crowd. Freed of their last fear regarding this man, the people broke into smiles and laughter. Curran, who suddenly saw the solution to his dilemma, readily joined in.

By dusk he was back at the keep and searching for Verony. He found her in the kitchens, seeing to final preparations for the evening meal. She looked up, surprised to see the man who was constantly in her thoughts but rarely in her sight. "My lord . . ."

"Come away from there," he said, seizing her hand and leading her toward the door. "The servants will finish up."

Delighted by his sudden desire for her company, Verony had no wish to argue. But she did regret his timing. Trust Curran to find her tired and disheveled, in wrinkled clothes with a smear of flour on her nose. Using her free hand to unobtrusively tidy herself, Verony trailed after him.

At this time of day, there were few places in the keep where they could be alone. But Curran managed nonetheless. His guess that the chapel would be empty proved correct. Guiding her inside, he shut the door firmly behind them.

For a moment he did no more than stare at her,

letting his eyes drink in the loveliness of red-gold hair, sparkling indigo eyes, perfect skin and a figure whose beauty was in no way disguised by her forest-green tunic and amber mantle.

Under his scrutiny, Verony flushed. She had no idea what he wanted, but she was determined to make the most of this opportunity. Empty, frustrated nights had convinced her she would be a fool to do otherwise. The memory of his passionate caresses and her own unbridled response gave her courage.

Taking a step toward him, she said softly, "I have missed you, my lord."

Curran's smile faded. His expression was serious, his hands gentle as he drew her to him. "And I have missed you, my lady. For too long."

His dark head blotted out the light as he bent to kiss her. Their lips touched tentatively, barely brushing. Verony trembled as a fire ignited within her, threatening to rage out of control. Curran's breath grew labored, so intent was he on restraining the full force of his desire. Determinedly, he reminded himself he was bent on persuasion rather than seduction. There would be time enough for that when he had her safely wed.

Drawing back, he muttered thickly: "You intoxicate me, Verony, far more potently than any wine."

She took a deep breath to still her own raging need before grinning up at him mischievously. "With less destructive effect, I hope."

"With quite the opposite effect," he assured her. The truth of these words struck him forcibly. Her nearness and that single fleeting kiss were enough to arouse him achingly. Thinking it wise to put some distance between them, he led her to a bench against one wall.

Verony sank onto it gratefully. Her knees shook, and her legs threatened to give way. Even as she marveled at the impact he had on her, she wondered how quickly they could contrive to assuage the yearning she was now sure pounded through them both. Nothing in her training had prepared her to tell a man she wished to be his mistress.

Curran did not help her. He was too busy grappling with his own thoughts. Knowing he had to strike just the right note with her robbed him of the natural eloquence he showed in every other situation. As dumbstruck as a young boy, he faced her warily.

"Curran . . ."

"Verony . . ."

They broke off, laughing self-consciously. Curran was willing enough to let her go first, anything to gain himself more time. But Verony deferred to him. Sitting with hands clasped tightly in her lap, eyes lowered, she waited for him to speak.

Confronted with what was easily the greatest challenge of his life, far beyond any battle or political intrigue, Curran drew on his deepest reserves of courage. His face pale but composed, he said the words he had never thought to utter with only the barest tremor. "Verony, I want you to marry me."

Her head shot up, indigo eyes darkening in disbelief. Not that again! Vexed that he should return to such an impossible issue just when she thought they were making some progress, Verony snapped: "If you have dragged me from the kitchens to be the butt of a tasteless joke, I will take my leave. Your humor is wanting."

Curran drew back slightly, an angry flush darkening his cheeks. "This is hardly a joke," he said stiffly. "I am not in the habit of asking women to marry me."

"Obviously not, since you don't even know *who* to ask!" Tears scalding her eyes, Verony jumped up. "I won't listen to this . . . I can't . . ." She turned to flee, but Curran, having come this far, could not let her go without at least making her realize he was serious. Catching her around the waist, he set the angry young girl firmly on his lap.

"You will listen, whether you want to or not. This is far too important to both of us for you to just run off." Tightening his grip on the squirming bundle of delicious femininity, his voice softened. "First, let's get one point clear. I am absolutely sincere about this. I've given it a great deal of thought, in fact I've hardly been able to think of anything else all week. Certainly an argument could be made against our marriage, but there are far more compelling reasons why we should wed. And soon," he added huskily.

"What reasons?" Verony demanded, trying hard to control the devastating effect of his nearness. Held so closely, it was impossible to ignore the sun-warmed scent of him mingling with the aroma of horses and leather, the heat radiating from his lean, powerful body, the iron strength of his arms clasping her so fiercely. She had no doubt he could feel her pounding heartbeat, perhaps even sense the growing languor of her body as she yearned to yield to him utterly.

Curran took a deep breath, fighting to bring his raging passion under control. He knew he had to speak clearly and reasonably if he was to have any hope of convincing her.

"You will agree," he began slowly, "that I am rightly expected to marry now that I hold so much land?"

Verony nodded grudgingly. She didn't really want to talk, but since her true desires could hardly be fulfilled in the chapel, she was willing to listen.

"Would you inflict some whey-faced court lady on me?" he demanded, only half mockingly. "Some pretty but brainless twit who will care for nothing but her own comforts? How many months do you think it would take for such a wife to destroy all the good you have done here? Why, the manor would be falling down around our very ears before my first heir was born."

Mention of Curran's child made Verony stiffen. The thought of another woman bearing his son or daughter was acutely painful to her. Upset by her own vulnerability, she sought refuge in dissembling. "Many young ladies are well trained in estate management. Your concern on that score is quite unnecessary."

Curran sighed. This was going to be even harder than he had thought. She was the most stubborn woman! A faint smile curved his mouth as he considered how, after marriage, he would woo her to greater docility.

"Perhaps you are right," he allowed, pleased by the glare that provocation earned. Soothingly he added: "But you have something to give which no other lady can claim: a dowry I consider vitally important to the welfare of this estate."

"*Dowry?*" Verony exclaimed, struggling to sit upright in his arms. "I don't understand what you mean. I have no dowry."

"Yes, you do, sweetling. Not property or wealth, but something just as important that can make my life pleasant or difficult according to your whim."

Now thoroughly bewildered, Verony stared at him. The gray-green eyes were as light as the sea on a calm summer day, which she already knew to mean he was in a good mood. The mouth she longed to touch with her own curved in a gentle smile that gave no hint of duplicity. His hands on her were firm but gentle, and the hard, male body pressed to hers showed only desire that was very much returned. Nothing about him suggested he was mocking her, or seeking to trap her in some way. Yet his words made no sense at all.

So absorbed was she by Curran's strange behavior that Verony did not notice when he reached into his tunic to withdraw a small package. He handed it to her, urging that she look inside. "Perhaps if you see what the peasants gave me today, you will understand why I speak of your dowry."

No nearer to understanding him, she nonetheless did as he said. A small gasp escaped her as she studied the statue. The loving care with which it was made brought tears to her eyes. "I am not worthy of this," she murmured brokenly.

"You are worth far more," Curran insisted. "The statue is only a symbol of something far greater." Gently he raised her head, compelling her to meet his loving gaze. "You hold the loyalty and trust of your people. They would do anything for you, even to risking their own lives. That is the dowry I wish from you." Tenderly his tanned finger stroked her cheek, finding its way to the tiny mole beside her lips. "What will it be, my heart? If you will not wed me, I must send you away lest I dishonor us both. How do you imagine your people will react to that? Surely they have too much sense to rise against me directly, but they can oppose me at every turn, break the forest laws, betray me in a thousand small ways. I will have no choice then but to rule harshly, hanging the worst offenders and hacking off the hands or arms of the others. Is that what you wish?"

Ashen-faced, Verony shook her head quickly. Such subversion and consequent brutality were just what she wanted to avoid.

"Then it need not happen," Curran assured her. "With you at my side, I can keep the peace gently. The people here will accept my rule and, in turn, I will be able to treat them well. It wants only your agreement."

Verony knew he exaggerated the case. The thought of having to leave her land and people was a cold stone in her heart, but before she went she could talk privately with those peasants most respected by their peers. Some understanding might be reached whereby opposition to Curran was minimized. But there was still a chance that some of the horrors he predicted could happen. Desperately wanting to believe him, she whispered, "You truly mean this? You really think I have something of worth to give you?"

"Something no one else can ever give me," Curran agreed vehemently. Sensing victory, he allowed himself to tenderly nuzzle her throat as he muttered: "Marry me, Verony. For both our sakes and the sake of all the people on this land. Be my wife."

His throaty plea and the fire his caresses unleashed within her sent hope surging through Verony. She turned to him lovingly, meeting his passion with her own. "Oh, Curran, I do so wish to share your life. I thought . . . since you seemed to want me . . . I thought I would be your mistress. Never did I let myself dream we could marry."

"Mistress? Did you think I would be satisfied to have only your body? I want all of you. Your spirit, your intelligence, your courage that could put any man to shame." A teasing glint darkened the eyes that caressed her gently. "Besides, I wish our children to be my heirs. No doubt we shall have remarkable sons, my lady, fiercely proud and independent."

Through tears of relief and happiness greater than any she had ever known, Verony still managed to answer him provocatively. "And what about our daughters, my lord? Do you count them worth any less?"

"On the contrary," Curran assured her hastily, "I shall value them all the more, especially if they have red-gold hair and their mother's astonishing eyes. But," he added as his hands moved up to cup her breasts, "I will need sons first, to help me protect our lovely girls." Lean, skilled fingers teased her nipples as he murmured: "Does all this talk of children mean you agree to wed me, my lady?"

Shivers of delight darting through her drove Verony's final doubts from her mind. "Y-yes . . ." she gasped, "oh, yes!"

A triumphant growl broke from him as his mouth closed on hers. In the dimly lit sanctuary, they came to each other joyfully, giving some slight release to their ardor as they counted the hours until they could be fully satisfied.

Chapter Six

How LONG DID IT USUALLY TAKE TO ARRANGE A
wedding, Verony wondered two days later as she
watched Hilda put the final touches on her marriage
robes. Surely few had been organized more quickly?
Barely had she and Curran left the chapel than their
intentions seemed known to everyone. From the
lowliest scullery maid right up to Sir Lyle, the entire
manor threw itself into fervid preparations for the
marriage.

Since there would be no family present on either
side, the ceremony itself would be fairly simple.
Father Dermond had already drawn up the nuptial
agreement, which Curran—in his position as both
groom and Verony's de facto guardian—signed for
them both. With his signature in place, he had
insisted she read the terms. Verony paled at the
memory of all he had ceded as her bridal gift; large

tracts of land, the taxes on two ports within his holdings, a mill and even a house in London he promised they would shortly visit.

She had tried to argue him out of it, saying his gifts were far too much, but Curran was adamant. He understood too well how she must have felt to be stripped of all property and wanted to make sure she would never again know such vulnerability.

For her part, Verony had spent the last two days laboriously stitching a shirt for Curran from the finest linen woven on the estate, intricately embroidering the cuffs and collar with ancient symbols of good fortune. Watching the slender form bent hour after hour over the meticulous sewing, Hilda had bitten her tongue to keep from suggesting a bride might be wiser to get more rest or spend her energies on her own apparel. But the clear pleasure Verony took in her task convinced the old nurse to keep silent. She only smiled fondly and thanked God for the mercy of love.

Meanwhile, the kitchens were thrown into turmoil as a great feast was prepared in which everyone on the demesne would share. Thanks to the hunting skill of Curran and his men, and his open-handed generosity, there was no lack of food. Three large pigs and dozens of fowl were slaughtered, fish brought from the freshwater pond, numerous loaves of white and black bread baked, venison and boar dressed, and all manner of other dishes readied.

The keep was swept throughout, fresh rushes laid on every floor and the chimneys cleaned. The chapel was decorated with fresh flowers. Servants and retainers alike sported their finest clothes. The hall was filled with trestle tables covered with snowy linen, and even the household animals were bathed. Only one item usual to a wedding was apparently overlooked; no effort was made to prepare a bridal chamber within the keep.

There was some concern that Verony might notice the omission. But she went through the days thinking only of the joy come so suddenly into a life that had known little but danger and struggle. Nothing penetrated the haze of her happiness until the morning of her bridal. Barely had she put the last stitches in Curran's shirt and dispatched it to him than Hilda put aside her own work to admit two serving women carrying a tub. Others followed with ewers of steaming water, fresh towels and a porcelain bottle containing rare attar of roses.

Watching the elaborate preparations for her bath, the full impact of what she was about to do struck Verony for the first time. She was marrying the powerful, wealthy son of one of the most important families in England, without the knowledge of either his parents or the king himself. For all Curran's talk of her dowry, she brought no tangible addition to his holdings nor could she claim to provide any useful political alliance.

When he wed her, Curran would be linking himself with a woman who had defied the royal will and flouted all social convention, who had claimed the right to decide her own fate even at the cost of survival. The court would be aghast at such an inappropriate union, the king would be enraged, and the d'Arcy clan . . . The mere thought of their reaction made Verony tremble. It took all her courage to stand silently as Hilda and the serving women removed her clothes and assisted her into the tub.

The soft, perfumed water lapping against her silken skin relaxed her somewhat. But she was still filled with apprehension as she submitted to a thorough washing of her waist-length hair. The maids' admiring exclamations, likening her glistening curls to burnished copper, barely reached her. When they were finished, she automatically lathered herself with the jasmine-scented soap, giving no thought to the beauty of her slender arms, high, pointed breasts, tiny waist and gently rounded hips. One of the younger girls ventured a teasing comment about the night ahead, only to be cut off by Hilda who sensed her mistress' preoccupation.

When Verony was thoroughly dried, her alabaster skin rubbed with oil and her hair brushed smooth, the servants were shooed away. The old nurse reserved to herself the privilege of dressing the bride. Lovingly she dropped a cloud-soft chemise of pure white linen over Verony's head, followed by a tunic of indigo silk whose tightly fitted sleeves were fastened at the wrist by tiny pearls. A mantle of saffron velvet trimmed in sable followed.

The brush of fur against her limbs jolted Verony from her thoughts. She gasped when she recognized the rarest of all pelts brought from the northernmost countries and restricted for use only by the highest nobility. Without having to ask, she knew the sable must have come from Curran, who was already in clear league with Hilda. Between the two of them, she had little choice but to accept what they deemed appropriate for her.

The mantle was tightly girded around her waist, the belt fastened by a gem-encrusted buckle. A transparent veil went over her hair, to be held in place by a coronet. It was the sight of that ornament that finally wrung a protest from Verony. The circlet of beaten gold was one she had worn before, but now it was transformed almost beyond recognition. Curran had somehow contrived in just two days to get it set with large, polished sapphires whose deep blue matched her eyes. "This is for a queen to wear," Verony insisted, trying to stop Hilda from placing the coronet on her head.

"Would you disappoint your lord?" the old nurse demanded gruffly. "He was so happy to have it ready on time, so certain it would please you. But if you are churlish enough to refuse his gift . . ."

"N-no . . ." Verony relented, knowing she could do nothing to hurt Curran. "I will wear it."

Hilda grunted her approval and refrained from noting that she had never had any intention of allowing her young mistress to leave the chamber without that symbol of her new rank. It might take Verony some time to get used to being the wife of an earl, but Hilda could adjust to Verony's change in status with no difficulty at all.

"Now sit down," Hilda directed, *carefully*. You don't want to get wrinkled."

Verony obeyed with a rueful smile. For all that it was her wedding day, she had rarely felt more like an uncertain child. The old nurse seemed to understand her need for comfort. After slipping soft leather shoes on her mistress' small feet, she handed her a cup of mulled wine with instructions to drink it all.

"You're too pale," Hilda noted critically, "but otherwise you'll do." Privately she thought no young woman had ever looked more beautiful. Her sentiment was shared by the small group waiting in the chapel a short time later when Verony entered on Sir Lyle's arm. The sight of her radiant loveliness, made all the more tantalizing by an air of vulnerability, brought a collective indrawing of breath.

Their admiration left Verony unmoved. She was aware of nothing but the frantic pounding of her heart and the growing fear that her legs would not be strong enough to support her as far as the altar. Only the sight of Curran waiting there gave her the courage to go on.

Had any man ever looked so breathtakingly handsome and virile, Verony wondered dazedly. His raven hair was freshly trimmed around his well-shaped head, with only a single unruly lock falling across his brow. His rugged features, which could appear so stern, were gently set. Though he was slightly pale beneath his tan, his gray-green eyes glowed with fiercely tender passion.

Across the broad sweep of his chest, he wore the shirt she had so lovingly stitched beneath a tourmaline silk tunic and surcoat of midnight blue. The hilt of his dress sword, held in place by a richly embroidered baldric, was encrusted with precious gems, as were the gold bands gleaming at his wrists and upper arms. His long, sinewy legs were clad in finely spun chausses ending in boots of etched leather.

At her first sight of him, radiating unmistakable eagerness deepened by his clearly somber regard for the step they were about to take, Verony lost all consciousness of everyone and everything else. The chapel decorated with freshly cut boughs and pure-white candles, the proud retainers and men-at-arms wearing polished iron and carrying unsheathed swords as a sign of respect, even the gently smiling Father Dermond were all lost to her. She knew only the reassuring touch of Curran's warm hand as he took hers, guiding her the last steps to the altar where they knelt beneath the care cloth, a privilege traditionally reserved for virgin brides. Dimly Verony realized the surprise the appearance of that sign of purity must have caused among the congregation, which had presumed she and Curran were already lovers. She did not doubt it was present by his insistence, a clear warning that he would tolerate no speculation about her honor.

As Father Dermond completed the blessing over them, Curran slipped onto her finger the ring that would normally have been given at betrothal. Staring down at the blood-red ruby surrounded by his family crest, Verony blinked back tears. She met his loving smile with her own as they both sipped from the garlanded bridal cup offered by Sir Lyle.

With that last ritual observed, the company was free to express its approval of the union. Verony and Curran were surrounded by his beaming men, each eager to outdo the rest in wishing the new couple long life and happiness. Escorted by that raucous bunch, they proceeded to the Center Hall where a great feast waited.

Surely not even the cooks and bakers of the royal household could have put together a grander celebration in such a short time. Trestle tables set at right angles to the slightly raised High Table ran the length of the hall. They groaned under a multitude of dishes from roast pork and venison to swan and capon cooked in flaky pastry, rabbit and quail stews, polished apples and golden cheeses, breads and rolls, even a cake of dried fruits glazed with honey. Against one wall, kegs of ale, cider and mead were piled high. Servants hurried about, filling goblets and bringing in yet more food. Minstrels tuned their instruments and began the first of what promised to be increasingly bawdy songs. Outside the hall, the last wagons were just returning empty of the largess Curran had sent to the village to ensure that everyone on his demesne shared his happiness in the day.

Before she had taken the slightest sip from her goblet, Verony felt intoxicated. The rush of blazing lights, vivid colors, trilling music, chattering people, laughter, shouts, smells . . . all combined to send her mind whirling. Dazzled by that most potent mixture of profound joy and the anticipation of even greater delight to come, she could do little more than pick at the food set before her. The wine she ignored all together, except for the obligatory toasts.

Seated beside her, his eyes rarely leaving her glowing face, Curran was at once a calming presence and a constant reminder of all that was yet to be. Midway through the meal, Verony started when she realized she had made no preparations for the bedding. Usually it would have been left to the ladies of her family to prepare the bridal chamber, escort the bride to it and ready her for the night before the groom was admitted. But there was no such women present at the keep, and she doubted even as independent a servant as Hilda would have thought to take that duty on herself. A blush darkened her cheeks as she wondered how she and Curran could extricate themselves from the assembly without the accustomed ritual to ease the way.

She glanced at him worriedly, only to guess by the gleam in his sea-green eyes that he knew perfectly well what was going through her mind. Her blush deepening, Verony dropped her gaze. She kept it assiduously averted until the final course was served and the tables cleared.

That done, Curran waited barely a decent interval. When each goblet was refilled and the company settled down for some serious carousing, he rose. Drawing Verony with him, he announced matter-of-factly: "My friends, I thank you for sharing our happiness, and I invite you to take your ease here as long as you will. But I bid you excuse my lady and myself. Good night!"

The embarrassed rush of blood pounding in Verony's ears prevented her from hearing the appreciative laughter and good-natured suggestions of the company. When Curran lifted her boldly into his arms, she hid her face against his massive chest. The sounds of the hall faded behind them as he carried her rapidly away.

Pausing only to wrap Verony in a warm cloak held ready by an indulgently smiling servant, he slipped out of the keep and across the bailey. The guards stationed at the gate house nodded respectfully, restraining their ribald comments until their lord, his lady still nestled in his arms, was well past.

Walking carefully because of his precious bundle,

Curran took a narrow path leading deep within a copse of winter-gnarled trees. Free of observant eyes, Verony felt brave enough to look up. Wondering where they were going, she quickly recognized the route that had often taken her to her favorite childhood hideaway.

In the tiny, sheltered glen Curran stopped. He slid Verony gently to her feet, his arm remaining firm around her waist to hold her to him. His deep, soft voice was close against her ear as he murmured: "I found this place a few days ago. When Hilda mentioned how fond you were of it, I thought perhaps you would not object to spending our first night as man and wife here."

Verony nodded swiftly, her gaze on the small bower newly erected beneath the spreading oak trees. Made of rough-hewn logs still smelling of sap, the shelter was just large enough for lovers. Curran eased the door opened, then lifted Verony again to carry her over the threshold. Servants had already been there to light the charcoal braziers and perfume the air with the traditional thyme and rosemary. The warm glow of flames reflected off lush floor and wall coverings, piles of silk pillows and the burnished sheen of fox and sable pelts engulfing the bed.

But it was the sound of gurgling water that caught Verony's attention. She gasped as she realized the bower was patterned on the ancient Viking saunas often built directly over the place where a hot spring emerged from the earth. How many times had she sat beside it, dangling her feet in the mineral-rich warmth and wishing she could submerge herself entirely. Now it seemed that wish would be granted.

Smiling at the wantonness of her thoughts, Verony turned back to her husband. "Thank you, my lord," she murmured tenderly. "I can think of no more lovely place to become your wife."

Curran swallowed hard. The loving warmth of her eyes, the sheen of her perfect skin against which her ripe mouth pouted softly, the supple beauty of her body only lightly concealed by her robes engulfed him in a sensual daze. Even as his desire rose hard and urgent, a fierce sense of protectiveness surged through him. Never had a woman invoked such powerful feelings; never had he been so driven to give himself without reserve while treasuring everything a woman had to offer.

Aware that he could not wait much longer, and determined to make the experience perfect for her, Curran reached for his wife. With consummate tenderness, he removed each bridal garment until she stood before him clad only in the thin chemise, which hid little from his ardent gaze. Through the almost sheer linen, he could see her high-pointed breasts darkened at the tips by rosy areolas already hardening in desire, her small waist he could easily span with his hands, the ripe curve of her hips, and her slender thighs parted by a cluster of red-gold curls.

Verony bore his scrutiny with pride. She knew he found her desirable and relished the growing confidence he inspired in her own womanhood. Inexperienced though she was, it took only a glance at the lambent flames flaring in Curran's eyes, the faint tremor of his lean, powerful body to realize the extent of his need for her. Made bold by matching passion, she reached small, trembling hands toward the laces of his tunic.

In the end, Curran had to help her. She could not quite manage the weight of his clothing, and he could not bear to delay. By the time he was stripped down to his shirt and loincloth they were both laughing like happy children bent on some marvelous game.

The laughter caught in Verony's throat as she gently pushed the shirt from his massive shoulders, reveling in the touch of hair-roughened skin against her finger tips. His chest was covered by a thick mat of ebony curls tapering down his long, sinewy torso to disappear from her sight. For just an instant her gaze lingered on the thrusting bulge still hidden by his loincloth. Cheeks flaming, Verony forced her eyes downward to where dark hair covered his muscled thighs and well-shaped calves.

The sheer male beauty of her husband so enthralled her that she was barely aware of Curran raising the hem of her chemise. Only when his calloused but infinitely gentle hands stroked the silken smoothness of her buttocks did Verony grasp his intent. A low moan broke from her as he deftly removed her last garment, baring her fully to his regard.

"So beautiful," he muttered thickly. Cupping her swollen breasts, he drew her to him. Skilled fingers teased her aching nipples as his mouth claimed hers. Helpless to deny him anything, Verony's lips parted for his probing tongue. Curran tasted her sweetness avidly as her hands stroked down the long length of his back to urge his last remaining garment from him. When he understood her desire, he laughed deep in his throat. He was only too happy to oblige his eager wife whose natural voluptuousness delighted him.

Verony had seen naked men before, even some who were partially aroused. But never had she witnessed the full, driving readiness of one who meant to slake himself within her. A tiny dart of fear spread through her as Curran grasped her hips, pressing her to him intimately.

Where before there was only rampant desire, now a remnant of virgin dread made Verony stiffen. Instinctively her hands went to his broad chest, trying to push him away. "C-Curran . . . don't . . . please . . ."

He stopped instantly, allowing some slight distance between them. Soothing her with a tender caress, he murmured: "There's nothing to fear, my love. Trust me. I promise, nothing will happen until you're completely ready."

How could she doubt him, Verony thought dimly, when his every touch set off waves of fire pulsating inside her? A hot core of flame built at the center of her womanhood, radiating outward until her whole body was engulfed.

Caught between instinctive apprehension and the desperate need for something she could not yet define, Verony gasped. The sound was smothered by Curran's warm mouth as he lifted her onto the bed. Instead of laying her down amid the petal-soft furs, he sat her on the edge, tipping her back far enough so that she reclined with her feet still on the floor and her legs parted. Kneeling before her, he blazed a line of fiery kisses from her ripe breasts set off by velvet nipples down to the silken smoothness of her hips and belly. Shuddering uncontrollably, Verony tried to stop him, but Curran was not to be denied. His tongue tantalized the very core of her desire before stroking the satin skin of her inner thighs.

A low whimper of mingled dismay and need tore from Verony, inciting Curran even further. Pinning her flailing hands to the furs, he moved to engulf her most sensitive point. Undulating ripples of pleasure surged through her. A sheen of perspiration broke out on her alabaster skin as she desperately fought the vast, irresistible forces overwhelming all sense of consciousness and self. The pressure built and built until at last she could stand no more. Just when the cataclysm of pleasure seemed about to destroy her, she was seized by an explosion of ecstasy that hurled her beyond thought, reason and the last remnant of resistance.

She had no being apart from Curran, nor he from her. They were one, united as fully and surely as he joined their bodies. No sensation of fear or even pain touched the perfection of their melding. She welcomed the pulsating fullness of his possession joyfully, sheathing him in warm, moist velvet that rippled sinuously along every inch of his massive length.

Clinging to a thread of reason, only by grace of his intense care for her, Curran moved cautiously. He made absolutely certain she could accept all of him before delving within the haven she so ardently offered. Slowly, tenderly, drawing out her pleasure to the utmost, he brought Verony again to an explosion of fulfillment so intense that she screamed. Only then did Curran at last release himself, finding within her cherished womanhood a welcome more profound than any he had ever known.

Long, dazed moments passed before he recovered enough to lift her fully onto the bed and cover them both with the fur throws. Purring softly, Verony snuggled against him. Her eyelids fluttered once, twice, then were still. Curran gazed down at her tenderly. His smile lingered as he joined her in dreamless sleep.

Chapter Seven

IN THE FULL DEPTH OF THE NIGHT, VERONY AWOKE. She stirred slowly, coming reluctantly back to consciousness beneath the warm weight of the furs and her husband's body.

Curran lay with his arm around her, his chest against her breasts and their legs entwined. Memory returned hesitantly, bringing with it trembling disbelief at her own behavior.

In all the hard years of work and struggle that had made up her life to that moment, Verony had never suspected her own capacity for passion. Always she had viewed marriage as a necessary evil that, if she was no luckier than her mother and many other women, would put her in thrall to a brutal, callous male.

That men and women could find mutual pleasure in lovemaking she had heard but scarcely credited.

Until Curran set off the first stirrings of her body that merely hinted at what was to come. Yet she had still been totally unprepared for the heights of ecstasy he could drive her to or the vast reservoir of emotion he so effortlessly tapped.

Trembling, she gazed at the man who had revealed a part of herself she had never even suspected might exist. Asleep he looked younger and unexpectedly vulnerable. His rugged features were relaxed, the chiseled lips parted slightly. His hair tumbled in an unruly mass across his forehead, almost to the thick dusting of lashes brushing his high-boned cheeks. One powerful arm was thrown out over the covers, the bunched muscles and corded sinew unmistakable even at rest. The other lay loosely around her.

Daring greatly, Verony edged the cover down. Her gaze caressed his broad, hair-covered chest as she remembered how pleasant it felt beneath her touch. Almost of its own volition, a small hand reached out to stroke the sun-bronzed expanse.

When he still did not wake, Verony took hold of all her courage. She was overwhelmed by curiosity about this male being who had so transformed her. Wanting to know as much about his body as he obviously did of hers, she eased the covers from him entirely.

Sitting up, Verony allowed her gaze to move leisurely over her husband. Long of limb and torso, without an ounce of fat on him, he was broader and more powerfully built than the vast majority of men. Certainly his sheer size and strength gave him an immense advantage both on the training field and in battle. The thought of Curran fighting made her wince. In the dim light of the charcoal embers she could see a long, white scar on his chest and another on one thigh. Other, smaller marks gave silent witness to the challenges he had faced and conquered.

Considering the frequent violence of their lives, men were precariously made, Verony mused as her eyes lingered on his manhood. Even at rest, he looked unusually large. Astonishment warred with anticipation as she wondered how she had ever managed to accommodate him. Her eyes widened as that part of him that had so recently been deep within her stirred. Her breath shortened, and her body felt suffused by heat. Responses only recently wakened flexed again.

A low chuckle forced her gaze upward even as a dark blush stained her face and throat, down almost to the tips of her rapidly hardening breasts. Curran's gray-green eyes sparkled. He missed no sign of his wife's fascination or her arousal. Chuckling, he said: "Does what you see please you, my lady?"

Unable to meet his teasing look, Verony nodded mutely. She was rewarded by a deep laugh and the touch of Curran's hands warm on her shoulders. "And you please me, sweetling," he murmured gently, "far more than I would ever have thought possible."

His obvious sincerity was exactly the reassurance she needed. Grinning mischievously, she said: "If you are so well satisfied with me, my lord, perhaps you would do me some small service?"

"Anything," he informed her fervently, nuzzling

the silken skin of her throat. "You have only to name your desire, my love. I will endeavor my utmost to fulfill it."

"Good," Verony purred, hands stroking perilously close to the seat of his passion. Abruptly she declared: "I'm starved. Is there anything to eat?"

Chagrined but undeniably amused, Curran laughed. "Trust me to take care of *all* your appetites, my dear." He gestured toward a corner of the bower where a small table stood. "You should find some refreshment there."

Heedless of her nudity, she scampered from the bed. On a cloth-covered tray were joints of roasted meat, cheeses, breads and small bowls of custard dusted with precious cinnamon. An ewer of wine and another of water stood nearby beside two goblets.

Gleefully Verony turned to tell Curran of the bounty only to discover he had left the bed and was happily submerged in the mineral spring. Propped up against the natural rock formation that had been left in place when the bower was built, he grinned at her lewdly. "Bring my supper over here, wench. And be quick about it!"

Falling into his game, Verony obeyed. With all the self-possession of a fully dressed serving woman, she carried the tray to him. Deftly wielding the carving knife, she quickly sliced the joints before filling both goblets with a mixture of wine and water. Curran, still mistrustful of the more potent brew, made sure his was pale indeed.

Slipping into the spring beside him, she plucked a

slice of capon and held it to his mouth. "I hope you will find the service to your liking, my lord," she purred throatily.

Curran chewed and swallowed the meat without taking his gaze from her. What he saw delighted him. Her indigo eyes glowed and her skin had a pearly sheen an experienced man knew came from only one source. Despite the heat of the spring, her nipples were hardened peaks tempting his taste far more than any food. He sighed silently, resolving to give her more time to recover from her first experience with a man before initiating her into the long delights of lovemaking.

"This spring," Curran asked in an effort to distract himself, "has no one used it before?"

"A long time ago," Verony said, settling down in the deliciously soft water, "this was a place of worship for the pagan tribes. There is still a belief among the people here that it has healing properties. About a quarter mile behind us there is a cave where the spring also surfaces. The village ill are frequently taken there, or water is gathered in ewers and brought to them."

Hesitating, she added: "Father Dermond naturally doesn't approve of pagan worship. But he tries to understand the people's feelings and make them part of Christian worship. He has blessed the spring and water taken from it, sometimes even using it in the church."

She feared Curran might be shocked by what some would regard as sacrilege, but he merely nodded. "Father Dermond is a wise man. The old ways

105

cannot be completely forgotten, nor should they be. Especially while England was under interdict, our people needed all the comfort they could get."

A shiver rippled through Verony as she remembered those terrible years, making up most of her life, when the ineptitude and mulishness of King John so sparked the Pope's anger that the entire realm was deprived of holy sacrament. Only in the last two years had priests again been allowed to say Mass and give Communion.

The people were, of course, grateful to have such rituals restored, but Verony could not help but notice a certain diminishing of fervor in their worship. After the initial terror at the interdict passed and it was discovered that life went on, some began to wonder if everything the Church had been telling them was actually true.

For all that the Pope was supposed to represent God on earth, his removal of grace seemed to have no real effect. The sun still rose, the rains still came, crops grew and children were born. There was no more pestilence than usual, or reports of devils sighted. No dreadful omens appeared in the sky, nor did the earth shake as it had been said to do occasionally in ancient times.

Inevitably, as people began to doubt the true power of their faith, they came also to question other fundamental beliefs that had guided their lives. There was a new spirit abroad in the land. From the great earls such as Curran right down to the peasant toiling in the field, men and women were asking themselves if some change might not be called for in the social order.

106

So far, this burgeoning movement was manifest only in a multitude of little ways. Some nobles, including the d'Arcys, had refused to meet King John's latest excessive demands for taxes. They said he had already wasted far too much money in his unsuccessful wars on the continent and would do better to attend to the welfare of his realm. The braver members of the merchant class, taking courage from this example, were also withholding funds.

The clergy, led by the revered Archbishop of Canterbury, Stephen Langton, had made some discrete statements about the dignity of all men and their right to protection under the law. It was rumored that in private meetings with the nobility, the archbishop spoke out more firmly, going so far as to say that the power of the king needed limiting.

At the lowest level, there were reports of tentative insurgencies among peasants on a few demesnes who sought to take advantage of the general climate of change to better their own poor lots. Though brutally crushed, such rebellion deeply concerned every man of property. Curran was no exception. Verony knew he had hurried their marriage in part out of determination to keep the peace among his own people.

That he would succeed she did not doubt. Besides being a good and capable ruler, Curran had the advantage of replacing a brutal, callous lord who had done the serfs only harm. The comparison alone would make them cleave to the young earl, especially now that she was his lady. But as to what would happen in the kingdom as a whole, she could not begin to imagine. She was certain only of her wish to know more, and guessed there was but one place where such knowledge could be gained.

Sipping her wine, Verony eyed her husband above the rim of the goblet. Softly she asked: "Will we go to London soon?"

Luxuriating in the hot, foaming water, Curran did not respond immediately. When he did, it was with obvious regret. "We must go in a few months. Much as I would prefer to stay here, there are matters at court that cannot be ignored."

"You will take me with you?" Verony demanded hastily. No sooner were the words out than she bit her lip, wishing she had been more diplomatic. There was still much she did not know about Curran. Perhaps he was one of those men who needed to be coaxed and cajoled into granting any favor. What if he took umbrage at her presumption and decided to leave her behind . . . ?

Opening one eye, Curran regarded his wife balefully. "I'm not sure the court could cope with you just now, my lady."

In the next instant, as the color fled from Verony's face, Curran realized she had taken his teasing to heart. Contritely he reached out to draw her into the circle of his arms. "You are so beautiful," he murmured, nuzzling her throat, "so radiant. You will dazzle all the lords. No one will be able to remember why he is there or what he meant to be doing. Only I, accustomed by then to your charms, will be immune and therefore able to carry the day."

"Immune?" Verony squealed, her good humor swiftly restored. "If you expect to tire of me so quickly, my lord, perhaps I should just take myself off right now."

"Try it," Curran growled, "and you will not get far." His hands slipped beneath the water, tantalizing the heated smoothness of her skin. "Particularly not in your present delightful state of undress."

Remembering his determination to go slowly with her, Curran abruptly broke off his caress. But he did not remove his arm. Drawing her with him, they both reclined in the foaming water, feeding each other choice bits from the tray and talking softly.

As Curran spooned the last morsel of spiced custard into Verony's mouth, she stirred against him enticingly. It was all well and good to feed one's stomach, but she was becoming impatient with his restraint. Small hands caressed the bunched muscles and flat planes of his hair-covered chest, finger tips just brushing the hard ridges of his hips. She was rewarded when Curran leaned forward to lick an imaginary crumb from the mole beside her mouth.

"I am still hungry, my lord," Verony whispered huskily.

"So am I, my sweet," he admitted, lifting the shining globes of her breasts to suckle her gently. A taut breath rippled from Verony, only to break off as he teased: "Would you have me go back to the keep for more food?"

Sharp nails digging into his thigh, she countered: "Would you torment me, my lord? Deny me what we both so clearly want?" To prove her words, Verony allowed her hand to drift upward, cupping the heavy pouch of his manhood before instinctively skillful fingers stroked his arching tumescence.

"I would deny you nothing," Curran groaned, recognizing that the time for teasing—and for restraint—was past. Grasping her narrow waist, he lifted her almost clear of the water before setting her on the very tip of what she desired.

Verony gasped as his mouth closed over hers, his tongue probing the dark, moist recess with the same rhythm of his manhood pressing against her softness. Coming into her only the slightest way, Curran waited, patiently nourishing his young wife's passion until she could receive all of him.

There in the ancient, hallowed spring, nestled in the arms of her husband, Verony learned more about the varied nature of love and the marvels of both her body and Curran's. Ecstasy exhausted, she drifted off to sleep, barely aware when he lifted her from the water, gently toweled her dry and snuggled them both into the fur-covered bed.

They spent two days in the secluded bower, sleeping little, eating well thanks to the discrete servants who left ample trays just outside the door, and making love in joyful abandon.

On the second night, they woke together to a world engulfed in stillness. Standing at the tiny window, wrapped in Curran's warm embrace, Verony stared out at the hushed landscape.

A sense of foreboding rose within her as she considered how deceptive the look of peacefulness was in a land on the edge of turmoil. Regretting that they ever had to leave their lover's haven, she turned quickly to her husband, losing herself and all her fears in his tender care.

Chapter Eight

"You said a 'house,'" Verony murmured accusingly. "This is a fortress."

Muffled in her sable-lined cloak, the hood pulled up against the biting winter cold, she peered out warily. Ahead loomed a massive pile of stone fronting on the ice-encrusted river and framed side and back by empty fields. Such flagrant use of space in crowded London spoke eloquently of the d'Arcys' immense wealth and power, as well as the family's deep distrust of the monarchy.

Built by Curran's father, the Earl Garrett d'Arcy, the compound was strategically placed for maximum defense. Although the arches above the narrow windows and the tiled roof dotted by smoking chimneys hinted at homey comforts, it was impossible to mistake the chief purpose of a structure designed to protect those within.

Curran studied her with concern, as he had frequently during the arduous trip to London.

"Don't be misled by appearances. This is really four houses placed together. Common galleries run through them all to make passage easy, but there is still much privacy. My parents use the house in the back, overlooking a field on one side and the courtyard on the other. My eldest brother, Mark, and his wife, Arianna, have the house on the right. The one in front belongs to those of my brothers still unwed. The other is ours, or more correctly yours, since I deeded it to you in your bridal gift."

His gaze ran over her worriedly, taking in the pallor of her skin and the slender back held rigidly straight despite the long hours in the saddle. He knew she dreaded this meeting with his family, despite all his assurances that they would welcome her wholeheartedly. Verony persisted in believing the earl and his lady would disapprove of the marriage.

"I had no idea it was so grand," she admitted softly, reaching out a small, gloved hand to him.

Across the distance separating their horses, Curran smiled. "According to my mother, it is not. She complains of the damp and drafts, the noise and dirt of London, the poor quality of the markets and the general sense of confinement. Yet whenever my father must be at court, she insists on accompanying him."

A low laugh escaped Verony, bell-like on the frigid air. "I can sympathize with your mother, for I, too, dislike London."

"Have you been here often?" Curran asked. He

hoped to keep her distracted long enough for them to enter the compound and get through the initial meeting with his family.

"Only once, more than a year ago." A hint of bitterness in her tone made Curran look at her quizzically. Reluctant to elaborate, Verony hesitated before explaining: "My father decided I should marry, so he brought me here to attract a wealthy, powerful husband. Someone who would pay his debts and help fuel his grandiose schemes. Since that was a fate I did not relish, I made myself as unpleasant as possible. Father gave up after a few weeks and sent me back to Langford, with dire warnings about what he would do to me when he returned. But he never did."

Curran frowned at the thought of his wife being spared from punishment only because of her father's death in a drunken brawl.

He remembered the beautiful, proud girl who had flitted so briefly through the court. Some had called her sullen and spoiled. Those lords foolish enough to approach her quickly felt her sharp tongue and haughty stare. Few suspected her behavior sprang from determination not to be used in the way her father envisioned. But Curran could remember his mother commenting that it could not be easy to be de Langford's child.

"This time it will be different," he promised, squeezing her hand. "There is much to enjoy in London, even now. We will go to the markets where mummers and magicians perform year-round. I'll take you hunting, with your falcon, if you promise not to ride too fast."

He knew how fond she was of the fierce peregrine she had raised from a chick. Learning of the bird, Curran was pleased to return it to her shortly after their marriage. Brought along to London with his own larger gyrs, the perfectly trained hunter would need exercise.

"And there is much to amuse you at court," he continued, "if you tread carefully."

That earned him a frosty stare. Verony had no need of his warning. She was fully aware of the volatile political climate pitting an irate, unpredictable king against his nobles. Though some semblance of amicability was still maintained, she had no illusions what it would be like at court.

"'Amuse' is the wrong word, my lord. Interest, certainly, but there is far too much at risk to be amusing."

Curran sighed. After four months of marriage, Verony still tended to ruffle her feathers when he did no more than exercise what he regarded as proper husbandly prudence.

Her delectable, sensual body distracted him so easily that he had overlooked much. But on a number of occasions he felt driven to point out that she was no longer running wild in the forest or struggling to manage a manor around her father's brutality and sloth.

Verony did not take such reminders well. Fiercely independent and accustomed to relying only on herself, she continued to take on tasks he felt were too tiring or dangerous for her, make decisions he believed should have been left to him and generally behave in a manner not in keeping with the way he expected his wife to act.

This trip to London was a good example. Any sensible woman, burdened with child, would have stayed placidly at home, content with her needlework and simple tasks. But not Verony. When her reasoned efforts to convince him she should go along failed, she declared flatly that she would make the trip whether he wished it or not.

Curran threatened to leave her locked up but finally relented. His reluctance to be parted from her—and her obvious good health—undermined his resolve. But even as he gave in, he vowed Verony had won her last battle. From now on, she was going to learn to obey as any proper wife should.

Reining in before the gates of the d'Arcy compound, Curran called a greeting. A steely-eyed veteran peered from the narrow window of the guardhouse to confirm their identity before admitting them.

The weary party dismounted in the entry passage. The men-at-arms went off hastily in search of food and sleep as the few servants they had brought with them lingered to begin unpacking the baggage carts. About to tell them that could wait, Verony was pleased when household retainers arrived quickly to take over the task. Such consideration touched her. She could only hope Lady Emelie would be as understanding of her new daughter-in-law.

"You made better time than I expected," Sir Lyle said as he came forward to greet them. Having gone on ahead to London, he was able to inform them of recent events. After clapping Curran on the back and smiling at Verony, the old knight muttered: "And a good thing, too. The court is in worse turmoil than ever. Your father just got back from Canterbury, where he saw the archbishop again. He and your mother are in their chamber, but your brothers and the Lady Arianna are about somewhere."

"You've been reprieved," Curran whispered wickedly in her ear as they accompanied Sir Lyle through the courtyard at the center of the compound. "I doubt my father has been gone more than a few days, but he and mother hate being separated. It will be a while before we see them."

When the full meaning of his words reached her, Verony blushed. The Earl Garrett and his lady were such respected, even revered, figures that the image of them locked in sweet combat was unthinkable. Particularly when one considered that Lady Emelie was in her forties, well past the age most women felt they could do without the pleasures of lovemaking. Yet even as her pale skin darkened in embarrassment, Verony had to admit that, having tasted such delights herself, she would not be eager to give them up.

Walking beside her tall, powerfully built husband, she savored the look of pleasure on his rugged face. Despite the strain of the journey and the dangers awaiting them at court, Curran was clearly delighted to be back amid his family. His smile widened even further as he spied a slender, feminine figure poised on the steps above them.

"Arianna! More beautiful than ever. I trust my brother is taking proper care of you?"

"If he isn't, I'm sure you'll quickly set him straight," the girl teased, embracing Curran warmly.

Gazing at the exquisitely beautiful creature with hair like ripe wheat, sparkling hazel eyes and a perfect figure set off by an emerald silk tunic and mauve surcoat, Verony felt a stab of jealousy. Only the silent reminder that this was her sister-in-law, wife to the eldest d'Arcy son, kept her still.

"How did you get here so quickly?" Arianna asked. "I thought you were bringing your wife. You didn't leave her at home, Curran? It would be just like a d'Arcy to do that, or at least try."

"Hardly!" Curran laughed, drawing Verony out from where she stood behind Sir Lyle. "I can't bear to let her out of my sight for a moment, let alone put miles between us."

Arianna smiled a welcome. But her eyes were cautious as she studied Verony. What she saw must have satisfied her, for the smile quickly became warm.

"You are even lovelier than Sir Lyle told us," she said sincerely. "How do you manage to look so fresh after that horrible trip?"

"I don't feel very fresh," Verony laughed, her tension easing as she recognized the offer of friendship. "In fact, I suspect a good part of England is stuck to me."

"You'll want a bath," Arianna suggested. "The serving women are heating water." Linking an arm through Verony's, she drew her inside. "Your clothes will follow. Are you hungry? I could never get enough to eat when I was carrying."

Taken aback by the other girl's swift perception of her condition, Verony did not know how to respond. So far as she could tell, her pregnancy showed very little. Certainly the all-enveloping folds of her cloak hid the slight swelling of her belly. Yet Arianna had known instantly.

"How is my nephew?" Curran asked to cover her silence. "The last time I saw him he did little but sleep and eat."

"He says several words now," Arianna informed him proudly, "and is beginning to walk. Mark, of course, thinks he's the most wonderful baby ever. He will surely bore you with all sorts of stories about his offspring's prowess." She gestured toward the Main Hall. "James and Kevin are in there along with my lord. Go and join them. Your arrival will be ample reason to celebrate."

Satisfied that Verony was in good hands, and eager to see his brothers, Curran kissed her quickly and departed. Together, the two women followed the gallery leading from one house to the other. Along the way, Arianna gave a brief explanation of the domestic arrangements.

"The kitchens and storerooms are downstairs in the undercroft. Most of the cooking and baking is done in the Lady Emelie's house, since we all gather there for supper. But I find it useful to keep a small kitchen staff for Mark and myself, because he sometimes gets home at odd hours and I never know when he will want to be fed."

Pausing to allow Verony to admire the unusually large amount of light and air admitted by the gallery windows, Arianna continued: "Each house has two storys above ground, with room for men-at-arms on the first floor and a hall and family chambers above. Water is drawn from the well in the courtyard and collected in catch pans. The stables, poultry coops and pigsties are in the fields beyond, although they could be moved in here quickly should the need arise. I know most of the nobility depends on the markets while in London, but we try to be just as self-sufficient as we are at home. I don't imagine I have to explain why."

Verony shook her head. "I knew something about the political situation before Curran and I married, and since then he has explained much more. I understand why he is here."

"Good," Arianna said, stepping aside to allow Verony to precede her into what was to be her own home while in the capital.

A quick glance around showed that the house was in excellent order. Fresh rushes lay over the floors, the walls were newly whitewashed, there was no sign of any litter or debris, and even the ceiling rafters looked recently scraped and sanded.

"Lady Emelie wanted everything to be perfect for you," Arianna explained smilingly. "She's had the servants working nonstop for days to prepare the house, especially your chamber." Mounting the newel staircase nestled into the wide stone wall, she laughed: "I can't wait to show it to you. The furnishings are magnificent."

They were indeed, Verony thought dazedly a few moments later as she stood in the center of the most luxurious room she had ever seen. Large and airy with a high, beamed ceiling, the chamber was warmed by fireplaces at either end. A raised bed ample enough for half a dozen adults held a down-filled mattress and pillow bolster. As further protection from the cold, a brocade canopy stretched over the bed, and matching curtains hung at the four corners. Two small tables stood at either side, holding candles and flint. A larger table occupied almost all of one wall beneath a window which, since it looked out over the courtyard, was far larger than those facing the street. Beautifully carved chairs and chests completed the furnishings.

A vivid tapestry hung across from the bed, and embroidered seat covers were set on the chairs and a bench beneath a window. But it was the floor covering that most amazed Verony. Instead of the customary rushes, another larger tapestry lay over most of the flagstones. The thought of walking on such exquisite work appalled her, even as she was fascinated by such imaginative use.

"That is lovely," she began, pointing at the tapestry, "but surely we are not supposed to walk on it?"

"I'm afraid you are. It's called a rug. Lady Emelie first saw them in the East and decided to use the same idea here. They are much warmer and more comfortable."

So taken was she by the thing called a rug that Verony stared at it silently for several moments before Arianna's words fully reached her. "In the East, you said? Do you mean Lady Emelie has visited the Holy Land?"

"Oh, indeed! Hasn't Curran told you? No, I suppose you haven't had time yet, being practically newlyweds." Grinning at Verony's blush, Arianna went on: "The Earl Garrett and Lady Emelie were married in the East, during the crusade of Richard the Lionhearted twenty-five years ago. My husband, Mark, their eldest son, was born before they returned to England." Hazel eyes sparkled mischievously as she concluded: "Emelie can probably be persuaded to tell you the story herself, so I won't spoil it. Suffice to say you are not the first d'Arcy bride to wed under unusual circumstances."

"I hope that means the family will be able to accept me," Verony said in a burst of candor brought on by Arianna's friendliness. "I could hardly blame them if they did not."

"Of course they will!" Arianna exclaimed, helping Verony off with her cloak. "How could you think otherwise?"

"Quite easily. After all, I brought nothing to Curran except some hope of keeping the peace among our people. Surely his parents must have expected a wife who would bring him even greater wealth and power."

Opening the door to admit servants carrying a tub and Verony's wardrobe, Arianna giggled: "Truthfully, I think the earl and his lady had almost given up hope of getting any of their sons wed. Curran and Mark showed no interest in proper young court ladies, and the other two are even worse. Their father could have forced the issue, but since he himself married for love and has never had cause to regret it, he wished his sons to have the same happiness. Until Mark and I met, it must have seemed such patience would go unrewarded."

Somewhat reassured, Verony relaxed in the steaming bath water. As the serving women laid out fresh clothes, Arianna perched on the edge of the bed to keep her company. "You must be delighted to already be with child. How far along are you?"

"About four months," Verony said, then waited for the speculation she felt must inevitably come. So far as she could determine, the child she carried had been conceived during those two blissful days in the bower. But others might presume she was breeding before she was wed.

Arianna, however, showed no such suspicion. Laughing, she declared: "So Curran has lived up to the reputation of the d'Arcy men."

At Verony's puzzled look, she continued: "I don't think there's been one in a century and a half who hasn't managed to get himself an heir within little more than a year of marriage. It's become a family tradition."

One Curran had upheld with true fortitude, Verony mused as she soaped a slender leg. Barely a day had passed since their wedding that they had not managed to find the time and privacy for lovemaking. Since learning of the baby, their intimacy had become even more passionate and tender. Under Curran's loving care, Verony had blossomed into a confident, fulfilled woman. But motherhood still remained something of a mystery.

"I don't know very much about children," she admitted softly. "I've helped birth foals and calves, but never a baby."

"Don't be worrying about it," Arianna advised. "I'm sure Lady Emelie will arrange to attend you, as she did me. She's very knowledgeable. The earl's mother taught her much about childbirth that midwives either do not know or . . ." She broke off, glancing round to confirm that the serving women had left the room. ". . . or are afraid to use."

Verony's eyes widened. This latest bit of information, hinting as it did at practices that might at the least be impious, made Lady Emelie seem all the more formidable. How could she hope to win the approval of this epitome of all feminine grace, this tower of beauty and strength to whom all deferred, even the proud, stalwart men of her family? Sighing, Verony wished vainly that she might have a little more time before having to confront her remarkable mother-in-law, even as she knew such a further reprieve was not to be.

Having completed her bath and choked down a few morsels of the delicious repast set before her, Verony dressed with great care. As Arianna offered advice and encouragement, she selected a blue silk tunic which complemented her eyes and a crimson wool mantle, a daring choice with her dark-red hair, but which lent a welcome glow to the polished ivory of her skin. For jewelry, she chose only plain brooches, a simple gold circlet to hold her veil in place and Curran's ruby betrothal ring. Arianna agreed wholeheartedly with that decision, being so kind as to say her loveliness needed no ornament. Though she disclaimed such praise, Verony was glad of the reassurance. In Hilda's absence, the old nurse having been forced by stiffened bones and painful joints to remain at home, she needed all the support she could get.

All too soon she was dressed and ready. Taking a deep breath, Verony followed her sister-in-law from the room.

With the fast fading of the winter sun, torches were lit along both sides of the gallery. Dipped in the finest quality pitch, they smoked little and gave ample light. Arianna kept up a ready stream of chatter as they made their way to the Main Hall where the rest of the family was already gathered.

Verony instinctively sought out Curran, only to find him in the midst of a group of men clustered around a tall, powerfully built noble she guessed at once must be the Earl Garrett. His years, near fifty by Verony's count, in no way diminished the unmistakable aura of virility and determination surrounding him.

Rugged features very similar to Curran's were topped by the same raven-black hair lightly streaked by silver. A thin, white scar ran across the tanned skin of his jaw and throat, disappearing into the collar of a rich velvet tabard. Though made of costly materials and perfectly tailored to his heavily muscled length, the earl's clothes were sedate. Unlike many of the peacocks at court, he had no liking for excessive embroidery, lace trim or any of the other fopperies some men had recently affected.

The gleaming dress sword at his hip was his only ornament save for the old-style gold bands at his wrists. Very few of the nobility still wore those ancient symbols of authority handed down from the Norsemen. Verony wondered if they might have been in the family for a long time, and felt a sudden flash of liking for a man who would preserve such tradition. But it was the woman at his side who most commanded her attention.

Slender and small-boned, not quite reaching her husband's broad shoulders, the Lady Emelie was nonetheless a compelling figure. Verony had no doubt of who she was, although she looked far younger than might be expected. Thick, chestnut hair hung in waves to her tiny waist. Her features were delicate, set off by large, violet eyes and perfect skin as smooth as a young girl's.

Her amber silk tunic and golden mantle emphasized high, firm breasts and gently curved hips that were slender despite the four children she had borne. A warm smile curved her ripe mouth as she laughed easily, with an inner contentment Verony could not help but recognize.

The laugh broke off when she spied the two girls entering the hall. For just an instant, Verony felt the full impact of the Lady Emelie's acutely perceptive stare. Their eyes met and locked in a moment of silent but nonetheless intense contact. Verony recognized great intelligence coupled to rare courage and fortitude. Unconsciously she projected the same qualities in the proud straightening of her back, her uptilted chin and the steadiness of her sapphire gaze holding the countess'.

Around them, Arianna and the d'Arcy men were silent. They understood full well what was happening and saw no reason to interfere. The earl had already made his own evaluation of the radiantly beautiful girl who had captured his son's heart. He was smiling even before the Lady Emelie said: "Come in, my dear. You are very welcome."

Grateful for her long skirts, which hid the trembling of her slender legs, Verony went to stand beside Curran. Putting an arm around her waist to draw her even closer, he grinned complacently. "I told them all how lovely you are, but they had to see you before believing."

After formally introducing her to his parents, Curran presented his eldest brother, Mark, who turned out to be a slightly older and somewhat gentler version of Curran himself. They were of the same height and build and had their father's features, although Mark sported his mother's chestnut hair. The two younger boys, James and Kevin, were both raven-headed and green-eyed. In their late teens, they still had some inches to grow but already showed the brawny shoulders and muscular chests of their elders. Not at all shy or fumbling like many young men their age, James and Kevin welcomed her genially, kidding Curran that he did not deserve such luck.

Before their jokes could get out of hand, Lady Emelie declared: "The cooks have labored hard and will be put out if we don't sit down promptly."

Even on such short notice, a special supper was ready to celebrate their arrival. As the family took their places around the wide trestle table, the earl offered a toast.

"I confess to some concern when Curran sent word of his marriage, but having met my new daughter, I am once more reassured as to his discernment." Raising his goblet, he said gently:

"We are very glad to welcome you among us, Verony. May you and Curran have a long life together with great happiness."

Deeply touched, Verony could only murmur her thanks. The experience of being in the midst of a warm, loving family was completely new to her. Curran had already shown her some of what she had missed during the long, unhappy years with her brutal father. But as she listened to the d'Arcys' affectionate jokes and ready camaraderie, she began to realize how rich their lives really were. Whatever might happen in the world outside, they could trust and love each other unreservedly. The knowledge that these remarkable people now regarded her as one of their own made her feel acutely humble. Silently she promised herself she would do everything possible to live up to their faith and, most of all, to Curran's.

Certainly she could share his delight as he informed the family that there was further reason for rejoicing. "My nephew will shortly not be the only spoiled infant in this family. Come May, Verony will present me with an heir."

His presumption that the child would be male made her laugh even as the family's exclamations of pleasure warmed her greatly. Only Mark looked the least chagrined, and that good-naturedly.

"My lord knows he has been bested," Arianna explained teasingly. "Our son was born ten months after our wedding, a fact which has caused far too much crowing in certain quarters." Eyeing her husband fondly, she said: "It rests with your younger brothers to equal this record."

"We'll do our best," James promised with an ingenuous leer.

"But not for a while yet," Kevin chimed in. With the natural charm all the d'Arcys seemed to have in abundance, he added: "Since the two loveliest ladies in the kingdom are already wed, poor James and I will have to look long and hard to find anyone suitable."

"And you'll enjoy every moment of the search," Curran snorted, bringing laughter all around.

Inevitably, the talk turned to politics. Accepting a slice of pigeon pie, Arianna asked: "How is the archbishop? Still as determined?"

The earl nodded. "Publicly he continues to speak of the king as God's representative on earth and to refer to the sanctity of the monarchy, making it clear however that he means the institution rather than the man who presently occupies it. But, in private, he leaves no doubt that John must be bridled."

"Is it only John he wishes to restrain?" Emelie doubted. "Stephen Langton suspects all kings and has never made any secret that he thinks their power must be circumscribed."

"I think the archbishop must have a secret fondness for our scapegrace sovereign," Curran suggested. "After all, who else could rally the barons in common cause?"

"That's true," Mark agreed laughingly. "England's nobility has always preferred conflict to agreement. Put two lords together and they will argue everything from the color of the sky to the exact measure of a boundary. It's a wonder old William ever managed to get them over here. I'm surprised they didn't fall to blows on the Normandy beaches, fighting over who was to board the ships first."

"They may be a shortsighted and rowdy lot," Earl Garrett agreed, "but they have no trouble identifying their own interests. John, God bless him, has offended everyone more or less equally. That's a rare talent in any man. In a reigning monarch, it's a gift we would be foolish not to use well."

"Timing is the crucial element," Curran said, wiping his mouth on one of the squares of linen provided for that purpose. "Once the barons are fully unified, I doubt they could be held together very long. We must be ready to strike without delay."

Bemused by the array of comforts she had never before imagined, let alone actually seen, Verony had some trouble following the talk. In addition to the cloths, there were circles of glazed pottery at each place on which the food was set after being selected from serving platters. Small knives of beaten gold lay beside each plate. These were used for cutting and spearing choice morsels.

Despite the late season, when even the noblest households depended heavily on spices to mask the gaminess of aging food, everything Verony tasted was uniformly fresh. Lady Emelie clearly planned her menus carefully and ordered the frequent slaughtering of animals all year round. Certainly only the wealthiest families could afford such luxury. But the fact that others who might have managed it did not do so showed that more than wealth was involved. Only someone with an open mind who was not afraid to break with tradition could have devised such lavishness.

Busy wondering what other marvels the household might contain, it took Verony a moment to understand what Curran had just said. When his words finally reached her, she came down to earth abruptly.

"Are you saying you mean to rebel against the king?" she asked in a voice little more than a whisper.

Seeing her white face and strained manner, Curran longed to reassure his wife. But he could not lie. "We hope it will not come to that. If all the barons join with us, John will have no choice but to give in. But if it comes to an armed conflict, we will not retreat."

"But your oaths of fealty . . ." Verony began, only to break off as Lady Emelie insisted: "The king's utter disregard for his own responsibilities has made those oaths void. How can honorable men be expected to follow a weakling knave who has brought only shame to the crown from the day he first claimed it?"

Four months of living with Curran, who discussed all manor business with her and made it clear he expected to be challenged when she believed him wrong, gave Verony the courage to persist. "There have been poor kings before, even evil ones. Yet oaths were still respected and loyalty maintained. What has changed now?"

"What has changed," the earl said quietly, "is that now men are more angry than afraid. It used to be that the Church told us to obey our kings, who in turn obeyed the Pope. Believing that to do otherwise would displease God, we suffered all manner of royal abuse. But since the interdict, we have learned that God's displeasure, if it is in fact the same thing as the Pope's, shows itself in strange ways indeed. Since no calamity befell us then, it is reasonable to expect it will not now."

"But since John has submitted to Rome and got himself back in favor, isn't it likely that Pope Innocent would at least threaten to excommunicate any who rebel against him?"

"Innocent is no fool," Curran insisted. "He's fully aware that his excommunication of John and subsequent reinstatement did nothing but weaken the church in England. Papal wrath is no longer the weapon it once was. Rather than risk a total breakdown of holy authority, he will tolerate much."

"If you are right," Verony considered, "and neither the Pope nor the barons will support John, then what is to stop you from deposing him and putting one of your own in his place?"

The d'Arcy's looked at each other uncomfortably. They were no strangers to the charge of coveting the throne for themselves. But neither were they so unrealistic as to believe it within their grasp.

Mark cleared his throat before saying: "The Crown Prince Henry is still a child, but he already shows signs of being far different from his sire. He seems more like his grandfather, who was a hard but able ruler. Many who would not raise a finger to help John would act to protect the boy. Right now, he is the best alternative we have to the chaos of civil war."

"Unfortunately," Curran admitted, "not all the barons feel as we do. There are hotheads in any group, men who think the solution to every problem is a war. So far we have managed to control them, but I'm not sure how much longer that can last."

"It will have to last some months yet," the earl insisted. "John is hardly likely to give in at once, especially when he knows we could not fight until the weather improves. If I had my way, we would wait until early spring to challenge him."

Emelie reached across the table to touch his hand, her violet eyes dark with concern. "But that isn't likely, is it?"

The earl shook his head. "The barons have no patience. Their unity is a tenuous thing at best. Men I might count on today could well be gone tomorrow. So some action must be taken to keep them from breaking ranks."

The family absorbed this quietly, the men and Lady Emelie seeking some way around the problem while Arianna and Verony worried about the outcome. Part of the family and yet still outsiders, they could only pray the courage of their kin would lead to restraint rather than impulsiveness. Finally Curran asked: "Is that what you and the archbishop talked about this time?"

"It is. Stephen knows there must be action soon or we risk losing everything. Yet he is as reluctant as myself to provoke a showdown right now. Our emissaries in Rome are just beginning to make some progress with the Pope. In a few more months, they may have been able to convince Innocent that our cause is just."

Verony privately doubted there was a possibility of that. Whatever the Pope might think about the wisdom of restraining royal power, he had no particular reason to side with the barons. At least not as long as one of their principal leaders was Stephen Langton, the man Innocent had so vehemently supported for Archbishop of Canterbury only to later turn against. Innocent was not likely to forget that Stephen had dared to restore the sacrament to England without papal approval. Brilliant though he undoubtedly was, the Pope was also an egotistical man who did not easily forgive a slight to his authority. Verony suspected those who challenged the king would have to do so without his help.

Recognizing that the d'Arcys expected, even welcomed, debate in their midst, she might have voiced her thoughts. But some hint of the earl's profound concern stopped her. He was more worried than he cared to admit. Looking round the table, she saw that the family shared his doubts. Even Arianna's lovely face was grim as the meal finished in silence.

Chapter Nine

"Don't misunderstand me," Lady Emelie said as she drew her horse closer to Verony's. "I don't dislike Isabella. It's just that whatever principles or beliefs order her life are so different from my own that I can never understand anything she does."

"You are being unduly gracious to suggest she even has principles or beliefs," Arianna insisted. "Isabella thinks of nothing but her looks, her wardrobe and her latest lover."

Verony had heard other references to the queen's faithlessness, but she still found it hard to credit. After sixteen years of marriage, John remained infatuated with his former child bride, though that in no way stopped him from pursuing countless affairs of his own. Yet surely any man, no matter how enamored with a woman, would not ignore infidelity?

"I know Isabella likes to flirt, but does she really

go so far as to take lovers? After all, what if she were to conceive by one of them? How could John stand for even the possibility?"

Lady Emelie and Arianna looked at her tolerantly. They were both already very fond of the newest member of their family, but they thought her education sadly lacking in certain respects.

"The queen," Emelie explained patiently, "is very careful not to get pregnant, by the king or anyone. She values her figure far too much to have another child. If she ever has slipped, I'm sure she wasted no time getting rid of the problem."

Verony blanched. From her contact with the serf women, she knew that miscarriages could be induced. But the Church bitterly condemned such action, even when the mother was likely to die. Despite the recent weakening of faith, few were yet bold enough to deliberately end a pregnancy. Isabella, however, was not known for inhibitions. Petted and spoiled since childhood, betrothed to a great lord only to be willingly stolen from him by the besotted King John, she assumed a natural right to her own way.

"Even so . . . wouldn't John be jealous? He can't much like the idea of sharing his wife with others."

"On the contrary," Emelie declared, easily maneuvering her palfrey through the narrow street. Riding three abreast, with guards front and back, the women had to go carefully to avoid passers-by and rubble. Two-story townhouses of stone and plaster loomed above them, their gabled roofs almost touching across the cramped passage. Little sunlight reached the streets, but even so piles of garbage, carcasses of animals and bundles best left unidentified could be seen. Winter was both a blessing and a curse to London. The chill weather kept down much of the usual stench, but it also turned the city raw and depressing. Dank winds blew off the Thames and Fleet, leaden clouds hung over all, and even the great bays and arches of St. Paul's Cathedral looked sullen and unwelcoming.

"Strange though it may sound, there are some men who enjoy sharing those they bed. I have no idea how that can be, but Garrett suggested once that having the same woman might be a substitute for an even more unnatural form of intimacy." Emelie frowned in distaste. "He could be right, for Richard was a great one for sharing the boys who warmed his bed. John won't go quite that far, but he seems to like nothing better than to take another's woman, and he certainly raises little quarrel when his wife strays."

"Sometimes he does," Arianna cautioned, smiling sympathetically at Verony's stunned look. Coming from a household of well-informed, outspoken women, Mark's wife had little difficulty adjusting to his mother. But for Verony it was quite different. In the last few minutes, she had heard more about the darker side of human nature than she had ever thought to know. It would take some time before her equanimity returned.

"Why, just last year," Arianna went on, "John lost patience and had Isabella's current lover killed. I forget his name, but he was a pleasant young man . . . skilled with the lute, I believe. Anyway, Isabella woke up one morning to find his head dangling from her bedpost. Her only response was to look annoyed and complain about the bloodstains on the curtains. Didn't waste any time replacing the hapless gentleman, either. Although I imagine the next one was a bit harder to persuade."

In deference to the passers-by, Arianna kept her voice down. Despite the early hour, London was already bustling. Merchants, sailors, vendors, priests, students and all those come with business at the court crowded the twisting streets. Along the river bank, the huge public cook shop was in full swing, its aromas making Verony's temperamental stomach reel.

Feeding most of the city's visitors and a good portion of its permanent residents, the covered arcade of stalls offered fish, pork, beef and chicken prepared in all manner of dishes as well as breads, pies, wine, cider, ale and even a few precious vegetables.

Along with the teeming horse market just beyond the city walls, it was London's favorite meeting place. People came as much for the cock fighting, bear baiting and gossiping as for the food and drink.

Holding tight to her reins, Verony prayed she was not about to disgrace herself. Having recovered from one bout of sickness that morning, she was determined not to succumb to another. Only by concentrating fixedly on her surroundings was she able to control her spinning senses.

They were passing the outskirts of the Jewish Quarter, a warren of tiny lanes and nondescript houses that looked out over the frozen marsh north of the city. As London itself was guarded by seven double gates, the Quarter had its own entrance behind which all its occupants were expected to be by the eight o'clock curfew.

Verony knew nothing about the Jews, although she had often heard her father rail against them. That alone was enough to make her look favorably upon the people who somehow managed to endure despite the lack of a homeland. They were frequently blamed for every sort of calamity, but Verony doubted they were ever truly responsible. Far from being the perpetrators of evil, they seemed more often the victims. Well within the memory of many was the terrible outbreak of violence against the Jews that occurred at Richard's coronation. Uncounted hundreds, perhaps even thousands, had died in London, York and elsewhere. Their homes and shops were burned and their goods seized by a vengeful populace.

Since John's ascension, the Jews had faired a little better, but only because he found them so useful as a source of financing for his endless wars. Discriminatory taxes and legal burdens were heaped upon them in return for grudging tolerance.

Gesturing toward the Quarter, Verony asked: "Have you ever been in there?"

Emelie hesitated, glancing at Arianna before saying: "Occasionally. Why? Does it interest you?"

Despite her queasiness, Verony managed a smile. "Anything I don't know about interests me."

That won an approving nod from the formidable countess. "Then perhaps Garrett and I should arrange for you to meet some friends who live in the Quarter."

139

Verony was still puzzling over the oddity of a peer of the realm and his lady counting the despised Jews among their friends as they crossed the final distance to the royal keep.

Built on the east side of the city near a turn of the Thames, the massive White Tower of William the Conqueror commanded vital approaches by both water and land. Flanked by four turrets and surrounded by other, smaller towers with such picturesque names as Bloody, Belfrey and Broad Arrow, the tower was an unparalleled fortification. Not even Baynard and Montfichet Castles on the opposite side of the city could equal it.

Given the uncertain mood of Londoners, who were as likely to throw stones as to cheer, John's fondness for the tower was understandable. There he felt safe, if uncomfortable.

Dismounting before the main gate, Verony rubbed the small of her back surreptitiously as she followed the other women. It would not do to let them think her lagging. Lady Emelie had already suggested once that morning that she would be wise to remain in bed. Though the advice was kindly meant, from one who remembered well the discomfort of early pregnancy, Verony was not disposed to accept it. She was far too impatient to get to court, where she would at least be part of all that was happening.

Upon first entering the White Tower, up a steep wooden staircase and through a guard post, it was difficult to believe anything of great importance could occur there. Verony's initial impression was of chaos, with dozens of nobles, men-at-arms and servants milling about in seeming confusion. The sheer volume of noise almost overwhelmed her. With so many people, it was impossible to be heard without shouting. Certainly there was no opportunity to exchange confidences, but there was no such hindrance to arguments. As Verony watched in astonishment, one lord drew his sword on another as the crowd blandly drew aside to give them room.

This was hardly the way she remembered the court, where men at least did not fight each other in the king's own house. As the lords lunged at each other, both quickly drawing blood, Lady Emelie touched her arm.

"We will go upstairs. It is quieter there."

The second floor of the keep was given over to private family quarters and the women's solar. A few ladies already occupied the spacious room warmed by a large fireplace and scattered braziers. They nodded carefully at the new arrivals, but made no effort to join them.

"No one is quite sure who it is politic to speak to," Lady Emelie explained as she sat down on a bench. She removed her cloak, revealing a magnificent scarlet satin tunic and gold-embroidered surcoat. It was a costume befitting a queen, and Verony doubted even Isabella had anything as grand.

She and Arianna were dressed with equal care, if somewhat less regally. Their different coloring—one with a tumult of red-gold waves falling beneath her waist and the other with straight sun-washed strands worn in plaits—made them the perfect foil for each other, while their similar size had allowed them to combine wardrobes with good effect.

Arianna had brought Verony a delicate azure tunic she claimed did nothing for her complexion but would suit her new sister perfectly. In return, Verony had insisted Arianna wear the pure white wool she said made her look sallow. On Arianna, the mantle assumed angelic grace, an impression somewhat dispelled by a ready grin and gleaming eyes.

"Each lady hopes the others will talk first," she hissed in Verony's ear. "Rarely has a bunch of women been so reluctant to gossip."

"They never manage to hold out long," Emelie commented. "See, even now we are being approached."

A venerable matron copiously swathed in wimple, veil and mantle smiled at the countess with surprising warmth. "How nice to see you, my dear. And so early. Didn't Garrett get back from Canterbury?"

Matching the lady's assessing look, Emelie said smoothly: "May I have the honor of presenting my newest daughter-in-law, the Lady Verony. Verony, this is my old friend and sometimes ally, Lady Barbara. Her husband fought with Garrett in the Holy Land. You already know Arianna, don't you, Barbara?"

Emitting a sniff Verony took as agreement, the lady scrutinized her carefully. "You're de Langford's girl, aren't you? How did you end up married to a d'Arcy?"

"Mutual interest, ma'am," Verony said promptly. "We are both deeply attached to the same land, I through birth and he through possession. It seemed sensible to combine forces."

"Hrrmmph. I'd guess Curran stopped feeling sensible the minute he got a look at you. When you came to court last year with your father, you were quite beautiful. But now . . ." Lady Barbara allowed herself a slight smile. "I see your second son keeps his sire's ways, Emelie. If the other two fall no further from the tree, you will have more grandchildren than you can count."

"A pleasant fate. I always liked children."

"I seem to remember you were quite upset the first time you found yourself breeding," Lady Barbara intoned, adding her ample girth to the bench.

"Only because I wasn't married," Emelie retorted, ignoring Verony's start of surprise. "Nor did the prospect of matrimony please me."

Lady Barbara cackled. "Until Garrett talked you round. Is the dear man still as eloquent?" Her voice dropped. "Is he making any progress?"

"The situation is so complicated," Emelie hedged, "that it is difficult to tell exactly what constitutes progress."

"Don't bandy words with me. You know I'm not one of those simpering idiots who keeps her head neatly buried in the sand. Can he keep it together?"

"He thinks so," Emelie allowed. "Garrett, the archbishop and certain others are working very hard to make sure the lords stay in agreement, and that no one acts precipitously."

"I don't envy him," Lady Barbara muttered, "trying to keep those hotheads under control. The old ones waffle back and forth, unsure if they want to fight the king or each other, and the young ones

143

don't particularly care as long as they get to fight someone. Garrett will need all his skill to pull this one off."

"Where does your lord stand?" Arianna asked softly. "Last week he was firmly with us, but is that still the case?"

Lady Barbara sighed, a mournful sound well suited to the atmosphere. "He is one of the wafflers," she admitted. "But I am determined to hold him firm. We cannot turn back now."

"Have courage, old friend," Emelie murmured, patting the dowager's veined hand. "We have been through worse times."

"We were younger then," the lady snorted. She nodded at the two girls. "It should be up to alluring young things like that to see this out, not to weary travelers like you and me. Surely in the sunset of our years we deserve a little peace?"

Emelie choked back what sounded as though it might have been a very unladylike guffaw. "Careful, Barbara, or you will have me weeping. Is this the same shrinking flower who went marching off with the crusaders in a white silk tunic with feathers in her hair?"

The dowager smiled nostalgically. "It was a fetching outfit. Though I wager the tunic looked better on you than me. You had the hips for it." Glancing down, she added ruefully: "Still do."

"Garrett didn't find it appropriate at all," Emelie sighed fondly. "In fact, he wasted no time getting it . . ." She broke off, suddenly aware of the two younger women listening avidly. "Never mind. This is hardly the place for reminiscing. Does Isabella intend to remain in bed all day?"

"I doubt it," Lady Barbara chortled. "Not without someone to keep her company."

Emelie raised her eyebrows. "You know perfectly well she will be here for better reason than that. Isabella has no more faith in our sovereign than the rest of us."

"At least her boy's different," Barbara admitted grudgingly. "Smart little bugger, doesn't miss a thing."

Arianna shook her head sympathetically. "Poor child, though, to have such parents. Young as he is, I don't imagine Prince Henry has many illusions."

"Nor should he," Emelie said emphatically. "Not if he is to be a good king, please God. It's his father's illusions that have gotten him into so much trouble. John thinks the treasury is bottomless, the people's patience endless, and his lords paragons of endurance and selflessness. Has any man ever more deluded himself?"

"His misconceptions don't stop there," Barbara muttered. "Here comes the greatest of them all."

The women turned, in time to see Queen Isabella and her ladies enter the solar.

At thirty-one, the petite, fine-boned woman retained much of the incandescent beauty that had long ago won her the title of the loveliest lady in Christendom. That sobriquet was always an exaggeration, yet looking at her Verony could understand why men had waxed so eloquent.

Thick, gleaming hair pale as moonbeams tumbled

from a well-shaped head set off by large, tawny eyes and milk-white skin. High cheekbones framed a delicate, straight nose complemented by a ripe mouth and a small chin.

Her almost unlined throat was proudly displayed above an emerald tunic and scarlet mantle worn rather daringly low on alabaster shoulders. Isabella's breasts were still as high and firm as a young girl's, her waist small and her hips slender. She moved gracefully, and her voice, as it reached Verony, was soft and pleasant.

Given such attributes, Verony wondered why she did not find the queen attractive. Puzzled, she looked closer to see the faint tightness around Isabella's lovely mouth and the flinty hardness of her eyes. Her expression was haughty, and there was an air of condescension about her that seriously undermined her charms.

When she spotted Lady Emelie and her companions, the queen's manner became even more remote. Political realities forced her to nod stiffly, but they in no way gentled her tone as she demanded: "Are we expected to feel honored at such a plenitude of d'Arcys, madam? First I spy your husband downstairs with his sons in tow, all busy conspiring at God only knows what evil. And now I discover you in my own solar, stirring mischief I cannot bear to contemplate."

"No mischief, my lady," Emelie said placidly. "I came merely to present my new daughter-in-law. As for my lord, he hardly needs to conspire. Rather it is all he can do to keep order among those who seek to enmesh him in their own plots. Your court," she advised coldly, "is a veritable beehive of conspiracies, though I doubt the honey will prove sweet."

An angry flush mottled Isabella's complexion. Silently she reprimanded herself for forgetting just what a formidable opponent the Lady Emelie could be. Small hands clenched impotently at her sides as she realized a full-blown scene between them would only fuel the gossip mill.

"Your concern," the queen said coldly, "touches me. However, it is misplaced. You would be wiser to attend to your own duties." Haughtily she reminded the countess: "Your daughter-in-law is waiting to be presented."

This was unfair. Verony was far too interested in the confrontation of two wily, stubborn women to wish attention shifted to herself. But she bore it in good form. Dropping a modest curtsy, she murmured: "Actually, ma'am, we have met before. My father presented me at court last year."

Isabella's flush darkened even as Emelie struggled to suppress a grin. "It is to be hoped," the queen snapped, "that you make a better impression this time. I remember you as quite ill-behaved."

"My apologies for any distress I may have caused," Verony offered quietly. "I'm certain you will be pleased to hear that my circumstances have now so improved that my temper could not help but follow suit."

A titter passed among the ladies attending Isabella, but their mistress did not share their amusement. Ice glinted in the narrowed eyes focused on Verony's slightly swollen belly. "Curran wasted no time, I see." The queen shrugged. "Of course, all the d'Arcy men fancy themselves great studs. A misbegotten conceit, if there ever was one."

Emelie's self-contained expression did not alter, but her voice went dangerously soft. "There was a time, my lady, when you held to a contrary opinion. Surely only the keenest frustration could spark such disenchantment."

The women around them gasped at the sudden, potentially disastrous turn the conversation had taken. Flashing Verony a warning look, Arianna hastened to intervene. "If you will excuse us, ma'am, I don't think it's wise for my new sister to remain standing like this. She has just completed an arduous journey and is naturally fatigued."

"Then she should have stayed home with the rest of you," Isabella muttered gracelessly. Suppressed rage trembled through her as she moved off with her ladies.

Steering her mother-in-law and Verony back to the bench, with a highly titillated Lady Barbara bringing up the rear, Arianna complained: "You do tread close to the edge. Would a showdown with Isabella really serve any good?"

"Of course not," Emelie admitted regretfully. "But after sixteen years of having to put up with that bitch, I am almost out of patience. It's not enough that she lusts after any good-looking man in the kingdom. When she went so far as to try to coax Garrett into her bed, we became enemies. We will never be anything else."

"It's not as though she succeeded," Lady Barbara soothed. "Garrett found the whole thing amusing. He turned her down with no hesitation at all and then, when she persisted, made sure the whole court knew about it. Can't remember the last time I had as good a laugh."

"I'm glad you enjoyed it," Emelie snapped, "but I did not. Nor was I pleased when she turned her attention to my son."

Facing Verony, the countess said: "You will hear this soon enough, so I think it best I tell you now. When Isabella discovered that Garrett was not available, she decided Curran would make an excellent substitute. Mark was already plainly infatuated with Arianna, and the other two didn't have enough experience for her jaded tastes. But Curran . . . well, the fact is he was rather wild. Oh, he never deliberately hurt anyone, but he was not averse to enjoying the ladies." A faint smile ruined Emelie's attempt at sternness. "He seemed to feel it was a case of 'the more the merrier.' But with Isabella he drew the line. Told her straight out he wouldn't bed another man's wife."

"Unfortunately," Lady Barbara chimed in, "that wasn't the end of it. While all this was going on, Curran had his eye on a particularly pleasing serving wench who had just arrived at court. John also found her most appealing. He decided to bed the girl first, believing rank has its privileges, and then looked forward to passing her on to Curran. But Emelie's dear son had other ideas. He made fast work of the lass, refusing the queen's bed in the process, and left both John and Isabella more than a bit put out."

"How disappointing for them," Verony muttered. She bore Curran no resentment for his past affairs, being realistic enough to know that his remarkable skill between the sheets could only have come from long, devoted practice. But were he to ever again betray the slightest interest in another woman . . .

"Now don't let this upset you," Emelie cautioned as an angry flush swept over her daughter-in-law's smooth cheeks.

"It will not," she snapped, "so long as no lady, particularly Isabella, so much as wiggles a hip in his direction. . . ."

"Calm down," Arianna advised quietly. "Our gentle queen would like nothing better than to hurt you, and she is looking this way right now."

Verony forced back her irate words. Smiling frigidly, she sat down beside Lady Barbara, who clucked consolingly, "Pay her no mind. She may lust after your husband, but she will never have him. Why would he take her when he has you?"

Because she is beautiful, Verony thought, and the queen, which is bound to flatter any man. And her body will not soon be misshapen with child. And he has not already lain with her night and day through four months. . . .

The pleasures of marriage, exquisite though they were, had not softened Verony's nature. A powerful streak of tensile steel still ran through her. She had not survived a brutal father, the plots of an unscrupulous king and months of trial in the forest only to be undone by another woman. Her chin stiffened as she silently resolved Curran would have neither the will nor the energy to look elsewhere.

Chapter Ten

PARTING FROM HIS FATHER AND BROTHERS IN THE
courtyard of the family compound, Curran made his
way to his own quarters slowly. The long, tension-
filled day at court had left him weary in mind and
body. Yet he did not doubt that the efforts of the
d'Arcy men were worthwhile.

In separate meetings with the king and the barons,
Earl Garrett had subtly managed to get his own way
while allowing all others to believe the victory theirs.
For the mutinous nobles, there was the knowledge
that a series of specific demands had at last been
presented to the sovereign. Having their ambitions
voiced in clear statements of policy calmed some
measure of their discontent.

For John, there was the carefully managed opportunity to pretend consideration of the proposals

while maneuvering for more time. Thinking over the meeting with the king, Curran wasn't quite sure how his father had managed to make John think the suggestion of a delay until Easter was his idea instead of the earl's. But the king had come away believing just that and no doubt congratulating himself on his cleverness.

A slight smile curved his hard mouth as Curran considered what this gain of time would mean to them. While plans were made to fight, should that prove necessary, efforts would continue in Rome to secure the support of the pope. The barons would still need scrupulous tending to keep them in line, but the chances of maintaining a united front through the spring were now greatly improved.

His mind still firmly on matters of state, Curran entered the bedchamber. What he saw drew him up abruptly. Far from being asleep as he had expected, Verony was awake and sitting up in bed. A brace of candles burned beside her, illuminating the perfection of ivory skin touched by a faint blush. She put down a missive she had been reading and smiled at him shyly.

"Good evening, my lord."

Curran's eyes remained fixed on her as he shut the door. Far from being annoyed at his long absence, as he had half feared, she welcomed him warmly. After the turmoil and deceit of the court, his wife offered a haven of peace he hardly dared to approach.

At his hesitation, she took a deep breath, which further swelled the curves of her luscious breasts above her low-cut sleeping robe. Leaving the bed, Verony moved toward him gracefully.

"You must be tired, my lord. Let me help you."

Slender, white hands were making quick work of the lacings of his surcoat before Curran recovered enough to speak. "That gown . . ." he muttered thickly. "I don't remember seeing it before."

"It is new," Verony informed him simply, continuing the pleasant task of removing his tunic. She saw no reason to explain that the sheer, midnight-blue silk creation was on loan from Arianna, who absolutely guaranteed its efficacy. From a plunging neckline that barely concealed the rosy velvet of her nipples, the gown clung to her narrow waist before flaring outward at the hips. Waves of cloud-soft silk floated about her as she moved, half revealing flashes of her alabaster skin. Her red-gold hair spilled in a tumult of satiny curls to her waist. The fragrance of jasmine mingling with some spice he could not identify rose to tantalize Curran's already spinning senses.

"Are you hungry?" Verony asked softly as she eased the tunic from his massive shoulders. "I could send for food."

In fact, there had been no opportunity to eat at court, and Curran's stomach was empty. But he could manage no thought of food as he stared at his wife. Exquisitely beautiful and desirable as always, there was yet something very different about her. It took him several moments to realize just what was changed.

Through the four months of their marriage, Verony had always responded to his lovemaking with unbridled passion that was everything a man could ask for. But she had never before made any but the most indirect advances to him. Their intimacy was always at his prompting. Now, suddenly, their roles were reversed.

In the flickering candlelight of their perfume-scented chamber, she became a temptress. Her wide, indigo eyes, veiled by thick lashes, glowed with a fire he had not seen before. Her ripe mouth parted slightly with the urgent rise and fall of her breasts. Beneath the transparent silk, he saw her nipples harden and marveled at the thought that his nearness alone could so move her.

He was hardly aware when soft hands on his bare torso eased him down on a bench. As Verony bent to remove his boots, the gown fell away to reveal the full glory of her breasts. They swayed and bobbed rhythmically as she bared first one foot and then the other.

Docile as a child, though his body already gave ample proof that he was anything but, he allowed himself to be stood again and stripped of his chausses. When nothing remained but his straining loincloth, Verony turned away from him. A devilish smile curved her lips as she scrupulously folded each article of clothing and put it neatly away.

The sight of her husband's long, tapered chest with its thick mat of ebony curls, his narrow hips and muscular thighs and the thrusting power of his manhood stirred her fiercely. But she hid her own desire, determined that this would be a night Curran would never forget. To assure that, his anticipation had to be drawn out to the utmost.

Tossing her head so that the thick waves of gleaming hair moved against her slender back, she drew his attention to the arching curve of her buttocks visible through the transparent gown. Curran's large hands clenched with the instant need to be filled by those glowing orbs. He took a step toward her.

"Perhaps you should lie down," Verony breathed, putting the bed between them. Drawing back the covers, she leaned forward to plump the bolster, providing another tantalizing display of her breasts.

"Only if you join me," Curran growled, reaching out for her. His need was becoming urgent. All thought of fatigue and hunger vanished as he concentrated solely on his wife.

She evaded his grasp laughingly. "So impatient, my lord?"

A low rumble of agreement emerged from deep within Curran. He considered that the game had gone on long enough. Long, lithe strides ate up the distance separating them as he tracked Verony around the bed. Her back was against the wall beside the headboard before he stopped. Heavily muscled arms shot out on either side to hold her trapped. "Come to bed, my lady, and we will seek to tame my impatience."

The lambent flame in his gray-green eyes warned that the first stage of preliminaries was over. But Verony was not distressed. She had much, much more planned for her ardent husband.

Lifted gently but determinedly into his embrace, she offered no resistance as Curran laid her down on the bed. But when he sought to remove her gown, Verony drew back. Kneeling before him, the silk held under her legs so that it could not be raised and her shoulders arched so that the bodice could not be pulled down, she teased: "I have been waiting all evening for you, my lord. The least you can do is allow me my way."

Unsure as to exactly what she intended, but more than willing to indulge her, Curran leaned back. He was rewarded by the soft brush of moist lips against his. Seeking to deepen the kiss, he was distracted by the sudden sharpness of her nails digging into his flesh.

"No," Verony demanded. "Lie still."

Astounded by her boldness, Curran obeyed. Curiosity mingled with desire as he studied the sensual witch his wife had suddenly become. Through hooded eyes, he watched as she removed his loincloth, freeing the arching fullness of his manhood.

A low purr of pleasure broke from Verony as she caressed the proof of his desire. Skillful fingertips barely brushed him in repeated strokes that quickly brought a sheen of perspiration to his bronzed length. "V-Verony . . ." he began, only to be stopped by a groan of delight.

The swollen globes of her breasts had replaced her hands, drawing him within a nest of sweetly scented skin thinly covered by silk. Dropping feather-light kisses across his flat, muscled abdomen, Verony rubbed a hardened nipple against him. Over and over she repeated the motion until Curran moaned. "E-enough . . ."

Again he reached for her, and again she evaded him. "Hardly enough, my lord. We have only begun."

Aching with desire, Curran was in no condition to

argue. He enjoyed love play as much as any man, but was used to being in control. This new experience was as unsettling as it was delicious.

Moving away from the bed, Verony at last gave in to his desire to have her unclothed. Slowly and seductively, she slipped the gown from her shoulders, baring first her ripe breasts, then her still slender waist, and finally the swelling mound of her belly and gently curved hips. Stepping free of the silken spill, she could almost feel the heat of Curran's gaze searing her.

His response was unmistakable. Already swollen in passion, his manhood hardened even further. Its prodigious size caused Verony a brief moment of fear for her own safety and that of the babe. But her concern vanished instantly. No matter how teased and tempted Curran might be, she knew he would never treat her with anything other than loving gentleness. Confidently she allowed the game to continue.

Through the haze of his throbbing need, it occurred to Curran that he was being well and truly seduced. In the brief moment before all thought became impossible, he felt a flicker of wonderment at the extraordinary instincts of the unleashed female.

Patiently, expertly, Verony coaxed and incited and aroused him to a point almost painful in intensity. Each time he tried to bring the loving torture to its rightful end, she stopped him. Each time he allowed her to go on, driven mindless by her determination to tempt him even higher.

In the past, he had lain with some undeniably

skillful women. But nothing had prepared him for Verony's enthralling onslaught. She required no graphic instruction in the workings of a man's body to know exactly what would most please him. Their lovemaking of the last four months had prepared her well to play the temptress. When she added to it loving perception of his every response and devoted determination to drive him to rapture, she could not be surpassed.

Every part of Curran's mind and body and spirit resonated to her touch. As she finally brought him within her, drawing out his release with exquisite sensuality, he was consumed by a firestorm of pleasure far beyond even his wildest imaginings. His climax was so powerful and so extended that his very soul seemed to shatter beneath its force.

Recalled slowly from the tumult of her own delight, no less complete than that experienced by her husband, Verony snuggled against him contentedly. She watched as utter relaxation carried him away into sleep before allowing her own eyes to close, after silently promising herself that his rest would be brief.

Curran awoke to the soothing touch of oil against his skin. He opened his eyes curiously, only to find the room plunged in darkness. Blinded by the heavy blanket of night, he could see nothing. But his other senses suffered no such disability.

Every inch of his lean, hard body came acutely alive as small, strong hands stroked him. He breathed in the heady scent of musk perfuming the oil. A low sigh of contentment broke from him as the muscles of his legs, chest and arms were slowly kneaded.

Then Verony began to talk. Her voice a dreamlike caress on the night air, she told him of the delight she found in his body, of how his lovemaking made her feel, of the way she thought of him when they were apart, of how each separate part of her responded to his look and touch.

Massaging the corded sinews of his thighs, she told him how it felt when his hardness filled her. She described her surprise when their first lovemaking brought no pain, and her embarrassed astonishment at her own ardor. She laughed as she confessed her susceptibility to wanton thoughts under the most awkward circumstances. Her words became a whisper against his heated skin as she spoke of their child, telling him of both the strangeness of finding life growing within her and the joy.

She fell silent only when his manhood rose again hard and urgent to give her tongue and lips better occupation.

This time, as their rapture grew, Curran resolved not to be outdone. Turning his wife in his arms, he kissed and nibbled the slender line of her back down to her dimpled buttocks and beyond. Arching against him, Verony moaned with pleasure. Curran had long ago discovered the sensitivity of her shoulder blades and the small of her back. Now he used that knowledge to good advantage, stroking and licking until she shivered in delight.

"C-Curran . . ." she murmured huskily, trying to turn over again and draw him to her.

A low masculine chuckle was his only reply. Holding her firmly face down on the soft mattress, he carefully lifted her hips. Rubbing his hardness against the silken smoothness of her inner thighs, he tenderly parted her legs and slowly, cautiously entered her.

One large hand cupped the swelling that sheltered their child as the other played over her engorged breast. A low whimper of pleasure tore from Verony before she gave herself up totally to her husband's impassioned care.

Much later, lying snuggled in his arms, she drifted contentedly back to sleep marveling at her own boldness and its delightful results.

That contentment remained with her through the early morning as she and Curran rose to dress, a process much prolonged by frequent pauses to touch and gaze at each other lovingly. Any lingering doubts she might have had about the wisdom of her plan were banished when Curran whispered against her ear: "My beautiful enchantress, you delight me! No man was ever more fortunate."

Blinking back tears of happiness, Verony kissed him lingeringly. They broke apart with regret only when sounds from the courtyard alerted them that the family was ready to depart for court.

Accompanied by her husband, whose eyes rarely left her glowing face, Verony entered the White Tower feeling far more confident and serene than she had the day before. Not even the sight of Isabella magnificently arrayed in cloth of gold could dampen her contentment. Let the queen ogle Curran all she liked. It was Verony's hand he held snug in his own and her body that still radiated the glory of his lovemaking.

With pressing political concerns briefly calmed, there was time for the social courtesies. As the crowd of men around the king gave way for the d'Arcys, Curran led Verony forward to present her to their sovereign.

"I have the honor, my lord," he said coldly, "to introduce my wife, the Lady Verony d'Arcy."

Hooded black eyes set in a heavily jowled face regarded her speculatively. At forty-three, John was far removed from the sullen, thin-chested boy so overshadowed by his far more favored brothers. Youngest son of the great King Henry and his Queen Eleanor, he had always seemed an unfortunate afterthought to his dazzling siblings. Only the most sardonic of fates could have decreed that death would clear the way for John to inherit the crown. His predecessor, the illustrious Richard the Lionhearted, had nurtured at least as many personal failings. But his glamour and daring made the darker side of his nature seem unimportant. The people had followed Richard gladly, but they felt no such infatuation for hapless John.

His numerous shortcomings stood out painfully. They were the stuff of public gossip on every street corner and in every tavern. About the best that could be said for the spendthrift, deceitful, inept ruler was that he had matured sufficiently to at least look like a king.

Of medium height and late but adequate muscular development emphasized by his carefully tailored brocade tunic and surcoat, he sported lackluster black hair trimmed low at the nape of the neck. A neat mustache and beard framed his sensual mouth, with his slumberous eyes the most clear-cut indication of his favorite pastime.

Under his blatant scrutiny, Verony flushed. She felt as though her mauve silk chemise and azure mantle were stripped from her, baring the most intimate secrets of her body. John's leering gaze on the high, firm breasts Curran had so recently caressed sickened her. When the king's eyes wandered lower, to the ripe mound of her belly, she shifted angrily.

Her distaste was shared by her husband. Taking a step forward, Curran put himself firmly between his wife and the king. John's swift, displeased look could not dislodge him. Curtly the monarch said: "You are welcome, my lady, although I will admit your presence is a surprise. We had no idea that you still lived, much less were married to d'Arcy."

Turning to Curran, he went on: "It is customary, my lord, to consult with me before contracting any noble marriage. Much as I can understand your haste"—the leering gaze passed over Verony again—"I must reprimand your disregard for the proprieties."

A muscle twitching in Curran's jaw was the only sign of the check he kept on his temper. Staring down at the king from his great height, he said: "Since Lady Verony's presence on my demesne put her within my care, I saw no reason to consult with anyone. Our marriage concerned no one but ourselves."

John frowned, but he had the sense not to pursue

the subject. At least not before he could think of some way to get Curran at a disadvantage. He hated all the d'Arcys, but this one in particular. Garrett and Emelie's second son was too virile, too noble and too compelling to be overlooked by his sovereign. He made John feel things he did not want to admit even to himself. For too long the royal thoughts had been distracted by the sight of raven hair and gray-green eyes, the sudden rumble of a deep voice and ready laugh, the flutter of women always surrounding the long-limbed, powerfully built young man. Now he judged it more than fair that the tables should be turned and Curran be the one discomfited.

The opportunity came only a short time later. Feeling the pressure of her pregnancy, Verony excused herself from the ladies gathering in the solar and went in search of the *garderobe*. Her departure did not go unnoticed. Seeing her coming down the stairs, the king slipped away from his nobles and followed her.

Ordinarily, John could not have moved about his court without being observed. But in the present concern and confusion, with everyone eager to talk to everyone else and the sovereign regarded as relatively unimportant compared to his opponents, it was possible for him to find some degree of privacy. The men who did see him go thought nothing of his departure. He might be off on any sort of mischief, and they had far more pressing concerns.

Walking swiftly down the corridor, John chuckled to himself. He did not for one moment doubt that his

suit would be successful. The only regal characteris-
tic he possessed in full measure was vanity. Never
averse to using his power and wealth to coax women
into his bed, he had utter faith in his persuasiveness.
The lovely Lady Verony, he was certain, would
prove easy prey.

A quick glance around the passageway assured
him they would be alone, except for a man-at-arms
who was brusquely dismissed. When Verony left the
garderobe, she found only the king lounging insouci-
antly against a pillar.

Instantly alert to the strangeness of his presence,
she regarded him warily. His lazy smile and appreciative scrutiny did nothing to reassure her. Courtesy
demanded that she speak. Attempting to edge
around him, Verony murmured: "Good day, my
lord."

John moved quickly to block her escape. His gaze
lingered on the rapid rise and fall of her breasts as
his smile widened. "Don't be in such a hurry. I
would speak with you."

Verony managed a distant look of puzzlement
even as she had a sinking feeling she knew why the
king had pursued her. Searching quickly for some
means of evading him, she could not prevent John
from grasping her arm and leading her to a nearby
bench. When she was seated he joined her, so
closely that his thigh pressed against hers.

Trying to put some distance between them, she
slid further down the bench, only to have the king
immediately follow. With her back against a wall,
Verony could no longer avoid his touch. John's eyes

laughed cruelly into hers as his long, hard leg felt the full length of her slender limb.

"Are you always so skittish, my lady?"

For all the present difficulties with the king, Verony knew she had to tread a fine line. He was, after all, the sovereign. Though the man might deserve only contempt, his office demanded deference.

"I am anxious to return to the solar, my lord," she said finally, "before I am missed."

The hint of warning in her words did not go unnoticed. John knew the d'Arcys were fiercely protective of their own. No matter how preoccupied the Lady Emelie might be, she would quickly notice her new daughter's absence. The countess would not wait long before informing Curran.

Taking a deep breath, the king spoke rapidly. "You must allow me this opportunity to tell you of my great admiration for you, my lady." His hand grasped hers, despite Verony's best efforts to wiggle free. "From the moment we were introduced, I was struck by your remarkable beauty. Never have I seen a lovelier woman, or one more courageous." He leaned closer, savoring the fragrant scent of her. "You deserve the best the world can offer . . . the finest jewels . . . the highest position . . . the richest garb . . ." His beard tickled the back of her hand as he raised it to his lips. ". . . the most proficient lover . . ."

A shiver of repulsion ran through Verony as she endured the touch of his mouth on her palm. John felt the motion and chose to interpret it as excitement. A pleased laugh broke from him. "Ah, Verony, how enchanting you are. No woman has ever provoked me like this. You make me feel a boy again, but with all the added advantage of a man's skill." A small, pink-tipped finger was sucked into his mouth as he wrapped an arm around her slender waist.

"I can feel the heat from you," John muttered thickly. "There's no doubt how you would be in bed . . . wild . . . tempestuous . . . insatiable . . ." He trembled eagerly, passion mounting at the mere thought of her spread out naked beneath him. "A boy can't satisfy you, my sweet. You need a real man. Someone skilled . . . imaginative. I can show you delights . . . exquisite pleasures . . . your own capacity for fulfillment will amaze you. . . ."

Bile rose in Verony's throat. King or not she could not stand his pawing an instant longer. Desperately she began to struggle. "Let me go! You have no right! I will not listen to this!"

"Verony . . . sshhh . . . don't take on so," the king murmured against her throat. Convinced she was merely playacting, he did not immediately take offense. "You don't have to pretend with me. I know women too well to be misled. Your husband won't be anywhere near as generous as I will . . . in bed and out. You will want for nothing. . . . Jewels, furs, the finest silks, they will all be yours. Those you befriend will prosper at court. With my favor, you will have power . . . real power, Verony. . . . You won't have to depend on your husband or his family. You won't be helpless like you were in the forest. You'll have everything you want. . . ." He leaned nearer, intent on kissing her.

"*No!* My God, don't you listen? I don't want you!" Vainly she tried to kick him. "Let me go! No man but my husband has the right to touch me."

Mindful of the passing time, John was becoming impatient. It was all well and good for a woman to mouth reluctance. That gave the game added spice. But his experience was that they always yielded. Marriages founded on no more than property were notoriously lax. Invariably greedy and ambitious, women did not hesitate to reach out for wealth and power when they were offered. He had no reason to believe Verony was any different. Still, he thought irately, her refusal was rather overdone. When all was settled and they were alone together, he would have to teach her better manners.

"Sweetling," the king crooned patiently, "remember you don't want to be missed. Much as I enjoy the chase, we must reach an understanding now. Come to me tonight, Verony. We will find a way. You won't be disappointed."

Managing at last to free her hands, Verony lashed out at him furiously. "You dolt! You unfeeling cur! I said *no!* I do not want you. You sicken me!"

This had really gone too far, John decided. The girl was completely out of line. Beautiful though she was, he was not about to tolerate such disrespect. "Madam," he snarled, "you have forgotten to whom you speak. I am your husband's liege lord. All that he controls is held in my name. His property is my property." Brutal hands closed on her hips, dragging her against him. "You will pleasure me, and be glad of it. If I am satisfied, I may still be generous. But your rudeness has angered me. It will require considerable effort from you before I will forgive."

He meant it, Verony realized in horror. He actually expected her to go to him. Horror clenched her stomach. Her small hands clenched into fists. The mere thought of another man touching her as Curran did made her want to vomit. "Never! Never will you have me! You are despicable! Everything they say about you is true. Everything!"

Rage turned John's eyes coal black. A dull flush spread over his heavy jowls. His temper, never under the best control, snapped. "You bitch! How dare you refuse me? You, your husband, his sly, conniving family are nothing! Dirt beneath my feet! I can crush you out of existence . . . turn your lives to hell . . . make you pray for death. I can . . ." His hand brushed across her swollen belly. John stiffened, abruptly reminded of her condition.

Slowly, holding her eyes with his own, he tightened his grip. Fear stabbed through Verony. "Curran's brat sleeps there . . . helpless . . . so easy to destroy. You wouldn't want that, would you? There are drugs, Verony, to slip into your food. Or ways of using you that would kill the baby. It would be so easy . . ."

A scream locked in Verony's throat. She had no doubt he meant exactly what he said. John knew not the slightest compassion or remorse. He saw her not as a woman but as an object to be conquered and subdued. Alone with him in the empty corridor, she was helpless. If she could not placate him quickly . . .

"Please, my lord," Verony breathed. "Do not . . . I was wrong . . . I am sorry. I should not have spoken so." Her small fingers tried unsuccessfully to pry his loose. John's grip continued to tighten until waves of dizziness washed over her. "D-don't . . ."

"Are you sorry, Verony?" he rasped, pressing his full weight against her. "Really sorry?"

His breath was fetid on her cheek, his free hand moving to cruelly clasp her breast. Through the thin silk of her robes, he squeezed and twisted a nipple until she moaned in anguish. "Yes! I am sorry! Truly!"

"You will come to me?"

"Please . . . let me go . . . !"

"When I summon you, you will obey?"

"Don't . . . the pain . . . p-please . . . !"

"You will do anything I order? Anything?"

"Oh, God, just let me go! You're hurting . . . the baby . . ."

The king's hand clenched into a fist aimed directly at her belly. *Will you come to me?*

"Yes! Oh God, please stop!"

Satisfied at last that she was properly repentant, John let her go abruptly. Verony slumped against the wall, sobbing softly. Never in her life had she felt so vulnerable. Fear for her child had overwhelmed even her pride.

"This needn't have happened," the king informed her coldly. "I was prepared to woo you gently. But you . . ." He caught hold of himself, knowing there was no time for a further tirade. Later, when he had her alone, she would know the full force of his rage.

Thought of the child she fought so desperately to protect made him even angrier. The world did not need another d'Arcy. He would see to it that this one would never be born alive. But in the meantime, he would use the baby as a weapon to control her.

Pulling Verony roughly to her feet, John warned: "If you want the brat to live, you will say nothing of this. Breathe a word of it to Curran or anyone else, and I will make your punishment tenfold." He shook her hard to emphasize the threat. "Do you understand?"

Mutely Verony nodded. She did not for an instant consider such a promise given under brutal coercion to be binding. But neither did she have an immediate plan for avoiding the king's attention. With the political situation so delicate, she did not dare tell Curran what had happened. His inevitable rage and the terrible actions that might stem from it could destroy the family.

Satisfied for the moment, John released her. He strode away grinning, anticipating the pleasure he would find in humiliating so beautiful and proud a woman.

Verony watched him go with wide, horror-filled eyes. The king's touch seemed to linger on her skin, making her cringe. Instinctively she wrapped slender arms around her belly as the child moved within. Terror reverberated through her, equaled only by rage so compelling as to make her tremble.

Never in her life had she felt so helpless. When she had only herself to consider, courage was second nature. But now that the fate of her babe, and perhaps even of the d'Arcy family, were tied to her own, she was powerless to act.

A sound halfway between a moan and a snarl broke from her. John chose his weapons well. He sensed enough of her character to know she would not dare report this confrontation any more than she could risk the safety of her child.

Repulsion at the mere thought, no matter how remote, that she might have to give in to him made her stomach heave. Waves of nausea washed over her as she slumped against a pillar.

She was huddled there, weeping softly, when Lady Barbara found her. Heading for the *garderobe,* that good matron was at first startled and then horrified to discover Verony on the bench. Fearing that something might have gone wrong with the baby, she rushed to her side.

"My dear! What is it? Are you in pain? Are you bleeding?" Gentle hands brushed back the spill of red-gold hair. At the sight of the young girl's ashen face, Lady Barbara inhaled sharply. "Don't move! I'm going for help. I'll be right back. Don't move!"

Long years of coping with all manner of emergencies had trained the lady well. Her broad girth sped down the corridor as she called out to the first servants she spotted. The unmistakable authority and purpose of her manner sent them racing to obey her orders. Within minutes, Lady Emelie was summoned from the solar along with Arianna, and Curran was brought from the Great Hall.

He reached her side first, steely arms engulfing her with utter tenderness as he drew her trembling body into the shelter of his own. "Verony, my love, what is it? The baby . . . ?"

"No . . . no . . . the baby is fine," she managed to reassure him. "I'm sorry . . . I didn't mean to disturb anyone. . . ."

Unconvinced, Curran studied her urgently. He took in the total absence of color in her face, her wide, dilated eyes, the quivering of her mouth. A gentle hand brushed her skin, feeling its coldness.

Determinedly he rose with her in his arms. Cradled against his massive chest, Verony hardly heard the swift words he exchanged with his mother, Arianna's anxious questions, the worried exclamations of the other lords and ladies who saw her carried swiftly from the keep.

Laid across Curran's saddle, still snug in his arms, she buried her face against him. For the short time it took to cover the distance from the White Tower to the d'Arcy family compound, she allowed herself to luxuriate in a sense of utter safety.

Murmuring soothing words, Curran mounted the steps to their chamber in rapid strides. Lady Emelie and Arianna followed as he laid her carefully on the bed. Her cloak was slipped from her and a warm blanket tucked around her slim form. Only then did Curran move away to make room for Lady Emelie.

Her still beautiful face suffused with concern, the older woman took Verony's hand gently. Managing somehow to keep her voice steady, she asked: "Can you tell us what happened? What you are feeling?"

At the love and worry so evident in her mother-in-law's tone, hot tears rose in Verony's eyes. She was just able to blink them back as her free hand clenched the coverlet. "I'm all right, really. . . . There's no reason to be concerned. . . . I'm so sorry I frightened you. . . ."

Lady Emelie exchanged a silent glance with her son. Neither thought Verony was telling them everything, but they could not imagine why she should do otherwise. Unless she felt some embarrassment at the natural physical problems that could occur with pregnancy.

"Are you certain?" Lady Emelie prodded gently. "There is no bleeding or contractions?"

"No . . . nothing at all," Verony insisted, appalled by how her voice trembled. "I just became dizzy . . . and a little sick to my stomach . . . that's all. . . ."

Lady Emelie studied her a moment longer before apparently deciding she was telling the truth. Remorsefully she said: "You have been doing far too much, and I blame myself for allowing it. After your exhausting trip to London, you should have done nothing but rest."

"It wasn't your fault," Verony protested. "Curran will tell you how stubborn I am and how eager I was to see the court again." A faint smile touched her pale lips. "I'm afraid I would not have seen reason, no matter how hard you tried."

"Well, you are certainly going to do so now," Lady Emelie proclaimed with loving sternness. "I don't want you to move out of that bed until we are absolutely certain everything is all right. And then you're going to take it very easy. No more rushing back and forth to court." Her hand tightened on Verony's. "You must allow us to care for you, my dear, not simply for the baby's sake, but for yours as well. You are already very dear to us."

Deeply touched, Verony could only nod silently. Unshed tears burned the back of her throat as she relaxed against the down-filled bolster. After assuring Curran that she really did think Verony was all right, but was not to be allowed to lift a finger, Lady Emelie took herself off. The memory of her own early months as a bride was still firm enough for her to know that her son and his young wife needed to be alone.

When the door closed behind her, Curran allowed the firm grip he had maintained on his self-control to ease. Beneath his tan, his rugged features were gray. A nerve pulsed near his square jaw, and his mouth was drawn in a hard, tight line. Strong, calloused hands shook as he sat down beside Verony.

"When I saw you there on the bench," he muttered thickly, "so pale and trembling . . . never have I felt such fear . . ."

Reproaching herself as much for having so alarmed him as for not being able to tell him the true cause behind her upset, Verony drew his powerful head close against her breast. Gently stroking his hair, she had to be content with admitting that perhaps his mother was right and she should rest more, even though she really was well and there was nothing wrong with the baby.

Hesitantly, Curran allowed himself to be convinced. From an acute pitch of dread more intense than any he had known in battle, he slowly regained composure. Verony still looked very strained and fragile, but some color had returned to her cheeks, and her skin was once more warm to the touch.

He stayed with her awhile longer, even after the lids had fluttered over her luminous eyes and she drifted into sleep. Not until he was certain she was resting comfortably did he slip quietly from the room.

Verony woke several hours later. Muted sounds filtering across the courtyard told her preparations were under way for the evening meal. Most of the servants would be busy in the kitchens and the Main Hall. Curran was most likely with his father and brothers, talking over the day's events at court. No one stirred in the house around her.

Grateful for the solitude, Verony sat up slowly. Her body still ached from the combined effects of severe tension and John's mauling, but she felt considerably more herself. Enough to understand full well the dangerous dilemma she faced.

Half regretting her decision not to tell Curran of the king's demands, even as she still believed her reasoning had been correct, she realized the moment for revealing the truth was past. Were she to speak now, her husband's rage might easily be directed at her as well as her assailant. She did not for an instant believe that Curran might harm her, and for far more reasons than simply the child she carried, but the mere thought of his displeasure sickened her. More than ever, she needed his love and comfort.

Yet if she did not speak, and John followed through on his threats, she would be helpless to protect either herself or the baby.

Slipping from the bed, Verony made her way cautiously to the washstand. She splashed cold water on her face and toweled it vigorously, trying to banish the fog of doubt and fear still clouding her thoughts.

Her best hope, she decided, was to maneuver for time. Her collapse at court provided an indisputable reason for her to remain safe within the walls of the family compound. If the king could not get at her, he might eventually lose interest.

Telling herself that strategy made sense, she wondered how long it would take before John decided she was not a worthwhile quarry. His mercurial temperament predisposed him to sudden fascinations and equally abrupt dismissals. Surely not very many weeks would have to pass before some other, more accommodating lady caught his eye.

Reassured that her problem might not be as great as it first appeared, Verony began to leave the chamber with the intention of joining the family for supper. But at the door she paused. Well-run though the d'Arcy household was, some slight chance lingered that John might have spies among the servants. Failing that, there could be some weak enough to be bribed for information. If her plan to remain within the compound was to succeed, she must play the invalid for all.

Returning to the bed, she resignedly slid back between the covers and propped herself up with the bolster. A quick search in the adjacent chest located her needlework. She was industriously, if not cheerfully, occupied when a light knock brought her upright.

Schooling her voice to sound weak, she called: "Who is it?"

The only answer was a faint creak as the door eased open. A serving woman slipped inside, eyeing Verony warily. "Beg pardon, m'lady, I didn't mean to disturb you."

Thinking the woman might have been sent to check on her welfare, Verony smiled kindly. "That's all right. I wasn't asleep."

The woman nodded but did not return the smile. She remained poised by the door. "I have a message for you, from one who thought you should receive it as quick as possible."

A frown marred the smoothness of Verony's brow. "What message?"

The woman came a few steps nearer, betraying her nervousness with twisting hands and quick looks back over her shoulder. "The gentleman you spoke with this afternoon wanted you to know he still looks forward to your company. He charges you to find some means of leaving here tomorrow when the rest of the family is at court. An escort will await you on the river road to bring you to him."

A leer twisted the woman's mouth, clear evidence of what she thought lay behind the message. If Curran d'Arcy's wife chose to play the whore, so be it. The servant was well paid by a messenger who wore the royal crest, and she was far too wily to question her betters.

Verony did not notice the woman's condemning stare. Sickened, she had turned her head into the bolster, her slender body heaving with fear and anger. The servant watched her for a moment, then shrugged and left. Let the lady solve her own problems. She had far too much to do as it was.

Much later, when she looked back on that time, Verony was never sure how she got through it. Not for a moment did she consider obeying the king's summons, but it took all her strength to keep from revealing her distress to Curran. The fact that she took her meals in the chamber and always pretended to be asleep when he returned from court helped. But even so, by the end of the week her endurance was almost gone.

Twice more the king sent word through the serving woman that he expected Verony to come to him. Each message was more sharply worded, hinting at dire punishment for her disobedience. But each she stalwartly ignored.

He will lose interest, she told herself, so repeatedly that the words became a prayerful chant. Sequestered in her chamber, bereft even of Lady Emelie or Arianna's company since they were in attendance to the queen, she wavered between dread and faintly flickering hope.

The messages were frightening, but the simple fact of their repetition seemed to indicate that the king could do nothing but sling words at her. He might be able to torment her mind, but he could not touch her body while she remained within the compound.

Slowly a tremulous sense of safety grew within her, only to be abruptly shattered five days after her removal from the tower.

On the morning of that day, John's patience ended. Driven to the brink and beyond by frustration and rage, he called his nobles together. Before them all, he announced that the marriage of Curran d'Arcy and Verony de Langford had taken place without his permission and was therefore invalid. The couple, he declared, were living together in contradiction of the laws of God and man. They must be separated at once.

Chapter Eleven

THE FLUSHED, ANGRY FACES OF THE D'ARCY MEN told the story even before they gathered the rest of the family together in the Main Hall to explain what had happened.

Curran stood beside Verony, his arm around her shoulders, as the Earl Garrett described the king's charges. "He seems quite serious," the older man said at length. He shook his dark head in bewilderment. "John has done some outrageous things in the past. He has never been a reasonable man and has always acted on impulse. But this . . ."

"How could this happen?" Lady Emelie murmured, her face white with concern. "There was no warning . . . no hint of what was to come. . . ." She looked at her husband. "You have not argued with him recently?"

"No, on the contrary, since the king 'suggested'

we delay any resolution of the nobility's demands until Easter, he has been very cordial. Why not? He thought he had won an important point. But then he suddenly launches this all-out attack against us. Such charges cannot be considered as anything less than a personal declaration of war."

"Perhaps," Mark offered hesitantly, "he was deliberately trying to provoke us." He glanced at his brother sympathetically. "John might have hoped such an announcement, made in your presence, would send you at his throat. If you had made a move toward him . . ."

"I would have instantly been cut down," Curran finished flatly. "Don't think I didn't consider it. But I also saw the guards positioned all around him. John chose his moment very well. If I had gone for him, I wouldn't have stood a chance, and all the rest of you would have paid for my attempt."

The Earl Garrett smiled faintly, glad that this second son of his, who had always been rather hotheaded, was gaining in wisdom. "It was still best for us not to linger. I have some experience dealing with John's maliciousness, yet even I found my temper sorely strained."

"And the other lords?" Arianna asked softly. "How did they react?"

"With shock," Curran told her, "but also with clear-cut sympathy for us. John managed to earn even greater enmity today."

"He is not a stupid man," Lady Emelie mused. "Surely he must have foreseen that this would only stiffen resistance to him?"

"You would think so," the Earl Garrett agreed.

"That's what makes the whole thing so incredible. Why should the king choose this time to threaten us? And why make the attack so personal? It makes no sense."

Instinctively the family turned toward Verony, as though hoping she might shed some light on the puzzle. Of them all, she was the only one to hear the news in silence. Now, with attention focused on her, she found it almost impossible to speak.

"I . . ." she began, her throat so dry that she had to pause and try again. "I believe the king thought himself . . . provoked. . . ."

The family continued to regard her inquiringly. Taking a deep breath, Verony plunged on. "His anger is not directed at you, but at me. . . . He wanted to . . . that is, he tried . . ."

"That day you were taken ill at court," Lady Emelie broke in, "John had something to do with it?"

Mutely Verony nodded. Slowly and painfully she reported the events of that afternoon. Before she got very far, her lord was roaring in rage. *"He did what?! That contemptible bastard! Guards or not, he dies!"* Frenzied anger gave way almost instantly to icy calm. With deadly implacability, Curran stated: "I'll kill him." He turned to stride from the hall.

Instantly his father and brothers hurled themselves after him. Curran resisted fiercely, but the combined force of the Earl Garrett, Mark and the other two boys was enough to overcome even his maddened strength. Gently but determinedly they shoved him onto a bench and held him there.

Kneeling before him, Verony clasped his hands in

hers. Tears flowed down her ashen cheeks as she pleaded: "You must not, my lord! I beg of you. The king would like nothing better than to cause your death."

"Listen to her," the earl said. "If you go anywhere near John in this mood he will take delight in having his guards hack you to pieces. You realized that this morning; remember it now!"

"There are better ways, Curran," Mark advised gently. "We will be avenged, but in the proper time and place."

"And in the meantime?" Curran grated, still straining against the hold of his father and brothers. A red mist rose before his eyes. He was blinded by rage more terrible than any he had ever felt. The knowledge that another man had dared to put his hands on his wife, to try first to seduce her and then threaten her into his bed, banished all reason. He knew only that he wanted to drown the insult in blood.

"Just what am I supposed to do while we wait for revenge? Smile at the king and bow and scrape while he lusts after my wife and labels her a whore?" This last ended in a snarl indicating his rage was about to burst all bounds.

Hastily the earl shook his head. "There is no reason for you to attend the court right now. Go to Canterbury, see Stephen and explain what has happened. The archbishop knows the law better than any man. He will find a way to prove your marriage is valid."

"Your father is right," Lady Emelie asserted. "No one in his right mind would believe the king's charges for a moment. But you cannot take the risk, especially not with a child already coming."

Verony's hands tightened on her husband's as she thought of their baby. Since the men's return from court, she had concentrated solely on the need to tell the family of John's lust and her worry over how they would react. Now, for the first time, she realized fully just what the king intended.

All the trials suffered during the years with her brutal father and later in the forest were as nothing compared to the chasm of horror that awaited her should she be separated from Curran. Without him, her life would be meaningless. Not even the child nestled in her womb, the baby John sought to condemn as a bastard, could console her.

A sob rose within her, only to be choked back as she caught sight of the steely glint in Curran's eyes. Trained on her, his gaze seemed to drill straight through to her soul. She flinched instinctively, trying to draw away from him, but his grip instantly tightened. Trapped on the floor before him, she was forced to endure his cold scrutiny through long, painful moments.

"Why," he demanded at last, "didn't you tell me of this when it happened?"

His voice was low but still the rest of the family could not help but hear it. Aware that they were inadvertently witnessing what should have been a strictly private confrontation, they looked away.

Verony's head drooped. Waves of red-gold hair tumbled over his bronzed hands. "I was afraid," she admitted softly. "I thought that if I told you while we were still at court, you might do something terrible."

Her wide, tear-filled eyes raised to his silently reminded him that his father and brothers had considered him capable of attacking the king. "Then later, when we returned here, I did not know what to say. The political situation is so delicate . . . it could so easily be overturned . . . it seemed that silence was best. When I began getting the messages from John, I believed they meant he could do nothing more than threaten. It never occurred to me that he could . . ." Her voice broke, the sob that would no longer be restrained breaking from her. Miserably she bent her head again, her tears falling like drops of fire against his skin.

It was all Curran could do not to console her. His hand ached to stroke her silken hair, to brush aside her tears. He longed to assure her that he forgave her failure to speak. But in all truth he did not, at least not yet. Much as he understood her reasoning, he could not lose sight of the fact that she had once again chosen to take matters into her own hands.

Gruffly he said: "You should have spoken. It is not for you to decide what I should or should not be told. I am your husband, and it is my right to know your thoughts."

Verony did not respond. The deep pain so evident in his voice forced her to realize how profoundly hurt he was by her unwillingness to confide in him. Overwhelmed by regret, she did not dare look at him again. If she had, she would have seen the piercing tenderness of his regard as he studied her bent head. But as it was, she knew only that Curran sighed softly before gently disengaging their hands. Without another word, he rose and left the hall.

The next few days passed slowly. With Curran en route to Canterbury, the rest of the d'Arcy men remained inside the compound to fortify it against a possible attack by the king. The wide trench between the outer walls and the surrounding streets was deepened. The drawbridge gears, always scrupulously maintained, were oiled once again. Additional guards were posted in the turrets that commanded a clear view of the city.

A troop of knights was sent to the earl's manor to bring back a large squad of men-at-arms to strengthen the compound force. But it would be some time before they could arrive. In the meanwhile, drills went on constantly as skills already well honed in battle were sharpened even further.

Under Lady Emelie's supervision, livestock was brought in from the nearby fields and housed in sheds set up in the courtyard. Some were butchered, the meat carefully smoked or salted. Unable to go to market herself, because the earl flatly refused to let any of the d'Arcy women set foot beyond the compound, she dispatched trusted servants to purchase large quantities of those few supplies not already well stocked. The grain bins were topped off, kegs of salted fish laid down in the cellars and barrels of cider and ale carefully stored for cooling.

Verony found some distraction from her unhappy thoughts in the work of provisioning the compound. But there were other, far less congenial preparations that forcibly reminded her of the danger lurking just upriver in the royal keep. Lady Emelie spent all of one day going carefully through her medical supplies, taking the opportunity to begin Verony's education in the healing arts. Bandages were rolled and splints cut, even as a prayer was said that they would not have to be used.

On the compound walls and in the courtyard below, pails of water were kept at the ready against an attack with flaming arrows. On the turrets above the drawbridge, vats of tar bubbled night and day, awaiting anyone foolish enough to try to storm the stronghold.

As well as keeping watch for unwelcome guests, the guards also scanned the surrounding area for the telltale signs of tunneling. That tactic was frequently used to undermine even the best protected fortress. A tunnel was dug to the base of one of the towers, where the stress points were greatest. Timbers supported the passage, and dried wood, flammable debris, grease, anything that would burn was packed into the end furthest from the attackers. When the tunnel was fired the timbers burned and the ground gave way, taking with it, if all went according to plan, a corner of the fortress. Through that chink in the defenses, the enemy then tried to enter.

In London, with so much cover provided by other buildings, a tunnel would be a more likely approach than an all-out attack. But if the idea occurred to John, there was no sign of it. Day followed day without the king daring to approach the d'Arcy stronghold.

Not that they were without visitors. A constant stream of the most exalted lords of the land came calling with their retinues. Carefully screened before admittance, they provided ample news and encouragement. To a man, the barons expressed outrage at the king's highhandedness and their support for the d'Arcys. The earl found some grim amusement in the fact that even a few who had not previously been eager to join the nobles' cause now came over to their side. In the privacy of his own chamber, alone with the Lady Emelie, he acknowledged his appreciation for their sovereign's stupidity. But he also continued to worry about where it would all lead.

There were, naturally enough, no further messages from the king. The serving woman who had accepted bribes to deliver them was gone. Verony knew better than to ask after her fate. Several other servants whose loyalty was suspect were also removed from the compound. Every possible effort was made to close even the slightest loophole in security.

But no such effort, however well managed, could succeed entirely. A tiny crack persisted in the defenses. The supplies being brought in from the market became so numerous that merchants had to send their own servants to help with deliveries. Such men were permitted within the walls on the understanding that they would not remain long. The Earl Garrett presumed that news of the measures being taken to strengthen the fortress would reach John through this route. He saw no harm in that, but neither did he guess that the king would dare use the conduit in reverse.

Verony was busy looking over several barrels of salted herring when the man found her. He was small and hunched, wearing the rough clothes of a laborer. His eyes, lingering on her beauty, were red-rimmed and watery. He scratched absentmindedly at the stubble of his beard, embedded with a few stray fleas, before he said: "Begging your pardon, lady. I have something for ye."

Surprised, Verony replaced the cover of the barrel she had just inspected before turning to him. They were alone in the undercroft, the other servants having returned to the courtyard. But she felt no fear. A single cry would bring dozens of men-at-arms down on the man, who undoubtedly would not survive their handling.

"What is it? I am very busy."

"Aye, but this is important." Dirt-encrusted fingers dug in a greasy pouch suspended by a cord around his waist. Gingerly he removed a small, cloth-wrapped parcel and held it out to her. When she hesitated to take it, he said: "Go on! Think I want to get caught with this?"

Reluctantly Verony accepted the package. Her hand shook slightly as she unwrapped it. At the first glimpse of the contents, bile rose in her throat. Hardly breathing, she stared at a gold-and-ruby ring still attached to the finger where she had last seen it.

The ring was a match to the one Curran had given her at their marriage, purchased some months later with funds from her bridal gift and given to him with great delight. He had worn it ever since, even as she wore hers.

Fighting down the urge to vomit, Verony became slowly aware that the man was reciting his carefully learned message. Curran had not reached Canter-

189

bury. Captured by the king's men, he was being held outside London. Unless Verony gave herself up to royal custody at once, he would die. If she was so unwise as to reveal this to the d'Arcys, Curran's death would be assured. He would perish by the slowest and most unpleasant methods that could be devised.

"Six hours, lady," the man concluded. "That's all ye've got. Be at the north entrance to the tower before then, or your lord dies." Gesturing at the severed member, he taunted: "That's only a sample of what they'll cut off 'fore he dies. He'll be praying for his end long 'fore it comes."

Every instinct in Verony screamed denial. She opened her mouth to summon the guards, to denounce the repulsive little man, to blurt out this latest outrage. No sound came. Fear for Curran's life kept her silent. Without the ring, she would not have believed him taken. But with it, she could only accept that he was in mortal danger and that she did not dare do anything that might cost his life.

Whereas only days before Verony would have sworn that she would never again keep anything important to herself, now she knew she had no choice. The earl would never permit her to leave the fortress even to save Curran's life. Her own well-being and that of the d'Arcy child she carried would outweigh even his great love for his son. But while she waited safe behind stone walls, what further horrors might occur?

Time was the crucial factor. She had to prevent Curran's immediate death while giving the family a chance to rally their forces and approach John in terms not even he could misunderstand.

Hurrying upstairs to that part of the compound used by Mark and Arianna, Verony carefully printed a note in block letters she knew her sister-in-law could read. The serving woman who watched her approach the cradle where her nephew slept saw nothing amiss in her interest. Nor did she notice when the tiny slip of paper was hidden inside the child's swaddling clothes. Arianna, Verony knew, reserved to herself the pleasure of bathing her son. Each evening she took delight in his excited squeals and splashes as she gently washed, dried and powdered him. It was a special time for them, but one that would be spoiled at least for that day. Arianna's shock when she found the note was easy to imagine, as was the swift action she would take to alert the family.

Convinced that she had done all possible to warn the d'Arcys without endangering Curran, Verony took firm hold of her courage. Wrapping herself in a warm cloak, she began looking for some way to leave the compound.

Chapter Twelve

A MAN WAS WAITING OUTSIDE THE WEST WALL OF the tower. Though wrapped in an all-enveloping cloak, his size and manner marked him a warrior. He strode back and forth impatiently. It was clear he had been there some time and was not pleased.

Verony approached warily. It had taken several hours for her to secure a safe way out of the d'Arcy residence. Only by hiding in one of the merchants' wagons and enduring the seemingly interminable delay until they departed was she able to slip unseen past the sentries.

By the time she jumped free of the wagon near the river road, she was stiff with cold. Her limbs ached, and a dull pain throbbed in her head, but neither slowed her pace. Unaccustomed to being by herself in a town of any size, she found the closely packed streets of London far more ominous than the familiar pathways of her forest. Good sense alone, even without her overriding dread of what might happen to Curran if she did not reach the king soon, made her hurry.

Treading carefully to avoid the piles of offal and debris, she kept her head down and her eyes away from the multitude of peddlers, gawkers, prostitutes and ne'er-do-wells pressing in at her from every side. Once a man reached out to grab her, but she managed to evade his touch. Several whores, out for the afternoon trade, noted her escape and laughed derisively. They lost no time approaching the man, who allowed himself to be consoled.

A drunk, stumbling from a tavern with the curses of the owner floating behind him, almost fell into her. But again Verony's swift reflexes served her well. She darted on, past the markets and public kitchens, beyond the separate quarters housing butchers, fishmongers, gravediggers, Jews and others who for one reason or another lived apart, through the warren of twisting lanes abutting the tower where the lawyers and scribners were housed, until she came at last to the small, secluded entrance set well back in a stone wall.

"Ye took long enough," the man snarled when he saw her.

Verony did not bother to answer or, in fact, to acknowledge his presence in any way. His sneering comment and the long, slow scrutiny of what little he could see of her body made his attitude clear. She was just one more of the king's women, little better than the whores she had seen earlier, and certainly entitled to no better treatment.

Her determined self-possession must have angered him. Grasping her arm cruelly, the man pulled her inside. "Don't go all high and mighty on me, girl," he ordered. "I know what you are, make no mistake. Many the time I've waited for some doxy the king fancies, and let me tell you, you're all the same. Whatever you've got between your legs he'll tire of quick enough. Then you might be glad of someone like me to keep you warm."

Verony's stomach lurched sickly. The man's touch on her coupled with the horrifying knowledge that she might shortly have to bear far more from John sapped her courage. Her legs trembled and, just for a moment, threatened to give way.

Pride came to her rescue. Not for the world would she allow such a churlish lout to see how he affected her. Verony drew herself up regally, her voice hard and cold. "You say you know who I am, but it doesn't seem to have occurred to you that the king might not appreciate my being delayed or"—she stared pointedly at his hand on her arm—"being handled by one such as you."

The man's small eyes widened. A harsh laugh broke from him. "Ye've got courage, I'll say that much. And maybe ye're even right. The great lord John never minded what happened to his women after he's done with 'em, but before . . . that might be another matter." He thought it over for an instant while Verony tried desperately to still the ragged beating of her heart. Finally the man said: "Come on then. Sooner he's had ye, sooner you and me can work something out." To emphasize the pleasure with which he contemplated this eventuality, the man pinched her bottom painfully.

Verony bit back her protest. Without the protection of an escort or even of her rank, she was utterly helpless to prevent anything the guard might choose to do. If he had been in the king's service long, the chances were good that he knew how to use a woman harshly without marking her. It would be only her word against his when she was brought to John.

Silently, she followed the guard across the open field inside the walls and up the steep wooden stairs to the royal keep. Once inside, they kept to the narrow, twisting passages used by the servants, avoiding those places where the nobility congregated. Verony was glad for the discretion. The thought of being recognized filled her with horror. A single careless instant could be enough to send word of her presence there racing back to the d'Arcy compound, and bring down the violent confrontation she hoped desperately to prevent.

In a small room set high in the keep, the guard left her. He pushed her inside, allowing his hands to once again linger on her body, gave a final leer and disappeared, locking the door behind him.

Verony stared at it for a long moment, her breath catching in her throat until her lungs constricted painfully. Only then did she ease her rigidly held body just enough to breathe with some semblance of normality. Looking around cautiously, she noted the room's spare furnishings, consisting of a table and chair and a bed.

The luxury John so enjoyed was not evident. The room, really no more than a cell, was not remotely part of the royal chambers. Isabella undoubtedly knew of its existence, but had her own reasons for overlooking what went on under her roof.

Shakily Verony sat down in the chair, keeping her eyes resolutely away from the bed. It took all her courage and strength to fight the tide of panic rising within her. What if her desperate ploy did not work? What if, no matter how great her sacrifice, Curran still died? If her note was not found . . . if the d'Arcy men could not locate him in time . . . Biting her lip hard to force back the tears that threatened, she refused to think of her ultimate fear: that her very presence in the king's house might already be useless. To the depths of her soul, Verony believed her husband still lived. But the possibility that she might be wrong did not elude her.

How long she waited she had no way of telling. From far below in the bailey she heard the shouts of the guards as one watch gave over to the other. Nobles, merchants, clergy, all manner of people having business at court came and went as the light slowly began to fade and the day gave way to dusk.

Her stomach growled emptily but the very thought of food made her nauseous. She did not doubt for a moment that John was deliberately drawing out her torment and could only be grateful he could not realize each passing moment was a victory for her.

Exhausted by tension and lack of nourishment, she struggled to stay awake. At last the effort proved too much and her head slumped, the silken fall of her red-gold hair falling forward to frame delicately strained features. Uneasy sleep claimed her, long enough for the last light to fade and night to settle over the city.

The sound of footsteps on the landing brought her abruptly awake. For a moment she had no idea where she was and glanced around in bewilderment. Then memory flooded back and she stiffened. The steps came nearer, pausing just outside the door.

Though her body ached from its uncomfortable posture and her legs trembled so much that she feared they could not hold her, she rose determinedly. When the door swung open, she was standing facing it.

John looked her over leisurely. He had come alone. Extravagantly dressed in rich blue velvet embroidered with gold thread, his lank black hair held in place by a jeweled circlet, he might have looked every inch the king to some. But Verony was not so easily fooled. She saw the calculating cruelty of his small eyes, the sullen set of his mouth and the overriding image of a man who found malicious pleasure in hurting others. Drawn up to her full height, she met his gaze coldly.

"I have heard so much of royal hospitality, my lord. Yet I find these accommodations singularly lacking."

Whatever John had expected her to say, it was not this. His eyes narrowed further in a puzzled frown. Taking a step closer, he muttered: "You are hardly here as a guest, madame."

Verony shrugged, managing a convincing semblance of unconcern. "However I came to be here, my lord, it was at your . . . urging." Steeling herself, she moved toward him. "You seemed eager enough for my attention, yet you have left me alone for hours." Glancing up through thick lashes, she pouted: "I have felt quite neglected."

John shook himself, as though not quite able to believe what he was hearing. The idea that a woman coerced into his presence by a grisly reminder of her husband's mortality would complain about being ignored was so at odds with his expectations that long moments passed before he could respond.

When he did so at last, Verony had to endure the touch of his hands on her shoulders as he drew her to him. His thick mouth parted in a leering grin. "My apologies, madame. I had no idea you so . . . avidly awaited me." His fingers tightened on her, digging cruelly into delicate skin as he added: "Our last meeting left me with the impression you were anything but willing."

Verony drew a deep breath. Every part of her screamed in revulsion at his touch, but she bore it stalwartly. To win time, she had to convince John he had more to gain than a resentful, uncooperative bedmate.

Lowering her eyes in what looked very much like remorse, she whispered: "I am so deeply ashamed of that, my lord. You have every right to think me stupid and unworthy of you. Yet if only you could understand . . ."

Her voice trailed off provocatively, leaving John with no choice but to demand: "Understand what?"

"What it has been like to be married to a d'Arcy. How empty and frightening my life has become."

May God forgive me, Verony prayed silently even as she told herself any lie was excusable if it helped secure Curran's safety.

Swallowing the bitter taste of bile, she raised her head. The full impact of luminous indigo eyes struck the king without warning. He swayed slightly, senses whirling. "I—I thought you were happily married?"

The bitter laugh that broke from Verony sprang from the torment of having to endure his nearness, but it sounded as though she was renouncing his impression of her marriage.

"Surely you know how vain all the d'Arcys are? Not for a moment would they allow anyone to think union with one of them was less than blissful. They are so arrogant . . . so proud . . . it was worth my life to say anything of my suffering."

John wanted to believe her. He was excited by the idea that Curran treated his wife cruelly and that in her misery she might turn to him as the better man. Such was his own vanity that he could easily envision a public spectacle in which Verony denounced her husband and threw herself on the mercy of the king. What greater balm to his own injured pride and frustration could there be?

But cynicism nurtured over a lifetime did not fade so easily. "That still does not explain why you turned away from me . . . claimed to hate me."

Verony was prepared for this complaint. Agilely she reassured him. "I thought someone was listening to us, my lord. One of my husband's spies. I feared that if I showed my true feelings for you, Curran might be provoked to even greater evil against the throne."

John straightened in surprise. "So you know how they challenge me? How they dare to subvert my authority?"

"I know very little," Verony claimed, not anxious to have him question her about the family's plans. "They consider me an outsider and do not speak in my presence. But I have heard things . . . rumors I could hardly credit at first but finally had to realize were true as I learned the full extent of their arrogance."

The crafty, scheming part of John wanted to hear more about what she might have learned. But he was too dominated by the sensual to concentrate on anything other than the beauty and vulnerability of the woman he held. Having possessed women beyond count, many of them remarkably lovely, he was still overcome by the challenge Verony represented. Astute enough to sense the passion within her, his self-love was so great as to allow him to believe he could unleash her desires.

Brushing his fingers across her full breasts, he murmured: "Later we will talk more of this. But now I would have you show me these feelings you claim. . . ."

Verony's nipples stiffened in fear and revulsion, but John took the response for lust. He laughed deep in his throat. "I guessed you would be hot, my lady. But don't worry. . . ." He licked his lips avidly. "I will give you what you need. . . ."

With one hand cupped over her breast and the

other still holding her firmly, he backed her toward the bed. Instinctively Verony resisted. Her hands pressed against his chest, trying vainly to hold him back. "Wait . . . my lord . . . just a moment . . . there is something . . ."

On the edge of despair, she spoke more severely than she had intended, enough to penetrate even the lecherous haze engulfing John. Annoyed, he halted. "What is it?"

"My husband . . . I want to know where he is . . . how he is. . . ."

Scowling, John forced her head up. He surveyed her features suspiciously. "What trick is this?"

"No trick," Verony said quickly. "I just want to see him . . . to know you really have him. . . ." Innocent though she was, some instinct told her that John was a man aroused by cruelty. The suggestion that she wanted to see her captive, mutilated husband would please him. He would be eager to believe her desires were as warped as his.

But Verony had underestimated the extent of John's taste for brutality. Though his breath came more quickly and his heart beat dangerously fast, the image of her confronting Curran was not enough. Perversely he wanted more and, being so driven, made a fundamental mistake. Staring into her indigo eyes, the king declared: "It is too late, my dear. Proud Curran has gone to his just reward. I took great pleasure in dispatching him."

A scream of denial rose in Verony's throat as the king went on to describe in graphic detail the manner of Curran's death. Inflamed by her nearness, he indulged in an item-by-item recitation of the tortures his victim suffered before death at last claimed him.

"Poor soul," John concluded with mock sympathy, "he had the misfortune to be uncommonly strong. He endured so much that in the end I was driven to pity and hastened the procedure." Smiling down at Verony benignly, he explained: "After his arms and legs and private parts were hacked away and yet he still lived, one of my men most skilled in the torments practiced by the Arabs inserted a rod into his anus and up through his body until it emerged from his mouth. Then we roasted him, as on a spit. He lasted only moments more, but it was worth it to see him suffer so."

The scream Verony had fought against through long, horror-filled minutes could no longer be denied. A dark film of madness closed over her mind. Driven beyond reason, beyond even the most elemental thought of her own or the baby's safety, all the hatred and repulsion she felt burst free.

The tortured sound that tore from her throat so stunned John that he did not at first realize the full impact of his words. Before he could move, Verony struck. With strength she had not known she possessed, she tore free of his grasp.

Seizing the only weapon that came to hand, a sturdy wooden stool, she lifted it over her head and whirled on the startled John. If some part of her shattered reason screamed that regicide was a crime far beyond the killing of a single man, she did not listen. Nothing mattered but that she wipe the satisfied smirk from the loathsome face confronting her . . . pound the dreadful, bestial voice into silence . . . hurt and punish and destroy the monster whose every breath was an offense to God and man.

For all his life of unbridled self-indulgence, John was a strong man. Given an instant to react, he would have had no difficulty stopping Verony. But she moved as one possessed by devils, driven by the image of Curran dying to overcome even the king's battle-trained reflexes.

The stool, smashing against his head, splintered. After the first blow, only a fragment remained clutched in Verony's hand. The diminishing of her weapon did not stop her. She struck again and again, using the heavy oak leg of the stool to beat John's head and shoulders into bloody pulp. Only when her maddened strength at last gave out did she stop.

Staring down at her work, Verony moaned. She knew no regret for her action, only revulsion at the spectacle before her. Coming on top of the hideous picture of Curran, it was too much. The bloodied weapon slid from her nerveless fingers as she turned to the door.

Through the waves of rage and panic and terror engulfing her, Verony fled. Behind her she could hear the shouts of men who, alerted by the strange noises from the tower room, discovered what remained of John. Stunned though they were, they were too well trained in every manner of violence not to respond instantly. Before Verony could reach the angled stairs leading to the Main Hall, they were after her.

Heedless of the danger of falling, she raced down the narrow steps, emerging breathless into the hall. Running smack into a startled servant, upsetting the tray he carried, she dashed past before the man could lift a hand against her. Avoiding the knots of lords and ladies in busy conversation, she darted into the shadows cast by wide stone pillars. Skills honed during her year in the forest served her well. No one among those who chased her could expect their quarry to be so elusive. Weapons drawn, they were just beginning to spread out through the hall as Verony sped from it, losing herself quickly among the crowds gathered in the bailey.

Fleeing more from John's fiendish words than from any threat to herself, she jumped the last steps from the tower wall to the street below. A faint cracking sound from her ankle was followed swiftly by searing pain which under different circumstances would have rendered her lame. But pain had no meaning in a world where Curran no longer lived. Without pause, Verony raced on.

The shouts from the royal keep faded behind her. In streets almost emptied by the winter cold and the gathering darkness there was no one to stop her. With sunset, Londoners retreated within their homes. The shops she sped past were shuttered, the lanes and winding passageways deserted. Only taverns and brothels remained open, and might have posed a danger to her. But since she was instinctively heading away from the city's center, she saw no one.

Not until she came up hard against a stone wall did Verony pause. Out of breath, her lungs on fire and her ankle throbbing, she looked round blankly. A rising moon showed that the barrier was not the ancient battlements surrounding the capital, but beyond that she could not see.

Closing her eyes, Verony leaned against the wall. Low sobs broke from her. She clutched her aching sides. Swept by despair more profound than any she could ever have imagined, she wept quietly.

The mere continuance of her life, the rush of blood within her body and the drawing of air into her lungs bewildered her. Why did she still live when Curran was gone? What vicious fate decreed that she should be left alone to endure the torment of his death?

Deep within her mind, Verony now understood why she had fought against loving him so totally. Bred by her father's cruelties and strengthened by her months of survival in the forest, the conviction that she could rely only on herself was not easily overcome.

But the vast, all-encompassing passion Curran set off in her drowned even the most bitter lessons. Her struggle to hold some part of herself separate from him was in vain. If Curran had died believing she never completely merged her will with his, always withholding that final degree of trust, he would have been wrong. Helplessly she acknowledged that he was so totally part of her that without him life itself would become the worst possible torture.

Through a gap in the wall, she made out the glittering ribbon of the river bathed in moonlight. Burdened by ice, it flowed slowly, the lazy motion seeming to beckon her. She took a step closer, only to be stopped by the sudden movement of the child within her.

Verony stopped, hands pressed to her hardening belly. Through the soul fire of grief, a glimmer of reason intervened. Curran was dead, but a tiny part of him remained nestled inside her. Torn between the desperate need to end her torment and the deeply rooted desire to protect the child, Verony stood frozen in place.

A chill wind whipped her slender body. The cloak she had tossed on hastily before leaving the d'Arcy compound offered little protection. Her hands and feet were already numb. A gust blew the hood back, revealing the glorious tumult of her red-gold hair. It glistened, silvered in the moonlight, matched by the sheen of tears against her alabaster cheeks.

Time passed without meaning. A rat scurried out from under the wall, paused to gaze at Verony, then scampered on. A scrawny cat darted by, intent on its prey. Off in the distance, a pack of the wild dogs that roamed the city set up a howl.

Verony stiffened, the sound recalling her abruptly to the peril she faced. It was madness to be out alone in London's streets at night. All manner of horrors awaited anyone so foolish as to be caught there, not to mention the threat of royal guards who might still be tracking her. Much as she might wish to court death, she would not condemn the babe she sheltered.

Yet with no idea of where she was, she could not begin to make her way back to the d'Arcy compound. Wearily, she huddled against the wall, seeking some protection from the cold. Long moments passed. Verony slipped into an exhausted doze, only to be shocked back to alertness by the sound of running steps.

Slipping into shadows offered by a stone niche,

she prayed she would not be seen. Whoever was approaching did so stealthily. The steps were light and paused several times, as though fearing pursuers. Some thief or worse, Verony thought and flattened herself even further against the wall. By the time the steps came round the corner closest to her, she was barely breathing.

But the small, skinny form hurrying past was too alert not to notice her. It paused, whirled to flee, then slowly turned back as though doubting the evidence of its own eyes. Slowly, warily, they faced each other.

Verony's breath left her in a relieved, if surprised sigh. The mysterious intruder was a child. A little boy, perhaps eight years old, stood before her. He had dark curling hair, eyes bright as onyx and olive skin, most of which was well wrapped in a heavy cloak.

Intelligence and alertness radiated from him, but so did curiosity. His bewilderment at finding a noblewoman in such unlikely circumstances overcame even the greatest caution.

"What are you doing here?" he hissed softly.

Verony hesitated. She needed help desperately but she was reluctant to involve one so young in her troubles. Not until the boy took a step forward, seemingly determined on a response, did she murmur: "I'm . . . lost. . . ."

He paused, thinking that over, then asked: "Where were you going?"

Again Verony pondered before answering. If the royal guards did follow her this far and discovered the child had spoken with her, he would suffer greatly. But even if she told him nothing, it could still go hard on him.

Slowly she said: "I was trying to get home . . . to my family. I am . . . Lady Verony d'Arcy."

The boy's head jerked back. Deep black eyes widened in a searing gaze that left her no doubt he recognized the name. "Lord Curran's wife."

"How did you know?" Verony blurted, stepping away from the wall in an effort to get a closer look at the child who seemed fully aware now of her identity.

The boy shrugged. "What difference does it make how I know? If you are who you say, it's enough that I've found you." Sternly, he added: "Don't you realize how dangerous it is to be out here at this hour?"

An almost hysterical laugh broke from Verony. She smothered it with her hand. "I . . . was running away . . ."

"Who from?"

She was about to answer, having decided that the child already knew too much to try to keep anything back, when pounding hoofbeats shattered the stillness. Certain that no one but the king's men would be about on such a night, Verony froze in terror. Having only just accepted the need to go on living for the sake of the child, she could not bear the thought that life was about to be ripped from her.

The boy reacted more practically. Gripping her hand, he lunged forward. "Come on!"

Verony's breath caught in her throat, making it impossible for her to ask where they were going. Though the child was far smaller than she, coming barely to her breast, she had to run to keep up with him. Her legs were leaden, the last of her strength almost gone, when he dragged her under a large piece of wood propped against the wall and through a chink in the stonework.

Once inside, they did not pause but continued hurrying through twisting lanes dwarfed by tightly packed, ramshackle houses. Verony barely had a chance to glance around before the boy pulled her into an entryway and pounded on an iron-studded door.

It opened almost immediately. Light from the inside, flooding into the darkness, temporarily blinded her. Verony raised a hand to her eyes, shielding them, as she stared at the man who stood glowering at her rescuer.

"Samuel! Where in the name of the Lord have you been? Your mother's been worried sick!"

Panting from their frenzied race through the narrow streets, the boy did not answer. Tugging Verony into the house, he stood for a moment getting his breath before grinning excitedly. "She's Lady Verony d'Arcy, Lord Curran's wife. I think it's the king's men after her, leastway sounded like them. Figured I'd better bring her here."

The adults in the room stared at her in stunned silence. Verony counted five of them in her own hurried glance at her new surroundings. Besides the tall, bearded man who had opened the door, there was a younger man sitting near the fireplace next to a girl cradling a baby. Another woman, older and with wisps of gray hair escaping from beneath her veil, tended a pot of what smelled like stew.

The room was small and sparsely furnished, but meticulously clean. Fresh rushes lay on the flagstone floor. A vibrant wall-hanging opposite the fire depicted a Biblical scene. Elaborately carved wooden chests were pushed neatly against the walls, leaving room for a trestle table, benches and several low-slung beds half hidden by curtains.

Her quick surveillance was enough to tell Verony that the family was relatively well off. Merchants most likely, for that would account for the boxes of spices she noted, the unusual embroidered shawl the older man wore, and the beautiful gold candelabrum set on one of the chests.

Their apparent occupation might also explain their surprising familiarity with the d'Arcys, since they could well have provided goods to the Earl Garrett and Lady Emelie. But it did not reveal why they were willing to help her, or why the boy Samuel seemed so certain she would be safe among them.

Honor demanded that she warn them of the danger following her. "The king's men," Verony said softly, "will be determined to catch me. If they come here . . ."

"They won't," the older man interrupted. Stepping out of the shadows cast by the fire, he looked her over carefully. What he saw seemed to reassure him. When he spoke again, his voice was gentler. "The soldiers will not go past the wall, my lady. At least not before daybreak."

"But why? They can go anywhere they please, and if they thought I came this way . . ."

"They still won't follow. Not while it's still dark. They . . . fear this place. . . ."

Verony did not understand. She saw nothing to fear in gentle, kindly people who gave every evidence of being hard working and decent. On the contrary, she was already counting herself fortunate to be among them. Surely there were few other places in London where a lone woman would be as safe as she seemed to be.

"I don't understand. . . ."

The man sighed. He glanced toward the older woman who, taking in the pallor of Verony's face and the shivers racking her delicate form, stepped forward quickly.

"Come and sit down, my lady," the woman murmured, drawing Verony close to the fire.

Behind her the older man began questioning Samuel. "Where did you find her?"

Quickly the boy explained. When he was finished, he looked round proudly, only to be abruptly brought down to earth by the younger man's demand that he explain his own absence. "And what were you doing outside the wall after curfew? Playing with those Sicilian brats again?"

"And why not?" Samuel demanded stalwartly. "I like them. They've been everywhere on their father's boat. They tell great stories about the places they've seen." His child's voice rose an octave in excitement. "Why, do you know they've even been to Jerusalem! Seen the ruin of Solomon's temple and so many other wonders I can hardly remember them all." Turning to the other man, he insisted: "How could I leave, Papa? I had to stay and listen."

The adults looked at each other in exasperation. "That's fine, but how do you expect to ever get to

Jerusalem yourself if you keep taking such foolish risks?" his father demanded angrily. "You know what the watch guard would have done if you'd been found outside the wall. We'd have been lucky to get you back by paying a big fine. Others haven't been so fortunate."

Samuel hung his head. For the first time since she encountered him in the wind-swept street, Verony saw the bravado that was a natural part of his eager, vivacious nature crack. Brushing away surreptitious tears, he murmured: "I-I'm sorry . . ."

His remorse penetrated even the dead weight of her terrible grief. Taking a quick step forward, she implored the older man: "Please don't be angry at him. I know no one should be wandering around this city at night, but if Samuel hadn't found me, I don't know what I would have done. I'm deeply grateful to him, and to all of you."

Even though I still don't know just who you are, Verony added silently. Something of her bewilderment must have shown on her face, for after a moment the man nodded. "As you say, my lady, Samuel has done well this night. Enough so that we must forgive his lack of discretion."

He smiled at her gently in an expression of welcome whose graceful warmth few noble lords could match. "I am Aaron ben Sharon, a merchant of spices and silks who has had the honor to serve your family." Gesturing to the other adults, he added: "This is my wife, Ruth, my oldest son, Mordecai, and his wife, Miriam."

For the first time since entering the house, Verony felt some small measure of tension leave her. Aaron's introductions told her at once where she was and why he was so confident she would be safe at least until morning.

Inside the Jewish Quarter, she could count on remaining undisturbed by royal guards until sunrise. While night still held, superstition and prejudice would combine to keep them away.

Remembering also that Lady Emelie had said she and the Earl Garrett counted friends among the ghetto population, Verony managed to return her host's smile. Her own was shaky but nonetheless warm.

"I thank you for your protection, Aaron ben Sharon. You are truly a light in the darkness."

Beneath his beard, the merchant blushed. He was not accustomed to compliments from exquisitely beautiful ladies, nor could he even yet believe he was actually sheltering one in his own home. Under no circumstances would he have turned her out to take her chances in the streets. But a quick glance at the ring she wore, emblazoned with the d'Arcy family crest, changed simple courtesy to genuine welcome. He would do everything in his power to help her. The scars he carried on his body were a lifelong reminder of the debt he owed the Earl Garrett, without whose timely intervention so many years before he would never have lived to see this day.

The knowledge that she was safe ended the blessed numbness that had engulfed her. Pain and grief returned in full measure, wringing a soft moan from Verony.

Aaron's wife, Ruth, was instantly at her side. "Sit

back, my lady. That's it. You've had a shock but everything will be all right. You'll be back among your family before very long."

In gently urging her back against the chair, the older woman's hand brushed Verony's rounded belly. Ruth glanced up at her husband worriedly. "I think we'd best get her into bed. She's with child, and whatever happened tonight could not have done it any good."

Strong arms lifted her carefully. Briefly held against a broad chest covered by soft wool, Verony breathed in the pleasant scents of ginger and cloves mingling with wood smoke. While Aaron held her, Ruth and Miriam hastened to make up a bed. Lowered to it and covered warmly by a fur blanket, Verony could not stop the flood of tears trickling silently down her ashen cheeks.

The women gathered round her comfortingly, trying to coax her into telling them what was wrong. But Verony could not. Giving voice to the terrible fact of Curran's death would make it a reality she was not yet ready to confront.

Reassured at least that her unexpected guest's ordeal had not brought on premature labor, Ruth carefully measured a dose of ground poppy into a broth. As Miriam helped her to sit up, Verony managed to swallow most of it. Her last thought was of kind faces creased with concern before merciful sleep claimed her.

Drifting in and out of sleep all through that night and the following day, Verony was dimly aware of people coming and going around her. Ruth or

Miriam paused often to make sure she was all right before continuing with their household duties. Once she woke to find Samuel watching her. He smiled gently and held her hand, urging her to go back to sleep.

Urgent whispers next drew her from unconsciousness. She opened her eyes to find Aaron and Ruth in close conversation.

"I don't think anyone suspects she's here," her host was saying. "I saw several of our neighbors this morning and none acted oddly."

"What about in the city?" Ruth asked. "Are the king's men still about?"

Aaron shook his head. "There's no sign of them. Even the usual guard has withdrawn inside the tower. Word is that the king will leave London shortly, maybe even today. But no one knows for sure."

"Have you been able to get in touch with any of her family? The Earl Garrett perhaps?"

"I'm trying," Aaron assured her. "But there's something strange going on there, too. The earl and his eldest son, Mark, rode out yesterday evening with a large force of men. They headed straight for the tower and took up position around it. A message was sent inside, but I've no idea of what it contained. Word is, though, that the earl is threatening to take the tower apart stone by stone unless John does whatever it is he's demanding. Crowds have gathered nearby to watch, some shops are staying closed, and there's a lot of wild talk."

Ruth paled. She knew full well what even the

slightest social disturbance could lead to. Not all that many years had passed since the coronation of Richard the Lionhearted was used as an excuse to burn the Jewish Quarter of York and other towns. Hundreds had died, including her own father. The memory remained like a blood-tipped thorn within her. "You don't think there'll be trouble?" she asked nervously.

Her husband looked away. He could offer little reassurance and had his own fears to confront. Grimly he said: "All I can do is try to see the earl. Once I get word to him of Lady Verony's whereabouts, it will be in his hands."

Ruth nodded, fighting back the impulse to ask him to stay inside where there might be some measure of safety. If the streets erupted in violence, Aaron would have little chance of making it back unharmed. The grim knowledge that their pleasant home offered only the illusion of protection kept her silent. Better he should go and take the chance that the earl would be able to shield him.

Toward midafternoon, Verony managed to get down some of the hearty soup Ruth urged on her. For once, the nausea that had plagued her since the beginning of her pregnancy did not occur.

Cloistered in a cocoon of numbing grief and hushed expectancy, the young girl found it a struggle to stay awake. She was annoyed by the unaccustomed weariness of her body and spirit, but found she could not hold the sweet release of sleep at bay for more than a few minutes. As a pelting rain began to fall against the timbered roof, she gave up the struggle.

It was still raining when she awoke. The neighing of horses and the slamming of a door drove away her dreams. Stirring reluctantly, she opened deep-blue eyes opalescent with repressed tears.

In the dim light of that gray afternoon, it was difficult to see. People were entering the house, large men wrapped in capes and wearing battle helmets. Ruth stood aside for them, then fiercely embraced Aaron, who had followed quickly.

Verony blinked, struggling to sit up. Because she was still not fully returned to consciousness, the scene before her had the strange quality of a waking dream. A soft exclamation of surprise broke from her as she recognized the Earl Garrett. He was staring at her silently, a frown creasing his proud features.

The door opened again. Another man entered; larger and more powerfully built than almost all the others. He exchanged a word with the earl before striding to the bed.

Verony stared up at him, her eyes opening wide in shock. Her heart skidded to a halt, hung for a moment suspended between life and death, then began to beat fiercely. The breath left her throat except in a low, strained moan.

Gray-green eyes turned almost black with rage met hers coldly. Powerful hands shot out to grip her shoulders. His voice low and feral, Curran snarled; "I could cheerfully wring your neck!"

Chapter Thirteen

THE TRIP BACK TO THE D'ARCY COMPOUND WAS MADE
in silence. Curran refused to let Verony ride.
Wrapped in a blanket, she lay across his saddle.
Strong arms that had always offered such comfort
were now only a further reminder of his immense
anger.

Dazed by the sudden release from terrible grief
and bewildered by her husband's coldness, Verony
remained mute. She spoke only to sincerely thank
Aaron and Ruth for their care. Their kindly faces
were tight with concern as they embraced her gently.

Lifted onto Curran's stallion, she was dimly aware
of the curious eyes peering from behind shutters and
around doorways. No one in the Jewish Quarter was
foolish enough to venture out among an armed
group of warriors whose presence was not explained.
But they could speculate among themselves, waiting
only until the last flick of a horse's tail disappeared

beyond the wall before descending on Aaron with eager questions.

Back inside the compound, Curran carried her upstairs to their room. Depositing her on the bed, he stood for a moment staring down at her, his expression dark and forbidding. Without a word he turned and strode from the room.

A low moan of anguish escaped from Verony, but was quickly stifled as Lady Emelie entered hard upon her son's departure. Her expression was one more surprise to the young girl's already overburdened system. For the first time in their acquaintance, Lady Emelie looked torn by doubt, her forthright, indomitable spirit burdened by questions she could not answer.

The sight of Verony's ashen face resolved at least a part of Lady Emelie's misgivings. She hesitated barely an instant before crossing the room to take her daughter-in-law in her arms. "There, there," she crooned softly, "you're safe now. There's nothing more to fear."

Even as she yielded to the gentle warmth of Lady Emelie's arms, Verony had to fight back a bitter laugh. It wasn't like her mother-in-law to traffic in falsehood. However much reassurance she might receive, Verony knew full well she still had a great deal to fear. Saved from both the king and the abysmal chasm of grief, she had yet to come to terms with her husband's inexplicable rage.

Nor was she given much chance to do so. Barely had she managed to dry her tears before Lady Emelie bustled Verony out of her wrinkled clothes and into a hot bath. Clean and dry, her hair brushed in glistening curls down her back, she was dressed in a petal-soft tunic of mauve wool under a lush velvet surcoat whose dark-blue sheen matched her eyes.

Verony tried to ask what could possibly require these elaborate preparations, but Lady Emelie was too busy instructing the serving women to answer. A jewel chest she recognized as her mother-in-law's arrived. From it, Lady Emelie selected a circlet of beaten gold whose intricate, feather-light design took Verony's breath away. Set over the transparent veil covering her hair, it made her look even more like a beautifully adorned enchantress.

A wide, long belt of woven gold matched the circlet. Wrapped several times around Verony's small waist, it emphasized the ripe curve of her breasts and hips. When it was in place, Lady Emelie stood back to study her. "You are far too pale, but otherwise quite exquisite."

Their eyes met briefly, Verony's full of questions, Lady Emelie's masked but not unkind. The eager compliments of the serving women broke the silence. Before Verony could insist on being told what was going on, she found herself escorted downstairs and into the Main Hall.

With the exception of Mark, whom Verony guessed must still be with the force at the tower, all the d'Arcy men were gathered there. Curran stood beside his father, talking quietly with Arianna. The young girl glanced up, saw Verony and Lady Emelie and excused herself to join them.

"You look lovely," she told Verony sincerely.

Sensing that Arianna would be more forthcoming than the formidable countess, Verony took advantage of the moment. "My note . . . I hope it did not distress you too much?"

Arianna's eyes clouded. She glanced at her mother-in-law for guidance. "It was a shock, of course."

Lady Emelie sniffed disparagingly at such understatement. She shot a reproachful look at Verony even as Arianna's self-containment snapped. Abruptly the young girl exclaimed: "Oh, Verony, how could you do such a foolish thing! The worry you caused and the danger! Don't you realize what could have happened?"

Verony stared at her dumbly. *Didn't she realize?* She had been threatened with rape by the king, tortured by a fiendish lie, driven to commit a capital crime and saved from certain death only by the miraculous intervention of unexpected allies. How could Arianna think for a moment that she didn't fully understand the gravity of her actions?

"Never mind that now," Lady Emelie snapped, cutting off any explanation she might have made. "The archbishop is waiting."

Verony's gaze was drawn to the tall, somber man in conversation with the Earl Garrett and Curran. At close to fifty years, Stephen Langton was so lean and fit that he looked much younger. As Archbishop of Canterbury and primate of the church in England, he had the right to wear elaborately ornate robes of office. But instead he was plainly garbed in a brown wool tunic with only a discreet wooden cross hung from his belt to mark his office.

The simplicity of his dress in no way detracted from the innate authority of his presence. Even

Curran and the earl, accustomed though they were to receiving deference, accorded him a full measure of respect.

For just an instant the archbishop's eyes met Verony's, long enough to allow her a glimpse behind the solemn visage surrounded by neatly trimmed white hair and a beard. There was compassion in Stephen Langton and a far-sighted perceptiveness beyond anything she had encountered even among the acutely intelligent d'Arcys.

Distantly Verony remembered the stories she had heard of him. He was the spiritual leader of the rebellious nobles, the guiding force in the struggle for greater justice and freedom throughout England. She supposed his role in the political struggle explained his presence, but in that she was wrong.

"The archbishop cannot stay long," Lady Emelie said. "He is only here as a favor to Curran."

Her mother-in-law's hand on her arm guided Verony toward her husband. He did not appear pleased to see her. A scowl darkened his broad forehead. The shadow of a night's stubble hid the clean line of his jaw. His eyes were red, and there were deep lines of fatigue and tension carved on either side of his sensual mouth.

Curran's eyes, running over her dispassionately, made Verony tremble. If he saw her distress, he gave no sign. "You look very beautiful," he informed her frigidly. "But then you always do."

The bitterness in his voice appalled her. What could have happened to so turn him against her? Granted, he had every right to still be angry about her failure to tell him immediately of the king's lust.

And he undoubtedly thought she should not have gone off on her own to try to save him. But surely a loving wife could not be expected to simply stand by when her husband's life was endangered?

Biting her lip, Verony tried to still her own indignation. She had already suffered far too much to endure Curran's chastisement patiently. It was comfort she needed, not coldness.

At the end of her forbearance, Verony snapped: "If my presence is not required at this gathering, my lord, I would just as soon take my leave."

Curran's eyes hardened even further. A pulse beat erratically in his throat. The hand that grasped hers was bruising. "In a few minutes, my lady. Just now, your attendance is regrettably necessary."

His derision stung Verony. Pride alone made her hide the hurt he inflicted. Unbidden, the ironic thought that this was the man she had mourned so desperately a scant day ago rose to torment her. Never could she have envisioned that they would be facing each other as adversaries, separated by some force she could not begin to understand.

Masking her deep pain, Verony forced herself to face the archbishop calmly. She could not imagine why he might wish some word with her, but intended to get it over with as quickly as possible and escape back to her room.

When he began to speak, in his low, melodious voice, it took a moment for her to realize the significance of his words. When she did, Verony stiffened in disbelief. Turning on Curran, she blurted, "You don't mean to . . . I can't . . . !"

"I do and you will," he grated mercilessly, his

hand on her arm preventing her from fleeing. "Though the marriage performed by Father Dermond may well be legal, I will take no chances." His gaze drifted scornfully to her rounded belly. "The child you carry is too precious to me to risk labeling him a bastard. Otherwise, believe me, I would be anything but the eager bridegroom!"

"Curran . . ." the archbishop began, dismayed that any union should be solemnized in such hostility.

Verony was not aware of his intervention. All her attention focused on the desperate need to control the misery threatening to explode from her. Eyes averted, she went through the ceremony in silence. Only at the very end, when a response was required, did she look up.

Curran was regarding her enigmatically. There was still great rage in his scrutiny, but it was undercut by confusion and what looked very much like pain.

Puzzled by what she saw in his eyes, Verony mumbled her acceptance of the vows. This time there was no tender, lingering kiss to seal their union. As soon as the archbishop pronounced them wed, Curran dropped her hand. Turning his back, he walked over to the trestle table where the family shared its meals and poured himself a generous goblet of wine.

The d'Arcys, always inclined to forgive one of their own no matter what he or she might have done, glanced at each other worriedly. Lady Emelie said something inconsequential, as did Arianna, but their strained attempt at gaiety made no dent in the palpable air of tension engulfing the chamber.

As soon as she was decently able, Verony excused herself. She fled from the scene of her second marriage without a backward glance, wanting only the seclusion of her chamber where she could sob out her hurt undisturbed.

Her privacy proved shortlived. When the bedroom door swung open a few minutes later she looked up, intent on telling the serving woman or whoever else it might be that she wanted only to be left alone.

The words died in her throat. Curran crossed the threshold silently, closing the door firmly behind him and shooting the iron bolt into place.

Without a word, he went over to the low wooden stand where his chain mail and weapons were kept to await his squire's attention. Verony's throat closed achingly as he stripped off the shirt of metal links and unbuckled his longsword, laying it carefully aside.

Flames from the copper braziers glinted off his burnished skin as he removed the rest of his clothes. Naked, he walked to the bed where she lay and calmly slid under the covers.

Verony observed him in mingled disbelief and anger. After all his cruelty and coldness, he couldn't seriously expect to share her bed?

Indignation won out over caution. "Just what do you think you're doing?" she demanded.

One gray-green eye opened to regard her balefully. "Just what it looks like, sweet wife."

Determined not to shame herself in a childish display of temper, Verony hissed: "I don't want you here."

Curran let the words lie between them for a moment before he shrugged. "Too bad."

"Too bad? Why you . . . you unfeeling cur! How dare you come in here? When I think how you've treated me after I . . ."

Rearing up on the bed, Verony clenched her small hands as she faced him furiously. She held that position barely an instant before Curran's steely arms shot out. Grasping her shoulders, his fingers digging into the satin-soft skin, he turned her flat on her back under him.

Looming over her, his sinewy body pinned her to the bed. One powerful leg, thrown over hers, held her firmly in place as Curran snarled: "It's rare for a man to be given a second chance to start his marriage. I intend to take full advantage of it. Tonight you will learn once and for all what I should have made clear four months ago. There will be no more rash displays of independence when I'm through with you!"

Dark pools of sea-deep blue stared back at him in disbelief. "You c-can't mean to . . ."

"Enjoy your charms? Be assured, I do." Tauntingly, he trailed a hard finger down her ivory throat to the shadowy hollow between her breasts. "Your spirit may be unwomanly in the extreme, but your body is quite another matter. That pleases me, even if nothing else about you does."

His words stabbed her brutally, turning her voice thick with unshed tears. "I won't . . . not like this . . ." Desperately, her head tossed back and forth across the pillow, trying to evade his mocking lips.

She did not succeed. Curran's mouth found hers, closing on the soft flesh cruelly. His tongue stabbed inward, fully tasting her sweetness without thought to her comfort or pleasure.

A low moan tore from Verony. She could not struggle for fear of harming the child. But neither could she bear his contemptuous use of her body. "No! Don't . . . Curran, stop! I won't . . ."

She got no further. A hard hand tore open the laces of her surcoat. Through the thin tunic and chemise that were her only other covering, he fondled her breasts roughly.

At the same time, his other hand tugged at her skirts. Before she realized what was happening, the fabric was bunched around her waist and her womanhood was bare to his lustful gaze.

Verony shivered with revulsion as she realized he meant to take her like a whore crudely tumbled without thought or feeling. His heavy, hairroughened leg was forcing its way between her slender thighs when her cry of anguish stopped him.

Sobbing helplessly, Verony was only dimly aware of Curran looking down at her. Nor did she guess at the losing battle he fought to hold on to the all-consuming rage that engulfed him when he learned she had deliberately endangered herself and their child.

As a further example of her unseemly insistence on making her own decisions and acting for herself, it was the last straw. He vowed to bend her once and for all to his will. But not all the fury in the world could cause him to truly harm her.

The coldness drained slowly from his face as he gathered her into his arms. This time his touch was gentle, offering only comfort. Nestling her against him, his hands tenderly stroked her back and hair.

Verony struggled for control. When her sobs finally died away, Curran raised her head. She could not see his eyes, but there was no mistaking the rueful line of his mouth as he said: "You defeat me, my lady. I cannot hurt you."

Profoundly relieved, Verony was nonetheless still torn by confusion over why he should ever have wanted to do her harm. Hesitantly she said: "I don't understand your anger. I know I should have told you about the king's demands when he made them, but surely that failure was not enough to cause . . . this?"

A deep sigh escaped Curran. He turned on his back, away from her. "Of course not. I was hurt when you didn't confide in me at once, but I understood it sprang from your habit of depending only on yourself. I had hoped that by now you would have overcome that, learned to trust me, but I had no idea you would go so far beyond simply failing to tell me something."

"What choice did I have? When John sent that message, every moment was precious. I had to at least give the appearance of obeying to protect you."

"But if you were only willing to trust people more, to rely on someone other than yourself, you would have told my father of the message and let him respond as he thought best. Instead you went racing off, deliberately leaving word of your action where you knew it would not be found for hours." Lifting himself on one arm, Curran demanded: "Why, Verony? Why put yourself in such grave danger when there was no reason?"

"How can you say that? John threatened to kill you! There was the ring and that horrible . . . f-finger. . . ."

Curran sighed deeply. "The finger came from a cadaver, and as for the ring, . . . it was a copy. Several weeks ago Isabella made a show of admiring the original. She even insisted on making a sketch of it. I thought it just more of her senseless flirting and ignored her. Little did I guess she intended to order an exact copy and give it to John, to help him trick you."

"S-so you were never in his hands?"

"Never," Curran affirmed quickly. "I went to Canterbury, spoke with Stephen, and we agreed that to be on the safe side, you and I should go through another marriage ceremony. He accompanied me back here, arriving just in time to find the house in an uproar and my father threatening to tear the tower down and strangle the king himself if he didn't reveal my whereabouts. Naturally, they were all relieved to see me until we realized that you were still missing."

"I was at the tower waiting to see John. It was hours before he finally came and when he did . . . he . . ." Her voice broke, the king's monstrous lie returning to haunt her.

Curran's eyes closed slightly, hiding his expression. "What happened, Verony? What did John do?"

The barely controlled rage in his voice alerted Verony to what he believed had occurred. Swiftly she said: "He hardly touched me, Curran. I swear it. He had no chance to do more because . . . he told me you were dead. . . . He described . . . how you were killed. . . . Something snapped inside me . . . I didn't care about anything then. I just had to hurt him somehow. . . . So I picked up a stool. I hit him . . . over and over. . . . He wasn't expecting it, and I was too quick. He fell on the floor . . . but I kept hitting again and again . . . I couldn't stop. . . ."

There was no mistaking the depth of her pain and torment. It stabbed through Curran more savagely than any weapon. He could think only to gather her tight into his arms, holding her fiercely to him until the storm of her horror dimmed.

When she was at last able to speak again, Verony looked up fearfully. "I may have killed him, Curran! I hit him so hard."

"John lives," he assured her firmly. At the questioning wonder in her eyes, he explained: "The men we sent into the tower to demand your return saw him. Granted, he's covered with bruises and his head is bandaged. But he was sitting up, and he spoke to them directly, so he can't be all that badly injured." An appreciative laugh escaped him. "The word is that he fell down the stairs while drunk. And John is saying nothing to refute that. He's the last man on earth to want it known that a woman overcame him. Don't worry, sweetling, he can do nothing against you now."

The last of Verony's fear slipped from her. Safe in her husband's arms, she curled against him. His embrace was warm and gentle, his body a shelter from any storm.

For several minutes he held her tenderly, offering the comfort he understood she needed. But then Curran moved slightly away, looking down at her. "Much as I appreciate what you tried to do, Verony, I must leave no doubt in your mind that I do not approve. Your actions were impulsive and dangerous, to yourself and our child. Surely you can't believe I value my life more than both of yours?"

Verony met his eyes reluctantly. She resented his censure, for she still thought she had acted properly. "I could not run the risk that John would grow impatient and kill you. If I had gone to the earl . . ."

"He would have handled the situation better, in keeping with my own best interests and those of our family."

A deep sigh escaped him. "You have many good qualities which I admire, but your stubborn insistence on independence is a danger to us all. This business with John is a perfect example. Your initial refusal to confide in me paved the way for him to challenge our marriage. And your lack of faith in my father put you and our child in mortal peril."

Tipping her head back, he gazed deeply into her eyes. "You are a beautiful and brave woman. I am proud to call you mine and to know that my children will come from you. But until you learn to accept your proper role, I will feel you are not fully my wife."

Verony did not answer. She was deeply hurt by what seemed like a callous lack of appreciation for her courage. His insistence that she submit her will to the control of others rankled. It went smack up against the fierce pride and self-reliance that had sustained her life for so long.

Moreover, his suggestion that she was not completely the wife he wanted wounded her deeply. It appeared he was demanding she give up all of herself to become merely a vessel for his expectations.

Moving away from him, Verony turned on her side with her back toward her husband. The distance between them did not narrow as they spent an uneasy night in light sleep and sorrowful thought.

Chapter Fourteen

THE SPRING CAME LATE THAT YEAR. AT THE END OF
April, frost still lay on the ground. By May, the first
wildflowers were just beginning to appear. The long
wait for fair weather, after the harsh winter, further
strained the nerves of those tensely anticipating
the confrontation that could not be delayed much
longer.

In London, Verony watched the snow melt, the
frost disappear and the rivers swell. From the window of the solar, she could see the fields surrounding the d'Arcy compound. Serfs brought from the
family's main holding in the south moved through
them, preparing the land for new crops. Others
were busy tending the newborn sheep, cows, pigs
and horses who crowded the stables around the
bailey. Still more could be heard hammering and
sawing as the inevitable toll of winter was repaired.

It was a busy time, but one in which she took little

part. Her swollen belly was heavy and cumbersome. The child moved often, most frequently at night when she tried vainly to sleep. Her back ached and even the effort of climbing stairs or rising from a bench required assistance.

Verony sighed. She longed for the baby and loved it already, but she had to admit that pregnancy was even more of a trial than she had expected. With Curran's constant absence she had to look to Lady Emelie and Arianna for help and encouragement. They did everything possible, but she still missed her husband keenly.

Even the few times he was at home, he seemed more like a stranger than the warm, loving man she had briefly known. Since the night they were rewed, he had not spoken again of his pain at her inability to be completely the wife he wanted. But there seemed no doubt his feelings had not changed. They observed a wary truce that did nothing to bridge the gulf between them.

Verony deeply regretted their lack of closeness, but had no idea how to end it. Even as she privately admitted she had acted impulsively in the matter of John, she knew she could never be the docile, malleable wife Curran appeared to want. Nor did she believe for a moment such a woman would be truly capable of sharing his life. He would quickly tire of her, whether he cared to acknowledge it or not.

A compromise was needed. But with the great political events of the day rushing to their conclusion, private problems had to wait.

Verony sighed, making forlorn stabs at her bedraggled needlework. She was sick to death with waiting. To one accustomed to strength and agility in both mind and body, her present state was irritating in the extreme. While everyone else was gainfully occupied, she could do nothing but sit in the sunlight and confront her uneasy thoughts.

Certainly there was no opportunity to take part in the sweeping political machinations going on all around her. She had no choice but to rely on the other d'Arcy women for the latest news. As busy as they were, Lady Emelie and Arianna still found time to sit with her, sharing her solitude and bringing a breath of the wide world into her confinement.

"John is in Windsor this week," the countess was saying. "He's trying to convince the lords there to support him, but without success."

Verony shook her head bemusedly. Since abruptly leaving London four months before, the king had crisscrossed the country trying to convince his recalcitrant nobles to stand with him. Wherever he went—from Wessex to East Anglia, Northumbria to Mercia—he found at best cold refusal and frequently outright rage.

The d'Arcy's were doing their job well. Like the king, the Earl Garrett, Mark and Curran spent the late winter and early spring in constant movement around the country. Within a matter of weeks, they met with every nobleman of consequence in the kingdom, assuring that the barons remained firm in their struggle for reform. Everyone knew that the day was fast approaching when even John would no longer be able to deny their success.

"A few barons still follow him," Verony reminded her. "Though I cannot imagine why."

"Because he pays them," Arianna averred. "They are no more than mercenaries."

Lady Emelie nodded. "He won't be able to keep that up for long. All revenues due him from the lords are being withheld until he agrees to meet with them again and reach some accord."

Putting down her needlework, Verony asked: "How much longer do you think he can hold out? Surely he realizes that if he tries to delay much further, he may spark outright rebellion that could topple him from the throne."

"I think," the countess mused, "John's whole strategy these last months has centered on wearing the nobles down. He knows no one wants civil war, which is what we would come to if the monarchy is overturned. Every baron in the kingdom would be vying to take John's place, and the result would be bloodshed beyond anything we have ever seen. So there was a certain twisted logic about believing that the confrontation could be brought to a choice between accepting the system we have now or facing long, destructive conflict."

"But he counted on our determination being less than it is," Arianna said. "Surely John is incapable of anticipating the degree of fortitude and selflessness our own family has brought to this struggle. Throughout, the Earl Garrett, Mark and Curran have all said we will gain nothing but freedom from the abuses of the throne."

"Unfortunately, few barons were willing to accept such assurances on face value," Verony pointed out ruefully. "Each believed the earl secretly wanted to put himself in John's place. That's why it has been so hard to keep the coalition firm."

None of the women wanted to say that the goal had finally been achieved, but the smiles they shared and the ease of their talk showed their conviction that the long struggle was almost over.

Certainly the earl's message that he and his sons would be back in London at any moment had not come as a surprise. The time was fast approaching when the rebel forces would meet to decide on final terms.

Cut off from the rush of events, Verony chafed at her idleness. The day, which had begun slowly enough, seemed to drag on endlessly. When Lady Emelie and Arianna returned to their household tasks, she found some occupation in the weaving rooms but could not sit comfortably for any length of time and had to leave.

A walk in the gardens soothed her somewhat, until the activity all around her reminded Verony of everything she could not do. Seeking the quiet of her own room, she indulged in what had become an almost daily ritual, going lovingly through the blankets, shirts and swaddling clothes prepared for the baby.

Seated beside the window, pillows piled at her back, she relaxed at last as she stitched yet another petal-soft chemise so small it was difficult to believe anything could ever fit into it.

Touching her belly, Verony smiled. Curran was certain the child was a boy. Lady Emelie agreed, saying that the infant's frequent movements and the fact that Verony was carrying so low indicated she would bear a son.

She prayed it was true, and that Curran would be pleased. Anything that might help close the distance between them was welcome. Thinking of her husband, she frowned. She knew he was well because he said so in his frequent letters. What she knew of the most recent political developments indicated he was actually in less danger than earlier in the year, when the king had tried to provoke what could easily have been a bloody showdown. Certainly everything she heard pointed to a peaceful conclusion by summer. She could look forward to spending the most pleasant months of the year with her husband and child back on their own estates where she prayed their differences would finally be resolved.

Yet still she worried. There were rumors filtering up from the streets of London that concerned her deeply. The citizenry, tense with the long wait and made reckless by the conviction that the king would be forced to give up some of his power, showed signs of hoping to take advantage of the situation for themselves.

For the more intelligent and reasonable, it was enough that any diminishing of royal authority would open up freedoms that could not help but benefit them, whether or not they were explicitly mentioned in the final agreement.

But for the sullen poor, too long weighed down by the combined abuses of the king and certain of his rapacious nobles, the present situation fueled a tinderbox of resentment and violence needing only a spark to set it off.

Late that evening, just as the long spring twilight gentled into darkness, the firebrand fell.

Verony had returned to her chamber after sharing supper with the Lady Emelie and Arianna in the Great Hall. Even in the absence of all but the younger boys, the family retainers gathered at the long trestle tables were ever mindful of their manners.

A musician strummed his lute as a bard recited. No one was in a mood for song, but there was no objection to quiet listening.

Verony was pleasantly drowsy before the meal ended. She accepted Lady Emelie's company back to her chamber and the two women talked briefly before the countess departed for her own quarters.

Undressed by her serving women, the silken veil of her hair brushed to a coppery sheen, she slid into a long white sleeping robe and padded over to the bed. Glancing down the length of her body under the covers, Verony smiled ruefully. She thought she looked like a beached whale.

Only by lifting her head as far as possible could she catch a glimpse of her toes. They wiggled at her cheerfully as Hilda grumbled: "That's enough now! It's time you were asleep."

Verony relented with poor grace. Now that she was actually in bed, her contrary body no longer felt tired. Disappointment over Curran's continued absence gnawed at her.

The message received that morning had said the earl and his son would be home as quickly as possible, but that could mean the following morning or even perhaps several days hence. Her patience, already sorely tried, stretched almost to breaking.

Flopping over on her side, she tried vainly to get comfortable. Hilda bustled about, straightening her clothes and picking up the sewing left discarded by the window. The nurse gazed at her charge tenderly, wishing she could do more for her but knowing that only Curran's return would better her humor. Bidding her lady a fond good night, Hilda departed to find her own rest.

Half an hour later, Verony was still awake and growing more discontent by the moment. Experience had taught her that any effort to lie still and court sleep would fail. Rising with considerable difficulty, she pulled on a woolen robe and returned to the window.

The last light had almost faded. A pale crescent moon shone ghostly against scattered clouds. The fields surrounding the house were empty; no boats moved along the river. London was settling down for the night.

Drowsily, she leaned her head against the stone wall and thought of the men and women going about their lives in the narrow timber-frame houses. Children would be sound asleep by now, snuggled into their beds under the eaves. Tables would be clear of the debris from dinner, wiped down with sand and water and tucked against the wattle and daub walls where they were out of the way until morning. Pallets spread on the dirt or flagstone floors would offer some slight ease to weary servants whose final tasks of the day would include banking the fires beneath the wide stone chimneys.

With so many people packed so tightly together, the smoke of London's fireplaces could be seen miles away. During the winter, the chimneys were in constant use. Only with warm weather, such as that enjoyed during the past few weeks, could fuel be saved by extinguishing the fires when the day's cooking was done.

It was an economy no Londoner failed to take advantage of, so why then could she make out wisps of dark smoke rising from the west of the city?

Straightening, Verony stared intently out the window. She was not mistaken. Black smoke was pouring into the sky from the residential district near the river, and it was growing denser by the moment.

The Jewish Quarter! Comprehension slammed through Verony with the force of a blow. Turning, she raced from the room. As quickly as her cumbersome shape would allow, she negotiated the steep stone steps leading down to the courtyard, sped across the open field and hurried into Lady Emelie's house. The countess was already downstairs, her clothing hastily jerked on and her voice sharp as she rapped out orders.

"Leave twenty men to guard the compound. Take the rest with you. Find Aaron ben Sharon and offer your help. He will be in contact with the other Jewish leaders and will know what can be done."

"My lady," the man protested, "your safety must be my first concern. I cannot leave you here so poorly defended."

Lady Emelie straightened to her full height. Without rancor, with the simple calmness of one who expects to be obeyed, she said: "You will do as I order. Immediately."

For just a moment, the man looked as though he wished to argue further. He thought better of it. Decades of service to the d'Arcy clan had taught him that once the Lady Emelie made up her mind about something she could not be swayed. At least not by anyone other than the earl himself who, God pity them, was not at home.

With the men dispatched, Lady Emelie turned her attention to the two white-faced young women watching her. "We will need blankets, salves for burns, bandages, warm clothing. Get the servants busy setting up shelters in the bailey. What space there is inside will be used for the most seriously injured."

Numbly, Verony and Arianna nodded. Each was experienced in the aftereffects of battle and had a fair idea of what could be expected. But the knowledge that this time the victims were helpless men, women and children—rather than seasoned warriors—added a piercing sense of dread to what they would shortly confront.

As the twilight flickered and died, huge fires could be seen burning in the west. The entire quarter must be aflame, Verony thought dimly as she hastened about her tasks. There was mercifully little time to dwell on what was happening. Every bit of strength and concentration had to be given over to preparing for the injured and homeless who would be unlikely to find care anywhere else.

Not very far away, in the center of the ghetto, Curran also paused a moment to watch the flames. Despite the cool night, his face was streaked with grime and sweat. The heat of burning buildings seared his skin.

Along with his father and Mark, he had ridden hard all day in hope of reaching London before nightfall. After weeks in the saddle, he might have expected to feel some weariness. But the sight of a rampaging mob descending on the homes of unarmed, unprotected families sent a surge of rage tearing through him that banished all fatigue.

It was a relentless, implacable warrior who—in company with the other d'Arcy men and their escort—breached the wall of attackers around the ghetto, established a line of defense around the houses not yet afire and fought fiercely to stop the assault.

They were gravely outnumbered by the drunken, bloodthirsty mob carrying axes, picks, clubs and swords. But with the help of men from the quarter, whose desperate determination made up for their lack of training, they managed to turn the tide.

Fighting alongside a young, bearded rabbi who showed considerable natural talent with the shortsword, Curran led a defensive line that gradually pressed outward against the crowd.

Reclaiming one house not yet engulfed in flames, he dispatched a rampaging citizen about to hurl a howling infant out a second-story window. Returning the child to a sobbing young girl, only just saved from gang rape by the sudden arrival of the defenders, he left a small group to hold the recaptured ground while the rest fought on toward the main focal point of the attack, the synagogue.

It was already on fire when they arrived. All outer walls were aflame and the roof had begun to ignite.

No amount of effort could save the structure, but that did not prevent the young rabbi from racing inside.

Curran yelled at him to stop, without effect. Hesitating barely a moment, he ordered his men to stay where they were and followed.

Thick black smoke almost blinded him. A corner of his cloak wrapped around his face offered little protection. Shouting at the man to come back, he swallowed fumes that made him gag.

Stumbling and choking, Curran managed finally to reach the temple's inner sanctuary. Behind a burning curtain, the rabbi was frantically pulling large, cloth-wrapped scrolls from an ornate box. The man's smoke-reddened eyes opened wide with shock as he spied Curran. Unable to speak because of the thick clouds of smoke, he mutely acquiesced to let him help carry whatever it was he was trying so desperately to save.

Holding onto each other and the scrolls, they only just managed to make it back outside before the entire temple roof gave way in a rush of flame and the building fell in on itself.

Slumped on the ground, retching up blackened mucus, Curran was only dimly aware of his father and Aaron ben Sharon kneeling beside him. A cold cloth was pressed to his face as his helmet was pulled off.

Resisting the removal of his armor, Curran was stopped by the earl. "It's all right. It's over. The mob's been driven off."

When the words penetrated the haze of smoke and

blood and flame, Curran relented. He lay back long enough to allow his father to determine that he was not seriously injured, but rejected the suggestion that he rest for a few minutes.

"How many injured?" he demanded, standing up.

Aaron shook his head despondently. "We aren't sure yet. Dozens, at least. And as many dead. If it hadn't been for you and your father . . ."

"We will not speak of that, old friend," the Earl Garrett interrupted, "or I will be forced to remind you of the great service you only recently provided to my family."

Aaron did not try again to express his thanks, knowing that words were unnecessary. The look on the earl's face and on the faces of the other warriors slowly gathering round them was enough to silence him. He saw shock and more. In the eyes of lords and knights alike was great shame for what their fellow Christians had done. Later there would be time for Aaron to express his gratitude. Just then it was kinder to say nothing.

A line of wagons entering what remained of the ghetto from the direction of the d'Arcy compound caused no surprise.

Lady Emelie would have anticipated the need to transport the injured. But when the countess herself hopped lightly from one cart, the earl hurried forward in concern.

"You should not be here, Emelie. It's still far too dangerous."

His lady ignored him. Standing on tiptoe, she pressed a short, hard kiss to his lips before demanding briskly: "Let's not waste time in foolish argument, Garrett. We cannot care for the injured here. They must be moved at once. Verony and Arianna are waiting back at the compound with all the necessary supplies."

Glaring at the grin that passed between his sons, the earl gave in with poor grace.

The courtyard of the d'Arcy compound was ablaze with light. Every servant was awake and hurrying about their tasks under the watchful eyes of Verony and Arianna. Large vats stood ready with bandages being soaked in water and fat for the burned. Two reluctant surgeons dragged out of their beds by the countess's men readied their implements. A discomfited priest moved about, trying to determine which among the dead and injured he could legitimately succor.

No such hesitation afflicted the d'Arcy women as they threw themselves into the grisly business of sorting out those who could still benefit from help.

Verony steeled herself against the sight of a little girl, her face streaked with blood from a head injury, crying in the arms of her burned mother. Accepting the woman's insistence that the child be seen to first, she gently determined the extent of damage before cleaning and bandaging the wound. With rest and care, the little girl would recover.

But her mother was a different matter. Though the woman remained stoically silent throughout Verony's ministrations, she was clearly in great pain. One arm and shoulder were badly burned and there were lesser burns on her back and legs.

Remembering Lady Emelie's warning that burn victims were particularly susceptible to virulent inflammations, she took special care to apply all the medicines the countess recommended. That done, she wrapped the woman in blankets and eased her onto a pallet. A neighbor who had mercifully escaped with little more than bruises took up the watch beside her as Verony hurried on to others needing her attention.

The hours before dawn passed in a blur. After the initial horror, a welcome numbness set in. It was pierced only briefly, when she found Ruth and Miriam helping with the injured. The women embraced, sharing their sorrow even as Verony found profound relief in the knowledge that all members of the family that had sheltered her had come through the terrible night unharmed.

"Aaron is still with the earl," Ruth told her. "They are keeping watch over what's left of our homes and businesses, to prevent looting." She took a shaky breath, blinking back tears. "May the Lord protect them. If it hadn't been for Earl Garrett, his sons and his men, none of us would be alive."

"I thought we were doomed," Miriam admitted, "when I saw the mob coming. Our men would fight with all their strength and courage, but I knew it was only a matter of time before they were overcome." Her eyes darkened with remembered terror.

Ruth put an arm around her shoulders comfortingly. "Your husband deserves our special thanks," she told Verony. "He went into the burning temple after Rabbi Josephus to bring out the scrolls."

"The scrolls?" Verony repeated blankly.

"Our holy writings," Ruth explained. "To us they are as living things, the symbol of our belief. When scrolls are destroyed, we bury the remains just as we would a person. Their loss would have caused great sorrow throughout our community."

Glad though she was that Curran had been able to help their friends in some mysterious way, Verony was more concerned with his safety. He had yet to return from the Quarter, and though she knew his continued absence meant he was unharmed, she still needed reassurance of his well-being.

"Did you see him?" she asked.

Ruth smiled understandingly. "Only for a moment as we were leaving to come here. He was lifting children into the wagons and looked dirty and tired, but uninjured."

Verony thanked her softly. The worst of the casualties had been seen to, and activity in the courtyard was slowing down. A few people still moved around, checking on friends and relatives, but most lay quietly on straw pallets.

In the aftermath of terror, shock was settling in. Voices were muted, faces pale. Children whimpered fearfully in their sleep. Adults soothed them automatically, their minds still engulfed by the terror they had passed through.

Among the last left on their feet after that long, exhausting night were the d'Arcy women. Lady Emelie and Arianna were rolling up the few leftover bandages when Verony joined them. They were both white-faced and weary, but still had more strength than her burdened body could manage. It needed but a single look for the countess to order her off to bed.

"You've already worked far too hard and there's little more to be done here. Go and lie down before nature compels you to do so."

Only the knowledge that the last thing they needed was another patient forced Verony to obey. Wearily she trudged up the stairs to her chamber, where Hilda waited.

The old nurse, who had done more than her part in caring for the injured, was beside herself with dismay. Muttering dire comments about noble ladies' disregard for their well-being, she eased Verony's bloodstained clothes from her, washed her gently in warm water and slid a clean linen chemise over her head before tucking her into bed.

"Don't let me see you move, my lady," the nurse warned ominously. "You'll answer to me *and* Lord Curran if you do, and I've no doubt what he would say."

Verony smiled tiredly. She would be willing to listen to anything from Curran if only he was there to be with her. Hoping that he would soon return, she drifted into uneasy sleep.

Her rest did not last long. Before the sun was fully risen, a stabbing pain in her back woke her. Verony lay unmoving in the bed, hoping the discomfort would ease. It did, only to return within minutes.

A sheen of perspiration shone on her face as the pain came and went through the next hour. Each time it returned, the hurt was greater until finally a low anguished moan broke from her.

Hilda, who had remained near her mistress, was

instantly alert. She bent over Verony worriedly, taking in the ashen pallor of her skin and the contractions rippling through her swollen belly.

Squeezing the young girl's hand reassuringly, she hurried out to fetch Lady Emelie. While she was gone, Verony lay staring up at the beamed ceiling. No words had been needed to tell her that out of this night of blood and fire her child would be born.

Chapter Fifteen

VERONY FLOATED IN A SEA OF PAIN. FAR FROM ANY hope of rescue, she drifted under a burning sky. A relentless red sun seared her. Tossed on waves of agony, her body arched piteously, too weary even to cry out.

The women gathered in the room looked at each other helplessly. Through all the previous day and the long night, they had done everything within their skill to bring the child forth alive. Every remedy had been tried, and had failed. In the last desperate hours, even those ancient practices prohibited by the church were resurrected in a final, extreme attempt to save the life drifting away from them.

Nothing worked. Hour followed torturous hour, and still the child would not be born. Lady Emelie wondered if it even still lived. Not that it mattered.

Verony stood on the brink of death. Downstairs, watched over by his father and brothers, Curran was going slowly mad. Silently Lady Emelie told herself there would be other children. But only if Verony lived.

Stepping to a corner of the room, the countess motioned to Ruth ben Sharon. The two women spoke urgently for several minutes before nodding in agreement. Servants were sent for fresh towels and water. Hilda was dispatched to the kitchens after some herbal concoction it would take a good while to find. Miriam followed her to the door, making sure no priest was in sight.

Lady Emelie opened her medicine chest. She carefully removed the fitted trays holding ointments, tinctures and elixirs. Beneath the last, hidden under a false bottom, lay half a dozen steel implements. They bore no resemblance to the crude, often filthy tools used by the surgeons. Brought from the East, where medicine maintained an exacting standard free of religious interference, the blades, needles and forceps were meticulously honed and clean.

Even so, she took the precaution of carefully scrubbing her hands and purifying the tools in fire before returning to the bed. Sorrow gripped her as she stared down at the tormented face of her daughter-in-law. Silently she prayed that Verony would understand and forgive her.

Arianna eased the covers back. Her face tightened with pity as she moved Verony's legs apart. Ruth gripped her arms. Lady Emelie moved to the foot of the bed, her hand taut on the forceps. She paused just a moment, to go over carefully in her mind exactly what must be done.

Her hesitation lasted barely the length of a single breath, but in that instant Verony's eyes shot open. A low moan of protest broke from her, distracting the women who had thought her far beyond consciousness.

Verony's anguished mind, lying dazed and exhausted beneath a red haze of pain, still managed to grasp the meaning of what Lady Emelie held.

Her cracked lips parted. Breath rushed through her throat raw with screaming. "N-nooo . . . !"

Downstairs, Curran heard her. For the first time in hours, a tiny glimmer of hope darted through him. Verony was alive and at least semiconscious. Hard upon that relief came the knowledge that she was aware of her suffering. His self-control snapped.

He had waited too long, letting himself believe that others would be able to help her. They could not, and he could no longer bear for her to endure alone. Evading the well-meaning restraint of his father and brothers, he dashed up the steps.

The scene that confronted him as he burst into the room needed no explanation. He saw his wife, her belly still grotesquely swollen with the child, trying frantically to rise. Arianna and Miriam were struggling to stop her. Emelie stood uncertainly at the foot of the bed, white-faced and trembling. Ruth had an arm around her shoulders. Her other hand held the forceps Emelie had dropped in shock when Verony began to fight what must surely be inevitable.

"There is no other way," the countess said quickly when she saw her son. "If the child remains within her, she will die."

Curran did not reply. All his attention was focused on Verony. Pain twisted through him, made all the more acute by guilt over his part in her suffering. Arianna and Miriam stepped aside as he sat down on the bed, drawing his wife into his arms.

"P-please . . ." she murmured piteously, "don't let them . . . The baby . . . has to have a chance. . . . Don't let them . . ."

Curran looked at his mother questioningly. He did not blame her for what she intended to do. He understood full well that she would not have even considered it if it hadn't been absolutely necessary. But of all the people gathered in the room, he alone understood what Verony would go through if the child was killed to save her. Knowing the almost limitless extent of her love and compassion, he doubted she would be able to survive such sorrow.

"Is there any other way?" he asked softly.

Lady Emelie hesitated. All the signs indicated that Verony would die unless the baby was removed quickly. But she knew enough of human nature to understand that women such as her daughter-in-law were capable of extraordinary feats of courage and strength, especially if supported by a man she cherished.

"Ruth and I have both tried to bring the baby out," she explained. "But it is twisted in such a way that neither of us could manage. Verony's strength is almost gone. She can no longer bear down with the contractions to help force the child from her. She has lost a great deal of blood, and each moment this continues increases the chances that she will hemorrhage. One way or another, it must end."

Curran nodded slowly. He touched a gentle hand to his wife's face, feeling the cold clamminess of her skin. Her eyes, pools of suffering bright with the acceptance of her own mortality, locked with his. "D-don't listen to them . . . The baby must live. . . . Nothing else matters. . . ."

He swallowed hard, fighting down the aimless rage her words provoked. It would do no good to rail against the merciless fate that sought to take her from him. Nor would he argue with Verony herself. Profoundly touched by her selflessness, he still disagreed with it totally. Her life was vastly more important to him than that of the child who might or might not survive.

Only the torment of her pain-filled features stopped him from telling Lady Emelie to go ahead. In the severest test of his courage that he had ever faced, Curran reached a decision. He placed Verony's hand gently back beside her and moved to the foot of the bed.

"Let me try."

His mother wavered. She wanted desperately to believe that he might be able to help, but she doubted he could do more than increase Verony's torment and his own. "Your hands are too large . . ."

"Perhaps. But I will still try." Looking up, he held his wife's gaze with his own. "And Verony will help me. We'll bring this child forth together." He did not add that it no longer mattered to him whether the baby came out dead or alive. All that counted was that she trust him enough to cease all resistance and let him do what had to be done.

Through the burning cloud of her pain, Verony understood him. She knew this was the child's last chance, and perhaps hers as well. Some hard kernel of denial dissolved within her. She could feel her mind and spirit becoming fluid, barriers melting, merging slowly, effortlessly into the mind and spirit of the man who held all her attention.

The room, the other women, the pain itself all faded from her consciousness. There was only Curran, his strength and determination all that now stood between her and death.

His hands were carefully washed and oiled when he next approached the bed. Clean towels were laid beneath her. The women stood back, knowing they had no part in this final struggle for life.

At first, he believed his mother was correct. He could not reach inside her to find the child. But after a long painful moment, the bones of her body seemed to relax. He could feel them giving way before his gentle, careful probing even as his own hand seemed to reshape to fit her.

In the instant that he touched the child, Curran almost recoiled. His eyes closed in horror. What monster had he spawned? There were multiple arms and legs, all tangled together. His discovery must have shown on his face, for his mother made a quick motion, causing Arianna to step forward, blocking Verony's view.

The mass of limbs and torso finally gave way to a

small, smooth head. Closing his fingers around it, Curran pressed his other hand against Verony's abdomen. He pushed hard even as she summoned the last of her strength in a final, desperate effort to expel the child.

He was sweating profusely when a patch of dark, wet fuzz finally appeared. "It's coming," Lady Emelie breathed. "Careful now . . ." Ruth moved forward with a blanket to receive what they all feared would be a twisted parody of a human child.

Slowly, cautiously, Curran drew out the head. It was followed quickly by wide shoulders framed by sturdy arms . . . a long, glistening torso . . . and two robust legs ending in dimpled feet.

His mouth dropped open in blank amazement as he stared at his perfectly formed son who was already squalling noisily. The child looked, at least at a quick glance, to be completely normal. Certainly he was nothing like the atrocity his father had touched. What then could he possibly have felt inside his wife's overburdened womb?

The answer was not long in coming. A low mew of protest rippled from the almost unconscious Verony as yet another contraction wracked her body. With the path to the world at last unblocked, nothing could hold back the tiny but vigorous girl born just minutes after her brother.

Curran had little awareness of what happened next. He swayed slightly, prompting Lady Emelie to shove a stool under him from which he watched dazedly as the women sprang into action. Freed of the weight of impending tragedy, they lost no time staunching the small amount of blood that followed the afterbirth and getting Verony clean and comfortable as the babies were carefully washed and tucked into a nest of blankets.

"We'll have to fetch another from the storerooms," Lady Emelie murmured bemusedly, staring down at the crowded cradle, "but I don't suppose it will hurt them to share awhile longer since they've been doing just that these last nine months."

Arianna shook her head in wonderment. "Verony did seem to be getting awfully big. But I never guessed . . ."

"Neither did I," the befuddled countess admitted. "There was only a single heartbeat, and though I thought the child unusually vigorous, it never occured to me there were actually two of them!"

Ruth gazed down at the infants in the cradle. The boy was larger by far, but it was the girl who had her eyes opened and gave every appearance of already sizing up the strange place in which she found herself. "They shared a single birth sac," she pointed out, "and their hearts probably beat in unison, making you believe there was only one."

"But there wasn't," Curran muttered, coming out of his stupor sufficiently to stare at his children. "I can't believe it . . . twins . . ."

Rising shakily, he went to stand beside Verony. She was deeply asleep, her red-gold hair spread over the pillow and her lovely face already regaining something of its normal color. Infinite tenderness and gratitude filled him as he gently lifted her hand, pressing a long kiss into her palm.

A low sigh escaped him. Still holding her hand, he

sat down beside her. Despite the great fatigue following hard on the release of his terrible fear, he remained there throughout the day. No thought of rest could distract him from the slow rise and fall of her breath, surely the most precious sight in all the world.

Chapter Sixteen

"No sense seeing how tired you can get," Hilda said gruffly. Taking Verony's arm, she headed back toward her room. "You're a bad enough patient without letting you get cranky."

"I'm not any sort of patient. I'm a perfectly healthy woman who's sick and tired of staying in bed." Digging in her heels, Verony tried to hang back. Being allowed out of bed less than two hours a day was hardly enough to ease her restlessness.

Ignoring her young mistress's futile efforts, Hilda continued on determinedly. "If you'd seen how you looked three weeks ago . . ." She broke off abruptly. The memory of Verony's brush with death was still too acute to speak of it. Not even for the excellent purpose of getting her to rest more would Hilda dwell on those terrifying hours.

Resorting finally to the only method that seemed

to have any effect, she warned: "If you don't get back into bed right now, I won't bring the twins in."

Verony relented. Muttering to herself about the penalties of letting longtime servants get the upper hand, she removed her yellow-and-green robes, pleased to see that the tunic and surcoat once again fit perfectly. Her figure was almost completely restored, the only change being her larger breasts swollen with milk.

A smile curved her generous mouth as she looked forward to nursing her children. When Arianna opened the door, Verony was sitting up in bed, her arms held out eagerly.

"Here they are," her sister-in-law teased, "the world's most beautiful babies. Fresh from a nice bath and ready for their mother."

It was Catherine's turn to go first. Cradling her daughter to her, Verony gazed down adoringly at feather-soft hair dark as Curran's own. She laughed softly as the babe stared back at her solemnly. Her eyes were the same light blue as all infants', but already they showed signs of darkening to her mother's indigo.

She nursed avidly, despite Verony's joking reminder to leave something for her brother. It never ceased to amaze her that both twins had equally eager appetites. Ruefully, she admitted that Gawain's willingness to wait patiently for his sister to finish must be a virtue inherited from his father.

"Curran sent yet another messenger this morning," Arianna said as the babies were exchanged.

Hilda took Catherine into her lap to burp her, but not before chiding: "That man has to be reassured practically every hour that you and the babies are fine. Otherwise he's liable to come storming back here to see for himself." She chuckled softly, making it clear she approved totally of such husbandly devotion.

Verony sighed regretfully. She wished with all her heart that Curran would come back, but never would she voice that yearning. He had important duties to perform that were vital to her own and her children's future, as well as everyone else's. Not for the world would she want to try to hang on him at such a critical moment.

Has anything new been heard from the king?" she asked.

Arianna shook her head. "The earl, Mark and Stephen Langton are still at Windsor, trying to persuade him that he must meet with all the barons. With Curran holding the tower, it's hoped that John will be more reasonable."

Verony touched a gentle hand to her son's red-gold hair. She and Curran had shared such a short time together after the children's birth. Exhausted by all that had happened, she had slept through most of the following days, waking only occasionally to find her husband sitting beside her. If he ever left her, even briefly, she did not know. Each time her eyes opened he was there to touch her soothingly, murmuring gentle words of comfort and reassurance that penetrated even her weariness and pain.

There was no opportunity to speak of the extraordinary experience they had shared. Try though she did, Verony could not form the words to tell him how she felt or to discover his own thoughts. She had yet to learn how the full flowering of her love, freed at last from all doubt and mistrust, would be received.

Curran had delayed leaving her as long as possible. But in the end, the decision to take the tower could not be put off. Seizing the most important symbol of royal power was dangerous in the extreme. Yet no alternative remained. The riots that burned the Jewish Quarter and other parts of the city showed clearly that public authority was breaking down. Unless someone intervened quickly, the civil war the d'Arcy's so wanted to prevent would be inevitable.

In a desperate gamble, they sent their forces against the huge stone keep. Only the good sense of the men inside, who saw little reason to remain loyal to a deceitful, cowardly king, made possible an almost bloodless victory.

With the tower secure, the Earl Garrett lost no time heading for Windsor, in company with his eldest son and the archbishop. He left Curran to hold the most important stronghold in England, secure in the knowledge that his confidence was not misplaced.

Though only a mile now separated them, Verony and her husband had not seen each other since shortly after the children's birth. The political situation was far too uncertain for him to risk leaving the tower even briefly, nor would he permit her to enter its dank and potentially treacherous walls.

The messages they exchanged at least once a day were of necessity brief. Curran spoke of his concern for her and the twins. Verony assured him that all was well. She longed to say more, but could not. Part of her even welcomed the delay in confronting Curran, when she would learn if her love was still welcome. If it was not, if her final release from doubt and mistrust was not in time to preserve his own feelings for her, she had no idea how she would endure.

Still not as strong as she wanted to believe, Verony fell asleep again after nursing the twins. Arianna and Hilda tiptoed out, carrying the children. A soft breeze blew in through the shuttered windows. Verony's body, after being so long swollen, looked unusually slender and delicate beneath the thin covers. Her hair, unbraided and brushed to a silken sheen, drifted over the pillows. The dark shadows were fading from beneath her eyes, and her features no longer looked strained.

Although she viewed her appearance as no more than restored to what it had been before the twin's birth, in fact she was far lovelier. There was a new gentleness to her curved mouth and a radiant inner light to her translucent skin. Her body, once more slim and supple, was also riper and more rounded. Her breasts, engorged with milk and set off by dark, velvety nipples, fairly ached for Curran's touch.

Murmuring uneasily, she turned in the bed. Sounds from the bailey drew her slowly from her dreams. Someone had just arrived. There was eager talk, exclamations of surprise and pleasure, much hurrying to and fro.

Out of bed and across the room in a single, swift movement, Verony thrust the shutters opened. She leaned out eagerly, only to be disappointed. There was no sign of Curran, as she had hoped. Instead she saw only another messenger.

But whatever news he brought sparked a far from usual response. Listening to him, Lady Emelie positively glowed. Always beautiful, she looked at that moment restored to the loveliness of a young girl. Hugging Arianna, who looked equally happy, she summoned servants and hurried off about some task.

Unwilling to wait until someone decided she should be told what was happening, Verony dressed rapidly and sped downstairs. Carts were already pulling up in the courtyard, being loaded with household goods, bedding, even the large tents the family used when it traveled in good weather.

Lady Emelie was in the kitchens, supervising servants hastily packing baskets of supplies. She greeted Verony eagerly. "Wonderful news! The king has agreed to a meeting with the barons. Garrett is on his way there now with Mark and Stephen. Curran has left Sir Lyle in charge at the tower and has gone to secure the meeting site. The rest of us are to join them there."

"I hope that includes, me," Verony said instantly.

The countess smiled drily. "Are you strong enough?"

"Yes!"

"And eager to see Curran?"

"O-of course . . ." Her voice trailed off. Something of her pain and uncertainty must have shown in her eyes for Lady Emelie embraced her gently.

"Then you shall go, provided you agree to be sensible and ride in one of the wagons."

Verony hesitated. She was determined not to be left behind, but she hated the idea of being stuck in a lumbering cart instead of cantering along on her palfrey.

"You don't want to be all tired out when you get there, do you?" the countess demanded provocatively.

A faint blush suffused Verony's cheeks. If only she could look forward to a passionately loving reunion with her husband. Curran might indeed be glad to see her. Or he might take her sudden arrival as further proof of her headstrong insistence on independence.

For just a moment, Verony hesitated. Perhaps it would be wiser to remain in London and wait for him to come to her.

That thought faded almost the instant it arose. It was not in her nature to wait. If she had permanently damaged Curran's love for her, to the extent that he no longer wanted the close, trusting relationship she now craved, it would be better to find out at once.

To her surprise, riding in the cart turned out to be more comfortable than expected. Lined with straw-filled pallets covered by blankets, it proved a remarkably luxurious conveyance. Accompanying her, Hilda thoroughly enjoyed the indulgence.

"Mark my words, my lady," the nurse declared, "some day people will ride all over the place in wagons like this. Fitted out with every sort of comfort . . . seats . . . cushions . . . even roofs and walls to keep out the rain."

Verony laughed, peering into the padded basket where the twins slept peacefully. "How dull that would be. I like to see the world from horseback . . . feel the breeze on my face and the smooth rhythm of a well-trained steed carrying me along."

"Hmmph. All well and good at your age. But when you get older, when your joints get a bit stiff, you'll remember what I said. Then a bit of luxury like this will look very good indeed."

"I just hope Catherine and Gawain don't get the wrong idea. Heaven forbid they should always expect to travel in such comfort!"

Hilda snorted. "Don't talk to me about those two. They're already as stubborn as they come. And such energy! I expect to find them crawling any day now."

"Give them a few more months." Verony laughed. Modesty prevented her from mentioning that Catherine was already doing remarkably well at holding her head up and waving her chubby arms around. Gawain wasn't far behind, though he seemed willing to let his sister take the lead. After holding her back so long in the womb, it seemed a courtesy she deserved.

Both babies were fast asleep by the time the party reached the large meadow on the banks of the Thames near Windsor where the meeting between John and his barons would take place.

Verony's deep-blue eyes widened as she looked around. The meadow still called by its ancient name, Runnymede, was an unlikely scene of gaiety and boisterousness out of keeping with the somber tension of the moment.

Over ground vivid with ox-eye daisies and purple clover, some fifty tents were pitched. About two dozen of these housed England's greatest nobles, including all her barons. Proud banners fluttered from spear points, shields hung before the entranceways shone with fearsome emblems, and servants dressed in the colors of each noble house darted back and forth about their many tasks.

It looked for all the world as though preparations were under way for a tournament. Verony said as much to Lady Emelie, who snorted disparagingly.

"How else do you think Garrett could get all these louts here and make them hold still for several days? He's promised a great meet once the agreement is signed. Let's just pray that isn't too far off."

A large section of the meadow was cordoned off for the d'Arcys. With speed born of long practice, large, comfortable tents were quickly erected, folding tables and benches moved in along with bedding, and supplies set near the river where it was particularly cool.

The largest tent, intended for Earl Garrett and his lady, was also where the family would gather for meals. Around it smaller tents were put up for Verony and Curran, Arianna and Mark, and the younger boys.

When Hilda had at last convinced herself that the ground was not too damp, the breeze ruffling through the opened flap not too brisk and the interior as graciously appointed as was possible, she permitted Verony to enter.

"Now lie down and rest," she instructed. "The twins will sleep several hours yet, and you could do with a nap."

"I'm not tired. Do you think there's any chance of a bath?"

"A bath! Out here in the open with all manner of foul humors mucking up the air? Whatever are you thinking of?"

Verony grinned mischievously. "I'm not exactly planning to strip in the middle of the meadow, Hilda. I just want warm water and soap so that, in strict privacy of course, I can wash off some of this road dirt clinging to me."

"Hmmph! Well, perhaps . . ."

"Please," Verony cajoled. "I promise to rest as soon as I'm clean."

Won over, Hilda capitulated. She set a servant to heating water and took herself off to help unpack the foodstuffs and start supper.

Stripping off her dusty tunic and surcoat, Verony bathed leisurely. Drying herself on a soft towel, she rubbed scented oil into her skin before donning a fresh linen chemise. The day was growing warmer, so much so that she chose a thin tunic of lavender wool and left off the heavier surcoat that would usually have gone over it.

Her hair, protected during the journey by a veil, was quickly brushed clean. Not bothering to braid it, Verony let it hang free in thick waves to her waist. Smells from the open cooking fires made her stomach growl, but she preferred to wait before eating.

Sitting down on the narrow camp bed, she wondered how much longer it would be before Curran came. Tedious and demanding though the negotiations must be, he would surely take time out to greet her. In the dark recesses of her mind, the thought occurred that Curran might have more than just political intrigue to distract him.

During the months they were apart, Verony had to fight against the tormenting fear that such a virile, passionate man would not go long without a woman, especially if he believed himself saddled to a wife who disappointed him.

As that dread rose again to haunt her, she forced it down, telling herself Curran deserved all her trust and faith. But even as she told herself to believe, a remnant of doubt remained. Willing herself to patience, she nestled her head onto a folded blanket and closed her eyes.

When she woke, it was to find a large, shadowy form looming over the twin's cradle. Starting up, Verony almost cried out. In the shadows of early evening, she saw only that the man was immense and powerful. Not until he turned could she make out his features.

The sounds of the camp, the laughter and talk of men, the soft singing of women, faded. Curran straightened, his attention shifting abruptly from his children to his wife.

"I wasn't sure you would come," he murmured.

Still half dazed by sleep, Verony answered hesitantly. "I thought . . . it seemed safe enough . . . and you hadn't seen the twins in so long."

Curran smiled down at the babies. "They've grown so much. Hard to believe it's only been three weeks."

Verony barely heard him. She was too busy drinking in the sight of his long, lean body simply clad in a short tunic and cloak. His ebony hair was a little longer than usual, brushing the nape of his neck.

Evidence, she supposed, of the frantic activity of the last few months that had allowed little attention to personal matters.

His eyes, looking even more like deep, inscrutable pools, were brighter than ever. There was a hard glitter to them that made her shiver, even as she told herself it came from fatigue and irritation at the long-drawn-out talks.

Despite the rigorous trials he had endured all spring, his body was as powerful and muscular as she remembered. Broad chest gave way to a massive torso tapering to lean hips and long, sinewy legs. He was deeply tanned, his skin gleaming bronze in the fading light, and a dark stubble showed on his chiseled jaw.

A stab of longing darted through Verony. Biting her lip, she fought down the desire to reach out to him. Too much remained unsettled between them. If she gave in to her yearning to hold and caress him, he might well respond in kind. Glorious though their reunion would undoubtedly be, it would solve nothing.

Curran seemed to share her thoughts. He backed away slightly, increasing the distance between them as far as the confines of the small tent allowed.

His tanned fingers fiddled with the stem of a goblet as, his gaze averted from her, he asked: "Are you well?"

Verony pulled herself upright on the bed, feeling more secure when her feet were firmly on the ground. "Oh, yes. I can hardly take a step without your mother or Arianna or Hilda appearing to make sure I don't overdo. They've been wonderful about helping to look after the twins. Since their birth, I've done little but sleep and eat."

"That's as it should be," Curran muttered gruffly, still not looking after her. "When I think . . ." He did not continue. The pain was still too raw.

Verony's eyes darkened. She took a step forward. "Curran . . . I never had a chance to thank you. . . ."

"Thank me? For what? Getting you pregnant so that you nearly died?" Whirling on her, he forgot himself long enough to grip her arms and draw her close.

"Oh, Verony," he groaned deep in his throat, "if you hadn't survived . . ."

Staring up at him in mingled wonderment and hope, Verony thought she saw the first faint sign of what she longed for in his eyes. Daring greatly, she raised herself on tiptoe so that her lips brushed his. "But I didn't. I'm here and alive . . . and I've missed you so much . . ."

Her words trailed off, lost in the power of Curran's kiss. He claimed her mouth with fierce tenderness, delving deeply to taste all her hidden sweetness. Verony responded uninhibitedly. Forgetting her resolve that they must talk first, she gave herself without restraint. All the pent-up longing of months threatened to burst from her as she embraced him ardently.

Curran's self-control, so long maintained, shattered. His arms closed around her like a vise, drawing her against the full, hard length of his aroused body. His hand, insistent but tender, grasped the back of her head, tangling in the silken curls as he deepened the kiss even further.

Without her even being aware of it, he loosened the ties of her tunic and eased it from her along with the chemise. When her ivory shoulders were bare, he rained kisses along them, down into shadowed hollow between her breasts.

Stroking the ripe curve of her hips and buttocks passionately, his ardent mouth nuzzled aside the cloth still clinging to the tips of her swollen breasts. Large hands came up to grasp them gently as his tongue darted out to soothe one aching nipple and then the other.

A low moan tore from Verony. Arching her back, she pressed even closer to him. All hesitation dissolving, her hands moved over him, savoring the long-denied touch of his burnished muscles, the broad sweep of his powerful back, the long, tantalizing line of his steely thighs.

"C-Curran . . ." she breathed brokenly, some tiny part of her fevered mind remembering she had meant to talk. No words would come. Nor did he allow her to try again. Sliding her garments from her, Curran carried his wife to the bed.

He set her down gently before stepping away just long enough to strip off his own clothes. When he joined her again, Verony welcomed him joyously. Whatever she had wanted to say, she decided in the last moments before reason whirled away into the red mist of passion, it could wait.

She doubted that Curran would be able to do the

same. His engorged manhood, pressing against her, made her quiver with mingled delight and trepidation. Some tiny remnant of fear caused her to press her silken thighs together, only to have them lovingly but firmly parted by Curran's coaxing touch.

"V-Verony . . ." he groaned, "I've waited so long . . . let me . . ."

Beyond denying him anything, Verony lay back. Savoring each beautiful inch of her, Curran kissed and stroked and tasted until they were both on the verge of consuming ecstasy. Even then he delayed, restraining her efforts to draw her to him. With gentle insistence, his tongue found her most sensitive point, quickly sending her spiraling over the edge of fulfillment and beyond.

Her moans of pleasure were smothered by his mouth as he moved to complete their union. On the verge of penetrating her velvety depths, Curran hesitated. Sounds outside the tent pierced even the haze of his ardent need. Swamped by desire almost painfully intense, he tried desperately to ignore what he heard. But a sudden shout and the crunch of fists meeting bone compelled his attention.

Groaning, he swung his long legs off the cot. Lost in the glory of his touch, Verony could not bear such withdrawal. Her small hands gripped him determinedly as soft sighs of protest rippled from her. Shamelessly, she stroked the taut peaks of her breasts across his furred chest as her skillful fingers caressed the aching seat of his desire.

All thought of the desperate need to keep peace in the camp at least until an agreement could be signed fled from Curran. He reached for her hungrily, stretching his full length on her as they tumbled back across the bed.

"L-love me, Curran . . . don't stop . . . p-please . . ."

He was about to oblige, most willingly, when the wall of the tent fell in.

Chapter Seventeen

"EXCUSE ME WHILE I GO KILL SOMEONE," CURRAN rasped. Rising from the bed, he tossed a blanket over the supine form of his wife to shield her nakedness. Unconcerned about his own nudity, he stalked through the gapping wall of the tent to confront two squabbling barons.

"Montgomery! Debourgard! What the hell are you doing?"

The unmistakable ring of authority reached even those accustomed to commanding in their own right. Sweat-streaked and dirt-smeared, the assailants paused. They had started drinking early in the day, when boredom over the wait easily overcame their too brief patience. Their bellies full of ale and raw wine, their heads whirling with a mist of alcoholic fumes, neither could really remember what had sparked the present confrontation. But neither were they willing to stand down.

Only the fearsome sight of an enraged Curran d'Arcy made them pause. The befuddled barons were both big men, but Curran was larger by far. Naked and unarmed, he still appeared more than a match. And the fiery gleam in his eyes made it clear he was relishing the thought of pounding some sense into both their inebriated brains.

A quick glance at his tent told them just why Curran was so angry. Verony blushed fiercely as she dragged the blanket more tightly around herself. While the men were so distracted, Curran moved swiftly. Grasping each by the collar, he lifted them off the ground and shook them hard. "This little show would delight John! He'd like nothing better than for us to be at each other's throats just when we're about to win." Another shake. "If you can't control your tempers, I'll be glad to do it for you. A soak head-down in the horse troughs should help."

The threat penetrated even the combatants' sodden daze. Twisting wildly, they scrambled to get free. "Wasn't nothing . . . ! Just a little spat . . . could happen to anyone. . . . No reason t'get mad. . . . We'll just get out of your way. . . ."

With a disgusted snort, Curran released them. As swiftly as their wobbly legs could manage, they weaved their way among the tents and out of sight.

Shaking his head, Curran turned back to the downed wall. He was about to lift it into place when a drawled challenge stopped him.

"Who says the d'Arcys don't rule here?" demanded a tall, slender young man Verony recognized as a second or third son of one of the lesser houses. Dressed in full armor, the features beneath his battle helmet were spare and sullen. When he spoke, his narrow mouth curled back acrimoniously. "The Earl Garret and his whelps hide behind a mask of unity, yet still dare to order the very manner of our lives. Interfere with their pleasures"—his small eyes fell on Verony lewdly—"and they'll squash you like a flea."

Curran took a deep breath, fighting hard for self-control. With the king due in camp at any time, accord among the barons was vital. No matter how sorely tempers and patience might be tried, it was not a time for fighting. If John even sensed dissension among his rebel lords, he would seize the opportunity to undo everything the d'Arcys and others had labored for these many months.

Hoping for a quick, peaceful end to the challenge, Curran said softly: "You sound drunk, too, Fairleigh. Why don't you go sleep it off?"

"Drunk? I only wish I was." Straightening to his full, if unimpressive height, the young man sneered. "Maybe a belly full of wine is what it takes to make you lot tolerable. But as for me, I can hardly bear the stench of so many d'Arcys gathered in one place. It would take a full wind indeed to clear the air around here."

Onlookers gathered to enjoy Curran's handling of the drunken barons drew back slightly. It took no great wisdom to see this was a far different sort of confrontation. Sir Fairleigh was known to be arrogant and impetuous. He had an overweening love for himself and a deep hatred of anyone he thought more privileged. And he was just stupid enough to try something truly dangerous.

Curran was of the same opinion. He still hoped to convince the offensive youth to take himself off. But when Fairleigh abruptly drew his shortsword, that hope faded. Without armor or weapons, Curran was at a severe disadvantage. Verony watched in horror as his challenger advanced.

The crowd, always eager to witness a fight and having no great love for the d'Arcys, edged forward. No one made a move to help Curran as Fairleigh's sword thrust through the air only inches from his abdomen. But for his lightning reflexes honed through years of training and battle, he would have been severly wounded right then.

Circling warily, Curran managed to keep some distance between them. He rapidly sized up Fairleigh's weaknesses, of which there were many, and decided how best to disarm him. Flexing long, powerful legs, Curran was about to put an end to it when a rope trailing from one of the tents caught his foot and he went down heavily.

Verony screamed. Vicious dullard though he might be, Fairleigh knew a priceless opportunity when he saw it. In an instant, he was on Curran, his sword lifted high to slash through bone and sinew.

The blow never came. Leaping from the bed, Verony seized a mallet used to pound in the tent stakes and fairly flew across the small distance separating her from the struggling men. Without thought for her own safety, she ran directly at them.

In that terror-twisted instant, she felt just as she

had inside the small room high in the tower, listening to John brag about torturing Curran. Only this time the horror was even more immediate and the danger real.

Wearing full armor, Fairleigh was a difficult target. But in that breathless moment, as his sword hung suspended between the cobalt sky and Curran's exposed body, Verony spied a chance. Summoning all her strength, she rammed the hammer down against the back of his neck exposed between the helmet and the surcoat.

Fairleigh swayed. The blow was just enough to stun him, giving Curran the chance he so desperately needed. A long, muscle-hardened leg shot out, wrapping around the other man's pelvis in a wrestler's hold. Turning agilely, Curran managed to deflect the blow that would have cleaved his chest. At the same time, his steely arm grappled for the sword.

They struggled briefly. Fairleigh was willing enough to attack when he believed he held an insurmountable advantage. But with the contest turned more than equal, fear engulfed him. He saw the deadly implacability in Curran's eyes and knew what was to come.

Tense moments of frantic struggle did nothing to change the end result. Resisting the impulse to extend the man's torment, Curran moved swiftly. He did not even bother to use the sword, but simply bent his knee into Fairleigh's back, grasped him around the neck and pulled.

The younger man's backbone ruptured, sending splinters ricocheting into his brain. He died so swiftly that it took his body a moment to realize its fate. A low sigh broke from him and he crumpled to the ground.

Clutching the blanket to her, Verony stared down at him. She who had never willingly harmed anyone in her life had just helped kill a man. Yet she felt not the slightest regret. No hint of horror or dread touched the utter relief filling her. To save Curran, she would have gladly helped slay a hundred such.

The surprise darkening her sapphire eyes was familiar to her husband. He, too, understood what it was like to act with such absolute deliberation and certainty that there was no room left over afterward for even the faintest remorse. Nor could he find it in himself to feel anything but immense admiration for what his wife had done.

Taking her gently into his arms, he led her back to their tent. The crowd, stunned by what had happened, moved quickly to lift the wall back into place.

This latest evidence of the d'Arcys daring and ruthlessness, extending even to one of their ladies, made the barons acutely aware of how close they had come to disaster. If Curran had been harmed, the Earl Garrett would undoubtedly have exacted revenge against every man who stood by and let it happen. Breathing a silent prayer of thanks for the unexpected ending to the confrontation, they dispersed swiftly.

Seated on their bed, held close to Curran's massive chest, Verony shivered. She, too, was thinking of the crowd and what might have been. "They were like animals . . . standing there . . . cheering him on. . . . T-they wanted to see you die. . . ."

Several months before, when he did not know her as well, Curran would have tried to soften the harsher edges of reality. But now he paid her the compliment of being completely frank.

"They fear us greatly. Despite all we have said about not wanting to supplant John, many still believe we desire the throne for ourselves. Added to that is immense envy of our wealth and power. You are right to think that had I been killed out there, many of our so-called allies would have rejoiced. At least until they had a chance to discover all the results of such an act."

"But why then do you try to work with them? Why endure all these months of debate and negotiation . . . all the long, wearisome efforts to hold the barons together? If they are so unappreciative and distrustful, so filled with savage resentment, why try to help them?"

Curran sighed, running a hand through his rumpled hair. He felt wearier than he had in a long time. The weeks of effort and struggle were taking their toll. He longed to carry Verony and the children off to their own lands, where they might recapture at least a measure of the peace and happiness that was so briefly theirs.

Only the strongest respect for duty, drilled into him since childhood, forced him to stay to see the outcome of all their careful planning.

"We try," he explained slowly, "because whether we like it or not, our fate is linked to theirs. No matter how much power we have, we can still be hurt by the king. His authority is too far-reaching, too free of any control or restraint. That has to change, or we will always be potential victims for unscrupulous rulers."

Verony closed her eyes. She dreaded the thought that Curran's part in the conflict might deepen, but she felt compelled to say: "If one of you ruled, there would be justice for all."

Her husband laughed softly. He studied her with indulgent eyes. "Maybe, but there's no guarantee. We are men like everyone else. Better than some, worse than others. If we could take the throne, without provoking civil war, perhaps England would be better off for a while. But down the years, who's to say that we wouldn't breed inept, selfish rulers as bad as anything that's come before?"

Shaking his head, he stroked her cheek gently. "The system itself has to change. We must have a body of law that protects all men regardless of who happens to sit on the throne. Only then will we have any protection against abusive rulers like John."

"All men? Even the serfs?"

"Well . . . no . . . not yet at least." Glancing down at her, Curran smiled. "I know you think the peasants are as deserving of rights and privileges as the rest of us, but very few share your opinion. Someday perhaps the laws we're struggling for will be extended to everyone, but right now it's enough to protect those who hold property."

His tone made it clear he regarded her vision of a world in which all men—and women—would be dealt with equally as a fantasy not to be taken seriously. Verony was in no mood to argue with him just then, but privately she clung to the hope that whatever good came out of this encounter at Runnymede might one day be extended to people like those who protected and sheltered her when she was most in need.

Snuggled into the warmth of his chest, she blocked out the sounds of men outside carrying away Fairleigh's body. She supposed there would be some complaint from his family, but given the circumstances of his death, she doubted they would do anything but bluster. At any rate, she was not willing to worry about it.

There were far more immediate concerns. Despite all her resolve to be at least a little less independent and forceful, she had done it again. While Curran would certainly not have preferred her to stand by and watch him killed, he couldn't help but take her assault on Fairleigh as further proof of her "unwomanly" temperament.

While she yet had the opportunity, Verony resolved, she would do her best to convince him she was the equal of any female. But no sooner had she reached out a slender hand to stroke his thigh than fate once again intervened.

"What's this I hear?" the Earl Garrett demanded from just outside the tent. "My son has taken to fighting bare-ass naked, leaving it to my lovely daughter-in-law to rescue him?"

Snorting, Curran rose from the bed. He paused long enough to throw on a tunic before greeting his father. "If we have to stay here much longer, my gentle wife may reveal other skills I hadn't suspected." He looked back at her teasingly. "But right now, it's enough to know she can look after both herself *and me*."

Stepping into the tent, the earl studied Verony carefully. "Are you all right?"

She understood that he was asking after far more than just her physical safety. "I'm fine. If I had to do it over again, I wouldn't hesitate a moment."

Though he believed her readily enough, the earl also knew she was far too gentle and kind not to suffer some aftereffects from what she had done. But he was glad to know they would be no more than the normal revulsion that comes from confronting death.

Satisfied, he saw no reason to dwell on the near tragedy. "John is on his way. He should be here at any moment."

Curran reached immediately for the rest of his clothes. "I'll meet you in your tent, all right?"

His father nodded, turning to leave. He paused a moment to smile down at his newest grandchildren, still fast asleep despite all the turmoil. "I'll send your nurse to look after them," he told Verony, "so you can come along to see the king." A wicked gleam entered his gray-green eyes. "I think it's a sight you'll enjoy."

Verony wasn't sure exactly what he meant, but she hastened to ready herself. Great events were at least coming to their culmination, and she was determined to be part of whatever now happened. With Curran's help, she got herself into a soft blue tunic and navy surcoat trimmed with gold thread. Her hair was left free to fall down her back in glinting waves covered only by a transparent veil and jeweled circlet.

Waiting only long enough for Hilda to arrive, she hurried off to join Curran at the earl's tent. A large group was already there. Arianna and Mark, reunited after months apart, stood close together. They hurried up to Verony as soon as they saw her, exclaiming over what had happened.

"How brave of you," Arianna said. "Curran must be so proud."

"Proud, nothing," Mark teased. "He'll know to go carefully from now on and not do anything to make you mad!"

Verony managed to smile, though her heart wasn't in it. She told herself Curran had been kindness itself in the few moments they had alone in their tent. But her feelings and his were all mixed up with passion and fear and the tension of the long-drawn-out confrontation with the king.

She couldn't begin to guess how he would feel once he had a chance to consider what had happened. Her action against Fairleigh would surely make him realize, as it did her, that she was no closer to being the docile, malleable wife he seemed to want. It was not enough that Curran still desired her. If he could not accept that her pride and strength were as much a part of her as her love for him, she had no idea how she would endure.

Her fretful thoughts broke off as a trumpet blast announced the king's approach. Standing on tiptoe, Verony strained to catch sight of the man who had so abused and terrified her.

He looked rather the worse for wear. Beneath

gloriously embroidered velvet robes, his body seemed to have shrunk. Though he sat erect in the saddle of his caparisoned palfrey, he appeared weary and tense. Deep lines were etched into his face, particularly around his still sensual mouth and beneath his small, dark eyes.

Staring at him, Verony's lips parted in a soft exclamation of surprise. A long, white scar ran across John's forehead, mute evidence of her tormented response to his claim of having killed Curran. Grimly, she wondered what the king would say when he heard of Fairleigh's end. At least he couldn't pretend to be shocked.

For a ruler so given to ostentatious display, his escort was remarkably small. White-bearded Stephen Langton rode beside him, the archbishop's presence being solely to guarantee the king's. Verony had no doubt John would have been far happier without the prelate's company.

Behind John came the papal legate and beside him, the Grand Master of the Order of Templars. William Marshal, one of the most respected men in England, was also there. His rigid concept of loyalty demanded his attendance. But his expression made it clear he would rather be elsewhere.

Rounded out by a few lesser knights and bishops, the train was a poor show indeed for the arrogant John. But Verony found it heartening. There could be no more eloquent testament to the effectiveness of the d'Arcys' efforts over the last months. Though the barons' coalition was shaky, they had succeeded in isolating the sovereign and forcing him to this showdown.

The Earl Garrett went forward to greet him. Only years of discipline enabled him to keep his expression blank. No sign of the intense personal victory he felt showed in the careful regard of gray-green eyes sweeping over the man before him.

Most of the other nobles were not so circumspect. They pressed forward eagerly. Mocking sallies and daring insults, unthinkable just a few months before, filled the air.

John's face darkened ominously. He had accepted the necessity of negotiation, but that did not mean he was willing to see his overwheening pride ground into the dust.

Before the encounter could get out of hand, the earl intervened. "If you will join us inside, Highness," he said quietly, "we may begin."

John agreed stiffly. Flanked by the earl and Garrett, with Mark lingering to have a word with the archbishop, he disappeared into the blue-and-gold tent.

Only a very few of the more intelligent, rational nobles would actually take part in the discussions. The rest, easily bored by anything that did not hold the immediate promise of a good brawl, wandered away.

Lady Emelie, Arianna and Verony stood for a moment staring at the closed tent flap. Taut with anticipation, they wished desperately to be part of the talks. But that was impossible. Though Lady Emelie in particular had made her feelings clear in private conversation with her husband, no woman would be allowed any part in the final effort to keep England from civil war.

"We may as well make ourselves comfortable," the countess said at length. "I suspect this will take some time."

She proved more correct than she could have guessed. The talks dragged on for three days. Separate accommodations were raised for John some little distance from the main camp, but he spent almost all the time inside the earl's tent. What began as a general discussion of goals quickly gave way to precise listings of grievances and detailed demands for reform.

On the second day, snatches of written proposals began to emerge, to be avidly seized by the women. One such brought a snort of rage from Verony.

"It says here," she exclaimed waving the piece of parchment on which a scribe had hastily jotted down the latest provision, "that a woman's testimony can only be accepted in court in cases having to do with the murder of her husband. For all else, she remains unable to have any part in bringing justice be it for theft, the murder of someone not her spouse, or even an assault on her own person."

Emelie sighed. She rocked the cradle holding her youngest grandchildren as she said: "There would be no mention at all of women if I hadn't persuaded Garrett it was necessary. He knows neither the king nor the barons will ever agree to laws that make us anything but chattels of our fathers and husbands, but at least this provision opens the way for future gains."

"What about this one," Arianna commented, studying the parchment. Carefully, she read, " 'No widow shall be compelled to marry if she be desirous to live single.' That's a big concession for John, who's always been one for selling noble widows into new marriages or demanding money from them to refrain from doing so."

Verony was glad to hear of that, as well as the other provisions which guaranteed widows immediate access to their inheritances and kept their property from defilement. But remembering her own experiences, she wished there was more said about the protection of minors who might be orphaned before marriage.

As it was, the king retained the right to sell guardianships, but he was forced to approve provisions against the misuse of estates, which had sometimes left young wards impoverished when they finally came of age.

These and the other clauses dealing with the rights of debtors and those accused of other crimes reassured her that the d'Arcys' overall objectives were being realized. Slowly but surely, they were whittling away at royal power and in the process establishing a system of law that would protect all freemen.

Throughout the three days of talks the weather grew increasingly warm. On the first day, the prideful barons insisted on strutting about in full armor. By the second, some of the more sensible were removing their helmets. On the third, Verony noted with amusement that they had stripped down to tunics and little more, and were spending the better portion of their time either by the river or sloshing water from the horse troughs over each other.

Food and, more critically, drink grew short. The

earl and Stephen Langton had originally estimated the talks would not take more than two days. But John proved unexpectedly obdurate, picking at even the smallest points. As the hours plodded by, runners were sent out to buy beef, mutton, vegetables and large quantities of wine and beer to keep the barons content. Under strict orders to pay a fair price for all the provisions, they quickly became favorites of the surrounding merchants, who valued a windfall far more than any liberties that might come out of the talks.

By the end of the third day, rumors and predictions were racing through the camp: The king absolutely refused to accept the final, most important demands limiting his power to tax or seize property; Earl Garrett and the other negotiators had threatened to hold him captive and confiscate the royal treasury being held a short distance away in Windsor if he did not give in; John dared them to do anything that would provoke civil war, warning that their old nemesis, King Louis of France, would waste no time taking advantage of the situation and invading; England would be drenched in blood before the year was out.

Verony tried hard not to listen to the wilder claims circulating among the waiting nobles. She could credit John with any obduracy or deceit, but she did not for a moment believe the earl or his sons would rashly threaten any action that could lead to war. If only she could speak with Curran and learn the truth. But during the days of talks he never left the negotiating tent. Her worries about how the great clash of wills going on around her would end had to be satisfied by what little could be gleaned from the scribners' notes and cautious comments.

On a more personal side, she struggled with the still unsettled question of whether Curran had changed his mind about her unsuitability as his wife. The note of pride she thought she had heard in his voice when he spoke to the earl of her attack on Fairleigh gave her hope. But until she could hear from his own mouth that he truly loved and wanted her, she would remain doubtful of their future.

Not until the night of the third day did Curran emerge with most of the other men to seek a few hours of exhausted sleep. Verony, having retired early to tend the twins, was in their tent.

Gawain lay at her breast, suckling peacefully as Catherine slept beside them. Candlelight gleamed against the ivory perfection of Verony's skin. Her hair was loose and unveiled, falling in a silken cloud around her slender shoulders and long, tapering back. In deference to the warm weather and her task, she wore only a loose shift that did little to hide the ripe loveliness of her form.

Curran stood for a moment at the entrance of the tent drinking in his wife's beauty and the tender scene before him. He was wearier than he could ever remember being in his life. Not even weeks of forced marches and constant battle had so sapped his strength.

The long hours of talk, the haggling over each tiny point, the ever-present danger that John would suddenly back out and plunge the country into war, combined to bring all the negotiators to the very brink of their endurance.

Petty arguments broke out even among the allies who knew and respected each other well. John made no secret of the perverse satisfaction he derived from such bickering. Understanding that he would try to press it to the utmost, the earl quickly called a recess. After which, Curran prayed, the latest impasse threatening all they had so far gained would be overcome.

He entered the tent quietly, but Verony was nonetheless instantly aware of his presence. She looked up eagerly, her smile fading as she took in his exhaustion.

Setting Gawain in his cradle, she went to her husband and took his arm, guiding him to the bed. Curran sat down heavily, rubbing his face wearily.

Moving around to sit beside him, Verony touched a gentle hand to his shoulder. "It goes badly?"

He nodded mutely. Every bone and muscle in his body cried out for rest, but he knew that at most he could count on only a few hours' sleep. And tense as he was, he doubted they would do him much good.

"Do you want to talk about it?" Verony asked softly as she began to rub the bunched sinews of his back.

Curran hesitated. He was glad simply of her presence and didn't want to overburden her. But it would be good to speak of the problems plaguing him.

"There's not much to tell," he said slowly. "John is being fairly reasonable about most points, only because he knows he has no choice. But now we've hit a wall where he refuses to give an inch and we can't afford to back down."

Verony knew that the d'Arcys' basic strategy lay in getting the more minor points out of the way first, hoping that whatever concessions they agreed to there would lay the ground for John to be forced to accept their major goals without change. But she was not clear on the exact details of what they intended to demand.

"Why is he objecting so strenuously? He's already relinquished major rights to seize property and render judgment."

"This is different. I've said all along that whatever agreement we work out here would be meaningless unless there was some way of enforcing it. This informal coalition of the barons that my father managed to put together was enough to get us this far. But now we need something more."

Careful not to break the rhythm of her gentle massage, Verony asked: "What more can there be?"

Curran stretched languorously, the soothing motion of her hands already beginning to have effect. "We need an established body of men whose authority is recognized by both the nobles and the king. Much like the old Saxon Witan that served as a kind of intermediary between the throne and everyone else. Beyond that, we must have a clear procedure for pinpointing any future abuses of royal power and at least trying to get them rectified peacefully."

Verony's hands were momentarily stilled. She stared at her husband in surprise. Like everyone else, including Curran himself, she looked to the Earl Garrett as head of the family and leader of the coalition against John. His wisdom and strength could not be doubted. Serving him loyally, his sons tended to be somewhat eclipsed by him.

But now as she listened to Curran, she realized that it was her husband who more than the earl or even the revered Stephen Langton held the clearest vision of what might be. If his hope for a formal organization of nobles with recognized powers could be achieved, the way would be paved to assure true justice in fact as well as word.

In their violent, strife-torn world, differences of opinion were almost always settled by the sword. Even when outright bloodshed did not erupt, negotiated compromise came about only when costly war became a real threat. Runnymede meadow would be empty just then of all but grazing cows and nesting birds were this not true.

How wonderful it would be if there was some other way. Verony did not fool herself into thinking that any such effort would be easy. Certainly the barons would continue to fight among themselves, the king would work to undermine all of them, and hot tempers could turn even the simplest problem into armed conflict. But at least there would be a chance to stop the horrible, wasteful violence that went on year after year.

For just a moment, Verony allowed herself to imagine a world in which crops could be planted without wondering if they would ever be harvested, peasants could go to sleep at night not fearing that the morning would find their women raped and their own throats slit, children could grow up without the ever-present threat of violent death.

If such a miracle could ever come to pass, then the vast energy now expended on warfare could be turned to other things. Perhaps ways could be found to increase the yield of the earth so that poor weather did not automatically mean starvation for many. Maybe it would even be possible to discover ways of controlling the diseases that frequently carried away entire populations.

Impatiently, she shook her head. It was all very well and good to dream, but such indulgence achieved nothing. Her thoughts could be far better directed toward giving her husband whatever help she could.

Softly she murmured: "It sounds as though you don't think John will honor the agreement even after he signs it."

Curran offered no denial. "I don't believe I could ever really trust any king. The office itself seems to corrupt even the most noble. But in John's case . . . Let's just say I think we would be wise to always expect the worst. That way we will never be disappointed."

His speech was slightly slurred, as the full calming effects of her touch began to be felt. Gently, Verony urged him to lie down. Curran protested that he could not sleep long, but obeyed. Removing his tunic, he stretched out on his stomach, head cradled on his bronzed arms.

Verony studied him lovingly. Surely there could be no finer figure of sheer male beauty anywhere.

Despite all the hardships of the last months, he remained the epitome of virile strength and grace.

She longed to be able to reach out to him without the slightest hesitation or doubt. To know that the vast love she felt for him was truly returned. The thought that he might still regret their marriage made her bite back tears.

She was caught in a quandary from which there seemed no release. She could not be the wife he had said he wanted without destroying herself, and by that very destruction she would surely lose all hope of happiness.

Tired as she was, Verony was prey to dismal thoughts. Her mouth quivered as she imagined a future wherein she and Curran remained only formally wed for the sake of the children and convention while he sought another to fulfill his image of what the woman he loved should be.

Her hand stifled the sob of denial that rose within her. Whatever might happen between them, this was not the time to burden Curran with her fears. He would need all his strength to face the last, most treacherous phase of the struggle.

When she was certain he still slept, Verony lay down beside him. The warmth of his hard, lean body offered some comfort. She curled close against him, but did not close her eyes. Every moment they were together was to be savored. There might be all too few left.

Chapter Eighteen

A HAND SHOOK VERONY'S SHOULDER. SHE STARTED, instantly aware that the bed beside her was empty. It took a moment for her eyes to focus. When they did, she found Arianna bending over her.

"I'm sorry to wake you, but they're about to sign the document. Curran said you would not want to miss it."

"No . . . no, I wouldn't. . . . But what happened? I thought there was some problem? Something John was still arguing about." As she spoke, Verony rose hastily and began to dress.

"There was, but very early this morning he gave in. I'm not sure of the details, but I know the earl sent someone for Curran and Mark and the other lords. They wasted no time drafting the final provision, and now it's all ready to be signed."

"Thank the Lord," Verony breathed, following

her sister-in-law from the tent. Whatever suspicions John's sudden capitulation might spark could be chewed over later. Just then it was enough to know the days at Runnymede had not been in vain.

Lady Emelie was waiting for them near the Earl's blue-and-gold tent. She fairly glowed with excitement. "I can hardly believe it. Curran got exactly what he wanted. When I first heard he was demanding a council of twenty-five barons to oversee the keeping of the charter, I thought there was no hope of the king's agreement. But John must have mulled it over and decided it wasn't worth fighting about."

"Especially not if he intends to fight later anyway," Arianna suggested cynically.

Lady Emelie hushed her. "This isn't the place to say such things. Until the charter is signed and we are away from here, we must pretend to believe John means to honor it."

Verony followed their talk closely. She was reassured to learn that the d'Arcys were already planning for events beyond the signing of the charter. No matter how important the agreement might be, it would not be worth the paper it was written on if preparations were not made to promptly defend it against any challenge.

John, looking tired and sullen as he took his place at the table with his lords, was no doubt already planning how to undo what he was about to put his name to. He had a crafty glint to his eyes his small stock of self-control could not hide.

Verony smiled faintly. No doubt the venal monarch was congratulating himself on tricking Curran and the others. By accepting the last provision, he believed they would consider themselves the victors and let down their guard.

In fact, nothing could be further from the truth. The king's capitulation on such a major point was a clear sign that he intended to subvert the charter. The barons, rolling bleary-eyed from their tents, might seize the opportunity for celebration. But the d'Arcys' rejoicing would be far more restrained.

Looking around, Verony saw what John had failed to note. Baggage carts were pulled up behind the family's tents, and their possessions were already being loaded. Before the king himself could be gone, the d'Arcys would be on their way back to the impregnable fortresses where their superbly trained, utterly loyal men waited.

If it did come to battle, John was undoubtedly counting on dissension among the barons to weaken their defenses. But the d'Arcys would not wait for their contentious allies. Their forces would stand ready to thwart John's every move until either his will or his strength gave out. They would not rest until the charter was secure in deed as well as name.

The sight of the wagons brought home to Verony that her need to speak with Curran was fast becoming imperative. Searching among the group seated around the table, her eyes moved over him with reluctant intensity.

Despite the great occasion, he was simply dressed in a bleached wool tunic and heavy leather surcoat sturdy enough to deflect a sword blow. The clothing was what Curran and the other d'Arcy men who were similarly dressed wore for traveling.

Had John not been totally absorbed in himself, he would have wondered at their manner of dress. But self-centered as he was, Verony knew he was conscious only of his own plans.

For a moment so long in coming, the signing of what was being called Magna Carta, the Great Charter, passed very swiftly.

Stephen Langton made a brief statement about the agreement being reached through the grace of God and for the benefit of all free Englishmen. In a sop to the king's vanity, he praised John's wisdom in realizing that even kingly power had to bow to the rule of law. This earned an angry scowl from the monarch, which was pointedly ignored.

The Earl Garrett, as secular leader of the nobles, also spoke. His words were carefully chosen to emphasize once again that the actions taken at Runnymede this day of June 15, 1215, were for the good of all the barons and not just the d'Arcy clan.

His audience, elated over what to their simple minds seemed an easy victory, heard him out good-naturedly. They even cheered when he finished, a gesture that wrung a rueful smile from the man who had no delusions about their loyalty.

Banners fluttered in the breeze as the scribners moved forward. The senior man among them, a grizzled, stooped monk, laid a roll of parchment in the center of the oak table. Another set down a jar of ink and an ivory pen. A third stood by with melted wax.

The crowd pressed closer. John appeared to hesitate, but only for a moment. Having accepted the inevitability of the event, he wanted only to be finished and away. Slowly, as was to be expected from one not used to writing for himself, he penned his name. In a country where few could read and even less were capable of recognizing his signature, this was necessary but not sufficient.

Next, and far more important, he slipped the signet ring from his hand, dipped it in the melted wax, and firmly pressed the image to the base of the parchment.

A long sigh left the watchers. No great shouts of rejoicing went up. This was not like a battle where a man was raised to a peak of excitement, only to be either cast down in defeat or elated even higher by victory. Oblivious to the subtleties of diplomatic combat, the barons knew only that they were at last free to get on to better things.

As the parchment was carefully rolled and tied before being given to the archbishop for safe keeping, discussions broke out about the promised tournament. There was arguing over whether or not the fair weather would hold. The merits of various contestants were debated and bets laid down.

Saying a quick word to the countess and Arianna, Verony took her leave. Throughout the proceedings, she had kept a careful eye on her tent, making sure it was not dismantled. Even so, she arrived back just in time to stop eager servants who were about to pack it away in the cart.

"You can wait a few minutes," she told them firmly.

The small shelter offered the only privacy she

could find for her talk with Curran, and she wasn't about to give it up a moment before she had to.

As it was, she had little time to wait. Surprised at not finding her with his mother and sister-in-law, Curran hurriedly sought his wife. He meant to explain why they were leaving so suddenly and assure himself that she could make the trip comfortably. But he didn't get the chance.

"I understand all about that," Verony said the moment he began. "But before I go anywhere, we must talk." Her courage carried her thus far but no further. As her voice began to quaver, she broke off.

Puzzled, Curran took a step forward. Though he had much on his mind just then regarding what the next days and weeks would bring, he could not help but savor the beauty so long denied him. Even in the shadowy light filtering through the tent walls, he could make out the ripe swell of her breasts lightly covered by a thin blue tunic, the gentle curve of her slender waist, the tempting arch of her hips, the long, well-shaped line of her legs.

Curran took a deep breath. He wanted to reach out and take her into his arms, but some hint of stiffness in her made him stop.

Gathering all her strength, Verony tried again. "Are you going back to Langford?"

"Yes. I must drill the men, equip them with more arms, perhaps bring others into the force there. You see, we suspect that John will . . ."

Again Verony interrupted. "I know about that, too. Only an idiot would trust John to honor the charter. Of course you must go to Langford. But you

see . . . the problem is . . . I'm not sure I can go
with you."

Beneath his tan, Curran turned white. He tried to
tell himself he had not heard correctly, but her
meaning was unmistakable. Slowly, fighting the terrible pain gripping his heart, he asked: "I-is the
thought of life with me so . . . unbearable . . . ?"

"No! Well, perhaps . . . I don't know. . . . If
you loved me, I would never ask for anything but to
be at your side. But if you regret our marriage so
much . . . if I will always be less than what you
truly want . . . then I cannot bear it. No torment
could be worse than to see you every day knowing
you wish for another. The twins and I could live
with your parents until Gawain at least was old
enough to be with you, s-so we would not have
to see each other. . . ."

Anguished, Verony hid her face in her hands. She
could no longer stem the flood of tears that broke
from her at the thought of being separated from the
man she loved with all her being.

For a long, pain-filled moment, Curran said nothing. He reached out a hand to touch her, then pulled
back as though thinking he would be burned. As her
sobs continued, a steady, explicit stream of curses
left him.

Verony looked up in horror. She had expected her
proposal to be received with anger, but not this
unleashed rage that set a pulse to pounding in his
corded throat and clenched his fists into deadly
weapons.

"C-Curran . . ." she began, thinking to explain
herself further and plead for his understanding.

He leaped up, striding toward the door. "Wait there. Don't move. Not an inch!"

Verony shivered, staring after him wide-eyed. What could he mean to do? Had he gone for a lash to chastise her with? Or perhaps he meant to summon his father and the rest of the family to hear him denounce her?

Fresh tears rose to burn her indigo eyes before Curran speedily returned. He was carrying a small wooden box recovered from the baggage wagons. Crouched on the bed as far away from him as she could get, Verony did not at first want to accept it. But he pressed it into her hands, insisting that she look inside.

Trembling, she obeyed even as Curran said, gently now: "I've wanted to give this to you for weeks, but there hasn't been a chance." Ruefully, he ran a hand through his hair in a gesture she knew well. "And perhaps I was trying to put off this talk it seems we're finally having, hoping that somehow it wouldn't be necessary."

Tenderly he drew her closer. "I'm not normally a coward, not in battle or in the sort of treacherous negotiations we've just completed here. But when I thought about facing you . . . trying to get you to understand and . . . forgive . . ." He laughed disparagingly. "I seized every excuse to put it off. Even when you came here, instead of making the most of what little time we had together, I told myself the charter had to be worked out first. When in fact nothing in the world is more important to me than you and your feelings."

Tipping her head back, Curran stared into eyes

luminous with wonder. He gestured at the box. "I had this made, thinking it would tell you more eloquently than I can how precious you are to me."

Lifting his gift from its velvet-lined nest, he gently fastened it around Verony's ivory throat. Her hand followed his, her fingers brushing against the smooth coolness of large, perfectly matched pearls.

"I'll never be a poet," her husband went on softly, "and the last time I was stupid enough to speak to you of our marriage, I botched it royally. So I thought I'd take a clue from the bards."

He didn't have to explain further. Verony knew full well that the pearl was the exalted symbol of feminine loveliness and enduring love. Fresh tears filled her eyes, though for a far different reason, as she realized what Curran was trying to tell her.

Even so, she did not quite dare to believe. "You don't still think I'm too forward . . . too independent . . . ?"

"I think," Curran said firmly, nestling her against his massive chest, "you are the most beautiful, courageous, honorable woman I have ever known. And considering the standard set by my mother and other women of my family, that is saying quite something!"

Soft as the brush of a bird's wings, his lips moved down the smooth line of her cheek to find the tiny mole beside her mouth. "Whatever thoughts I had about the 'proper' role for a wife were cured once and for all when the twins were born. Even before then, I suspected I had done you a terrible wrong. But with all the rest that was happening, there was never any chance to get things straightened out between us."

He paused, his eyes darkening with remembered pain. "Then that night you were still in labor, I was so afraid I would lose you. Nothing else mattered except that you live. When I saw how you had held on, against such tremendous odds, so that the children could be born, I was humbled by your courage. I knew then that I would never exchange you for any weak, dependent wife who would undoubtedly make my life a misery!"

"But Curran," Verony protested, her voice muffled against his brawny torso, "that night when the twins were born I finally realized you were right about my not being able to fully trust anyone but myself, and that it was wrong for me to be that way. When you saved all three of us, it was as though some barrier that has always been inside me finally crumbled. I knew then that there were times when I would willingly defer to you, knowing your experience or judgment to be better under certain circumstances. But I couldn't be sure that discovery would be worth anything to you . . . if you would still want me . . ."

"Still want you? How could you doubt that for a moment?"

"I don't mean just physically. I want to be your wife in every sense of the word. To work beside you, to plan for the future together, to share your worries and your joys. But if I'm not what you want, then I can never really . . ."

"How could such an intelligent woman get such a

crazy notion in her head?" Curran growled against her ear.

"It's not crazy! You made it clear I wasn't what you expected in a wife."

"I had some very strange notions," he admitted soothingly while lowering her onto the bed. "I thought that a strong, capable woman was fine for someone like my father who was a match for such a mate. But since I believed my own strength was less than his, I unwittingly decided a docile wife would be far more suitable."

Verony tried vainly to sit up, glaring at him in astonishment. "How could you think such a stupid thing? You are every bit as courageous and strong and wise as your father. Why, the earl himself would be the first to say so. If he ever got wind of what you've been thinking, he would . . ."

"There's no need to bring him into this," Curran assured her laughingly. "Whatever else these last few months accomplished, they banished my doubts. I always knew I could handle myself in battle, but I thought that was just because of natural size and agility. Against John, no such advantages mattered. It became purely a question of personal strength and determination."

He smiled, remembering certain encounters with the earl. "I think my father suspected how I felt. After all, he, too, grew up under the influence of an unusually powerful sire. So he pushed me into situations such as taking the tower for him to make me realize my own capacity."

Silently Curran added that he was infinitely grateful for the earl's actions. He suspected that in the months to come all his new-found abilities and confidence would be tested to the limit. But he was not about to say so to Verony, not when they could be so much better occupied.

"My love," he breathed softly against the heated skin of her throat, "never think that you are less than everything to me. I will cherish you forever. You are the only woman who holds my heart and to whom my body can respond."

The long months of doubt and separation were catching up with them. Freed from her last fears about the completeness of her husband's love and faith, Verony moved against him languidly. Her slender arms reached up to embrace him as she pressed the rapidly hardening tips of her breasts into his chest.

"Curran . . . I know the servants are waiting to pack . . . but couldn't we . . . ?"

"Mmmm," he murmured, busy nuzzling his way past the thin cloth of her tunic.

Thought of anything beyond the magic circle of their love faded. The servants were too well trained to come back before they were called. And the family was far too wise not to guess what was behind the delay.

Slowly despite their great need, they drew out their excitement to a shattering peak. Naked in her husband's arms, Verony took intense delight in rediscovering every inch of his body even as he did hers. Hardness against softness, arching strength against yielding warmth, they came together exultantly.

The long months of abstinence might have taxed

Curran's control. But so great was his love that he drew out his wife's pleasure to the utmost before at last giving way to his own pulsating need.

Even then he did not leave her. The knowledge of how infinitely special and precious she was to him, combined with her soft cries of joy, aroused him again. Barely had they both descended from the pinnacle of ecstasy than they began to climb it again, this time reaching even higher and further than either had ever dreamed was possible.

In the aftermath of fulfillment, they lay close together on the storm-tossed cot. Sounds from the camp filtered gradually through the haze of their delight, reminding them that they had tarried almost as long as was possible. Soon they had to rise and dress for the long-delayed return to Langford.

But before they did so, Verony propped herself up on one arm to gaze lovingly at her husband. She would not darken such a precious moment with talk of fighting, but she wanted him to know she understood what might be just ahead and that she would do everything possible to support him.

"This 'Magna Carta' that was signed today, perhaps I exaggerate it in my mind, but it seems any price would not be too high to protect what you've won here."

Curran studied her quietly. He was just beginning to understand how much could be said with so few words, when two people knew each other on such a fundamental level. A flood of gratitude for her strength and courage filled him as he realized that if in the next few months he was driven to leave

Langford to defend the charter, she would not hinder him.

"We will do all we can," he agreed, "but the true worth of what happened here won't be known for generations. It will be up to our children and our children's children and all those who come afterward to value justice and freedom."

Epilogue

THE BELLS OF WORCHESTER CATHEDRAL TOLLED dolefully as the small crowd hurried out. The service had been lengthy, as befitted a king. Even one so hated.

Outside in the bright October sun, Verony and Curran made no effort to hide their relief. John was dead, little more than a year after the meeting in the meadow beside the Thames. But not, to their way of thinking, a moment too soon.

True to his deceitful nature, the king had no sooner signed Magna Carta than he began plotting to rescind it. Leading a mercenary force, he made war against his barons. Months of indecisive encounters and forced marches at last broke his strength. Denied even an honorable death in battle, he perished from fever.

Now the boy king, Henry III, sat the throne with

his conniving mother, Isabella, at his side and a bevy of advisors who were little more than greedy sycophants.

Only the night before, when she and Curran lay entwined in the aftermath of fulfilling passion, he warned Verony again that the struggle had to continue. "We've won too much to back down now, and there's still far too much left to be gained. No matter how difficult, the fight has to go on."

Looking up at him, standing so tall and strong in the sun, Verony's heart filled with joy. For just an instant, she allowed herself to wonder what the years ahead might hold. Not for them, whose love would endure even beyond their mortal forms. But for the long line of proud men and beautiful women who would carry the d'Arcy banner far into the future, and whose stories were as yet unwritten.

Then Curran said something, and all her attention shifted back to him. Smiling, Verony placed her hand in her husband's. Together they walked toward their horses to begin the journey home.

MAURA SEGER has been writing stories since childhood, but has only recently decided to make it a full-time career. She is the author of *Defiant Love*, a best-selling historical romance also published by Tapestry. A Connecticut resident, Maura credits the support and encouragement of her husband, Michael, for enabling her to fulfill the lifelong dream of becoming a writer.

Tapestry

HISTORICAL ROMANCES

Breathtaking New Tales

of love and adventure set against history's most exciting time and places. Featuring two novels by the finest authors in the field of romantic fiction—every <u>month</u>.

Next Month From Tapestry Romances

SWEETBRIAR
by Jude Deveraux

EMERALD AND SAPPHIRE
by Laura Parker

POCKET BOOKS

	45963	DEFIANT LOVE $2.50

_____ 45963   **DEFIANT LOVE** $2.50
Maura Seger

_____ 45962   **MARIELLE** $2.50
Ena Halliday

_____ 46195   **FLAMES OF PASSION** $2.50
Sheryl Flournoy

_____ 46194   **THE BLACK EARL** $2.50
Sharon Stephens

_____ 46137   **HIGH COUNTRY PRIDE** $2.50
Lynn Erickson

_____ 46186   **KINDRED SPIRITS** $2.50
DeAnn Patrick

_____ 46163   **CLOAK OF FATE** $2.50
Eleanor Howard

_____ 46053   **FORTUNE'S BRIDE** $2.50
Joy Gardner

_____ 46292   **LIBERTINE LADY** $2.50
Janet Joyce

_____ 46054   **LOVE CHASE** $2.50
Theresa Conway

_____ 46052   **IRON LACE** $2.50
Lorena Dureau

_____ 46165   **LYSETTE** $2.50
Ena Halliday

_____ 46379   **REBELLIOUS LOVE** $2.50
Maura Seger

_____ 46957   **EMBRACE THE STORM** $2.50
Lynda Trent

Tapestry

Pocket Books
Department TAP
1230 Avenue of the Americas
New York, New York 10020

Please send me the books I have checked above. I am enclosing
$_____ (please add 50¢ to cover postage and handling.
NYS and NYC residents please add appropriate sales tax. Send
check or money order—no cash, stamps, or CODs please. Allow
six weeks for delivery).

Name _____

Address _____

City_____ State/ZIP_____

531